2084

A Novel

By Bruce Blackie

2084

ALSO BY BRUCE BLACKIE

Gods of Goodness

Brass Cross

For Lynn

1

His rank and name aren't noteworthy. Colonel Wavering. It's the surname he was given; he didn't choose it, and he despises it. He has a square jaw, chiseled facial features, black hair with hints of gray. Even though hardly anyone knows him, and his position is confidential, he has a very important job. He sits in the pilot's seat in the cockpit of blue and white Air Force One. Today, his hands are on his lap, his eyes lazily skim the instruments in front of him. The plane flies itself, so he has no reason to worry, although he feels a vague obligation to make sure the autopilot is behaving.

He's satisfied the plane is holding at forty-three thousand feet and is on course. His mind has a tendency to flit about, he thinks of what it will be like in two years when he reaches mandatory retirement. He'll be 55 and should have a lot of years ahead of him to do what he likes. Maybe even get married, since he won't be flying or on call and won't have one girlfriend after another tell him to call them, which he does, but they don't call back. They're not about to share him with three hundred tons of flying machine that the president can call on at any time of the night or day, and when Wavering gets notice, he's jerked away to duty regardless of where he is or what he's doing. Or who he's with. He thought his dates would understand that. Maybe they do, but they run out of patience.

He's always mindful that behind the cockpit door lives the president and his flying presidential office with its wooden desk, large and hand carved fitting an emperor. A door from the office leads to the president's living quarters with king bed and a dozen TV screens. Behind those quarters are the conference room and roomettes for members of the presidential staff and cabinet. There are galleys with cabin attendants passing out whatever anyone wants to eat and drink, all on demand. Sometimes Wavering feels he's flying a palatial cruise ship catering to every passenger's needs. Everything but ballroom dancing on the lido deck. But for the president, his staff, and his cabinet, why not? They deserve it, don't they? When you join a service like the Air Force, you do what you are commanded. And the president is Commander-in-Chief.

Behind the presidential and cabinet accommodations, in the tail of the plane, press members pretended they were thankful for their quarters. With economy class airline seats and serve-yourself buffet, quite a step down from the presidential and cabinet digs, but good enough, according to the president. He's suggested from time to time that if he had the nerve the press wouldn't be there at all. But he's grudgingly given in to the fact that their presence is part of his job, even though they are a despised part of his job. On the other hand, though their biting criticism drives him to shouting tantrums, they do keep the public aware of him, of what he is doing, and, most important of all, that he is the president of the United States of America. Every American citizen needs to be reminded of that as often as possible. He is the president. There is no other.

It's déjà vu for Wavering and his flight and cabin crews to fly the president, his white house staff, cabinet members, and a gaggle of the press from the Key Largo 'Winter White House' to 'The White House' in Washington, DC. It's a weekly run that Wavering has become so accustomed to that the ninety billion neurons in his brain tend to wander aimlessly when the plane is on autopilot. He has to remind himself that he is responsible for all the lives behind him in the plane. If he allowed something to happen that caused the plane to crash, those lives would be less than happy with him.

Wavering is well into his mind-wandering retirement planning when he's jerked to attention by a voice behind him: "He pushed the button." Wavering knows the voice. It's Colonel Revere, the president's aide who carries the black briefcase that Colonel Revere explained contains a transmitter and keyboard for communicating codes to US military bases. The case is called 'the football.' Why they call it 'the football' has always eluded Wavering. He did ask once, but he couldn't make head nor tail of the answer.

The codes at the president's disposal are printed on a card the president carries in his suit. The card is called 'the biscuit.' That name has also eluded Wavering. And the combination of 'the football' and 'the biscuit?' Now, hearing he pressed the button, Wavering's mind spins, 'football' and 'biscuit' fly around in his head like bats in a cage.

A slight tension in Wavering's fluttering brain tells him he mustn't let his mind stumble off into panic, or he's liable to let Air Force One do something that would make his passengers displeased with him. But try as he might, he cannot swat down the bat he pressed the button. Wavering knows it's not really a button. There is no button on 'the football.' It's just a term that means the president typed codes off the biscuit into the football, and the United States launched a nuclear attack on some place in the world or most places in the world or…? Launched an attack? Really?

He pressed the button. Wavering tries to make the button connect with the gauges and dials in front of him, the blue sky he sees through the windshield, the throttle handles between his seat and the other pilot, the control yoke that he will grab if the autopilot tries anything bizarre, but the connection doesn't happen. What's flitting around in his brain is a world of its own. He pressed the button.

A strain of discomfort suggests that his plans for retirement might not be as solid as they were a few moments ago. He can't directly connect he pushed the button with his vision of a home he wouldn't have to leave on a moment's notice and then be absent for a week or so. It's possible the button will affect his dream of a beautiful wife and a happy life together, but he dismisses it. He's been so far from a home he could relax in and a wife and happy life together that he can't imagine what they would be like. Or if he could manage it.

Why did the president do that? Wavering asks himself. Why did the president punch codes into the football that launched an attack? There must be a reason. Launching a nuclear strike will do a lot of harm. It will blow up a lot of things. People won't like it. It's a big thing to do, if he actually did it. It will cause a lot of damage. People will die. Why did he do that?

Wavering hears Colonel Revere breathing heavily behind him. He pushed the button. The phrase keeps echoing in Wavering's head. No matter how hard he tries, he can't get it to go away. Yes, he says to himself, something big. Something big must've happened. The president thought we were in danger or he knew we were in danger, so he pushed the button. Wavering admits to himself that he doesn't know about those things. But the president does. He's very smart. He's told Wavering he's smart. He's told a lot of people he's smart. He says most people believe he's smart. Wavering idly speculates, if he's smart and he pushed the button, he had good reason to push the button.

Good reason? But what was it? When Wavering isn't flying, he watches TV, he looks at social media, sometimes he listens to the radio. But he can't recall hearing anything about a threat that would cause the president to push the button. Not that there aren't all kinds of wars going on. In Afghanistan, again. Iraq, again. Iran, again. Venezuela, Wavering knows the US's got troops there to keep the peace and sustain the flow of oil. Russia? he thinks. The

US has deployed new missiles in Europe and the Mediterranean. But Wavering has heard nothing about any threat coming from anywhere. He pushed the button. Why did he do that?

Wavering reminds himself of where he is. He's flying Air Force One with the president, his staff and cabinet, and members of the press, and he'd better keep his mind on the plane and not let the football, the biscuit and he pushed the button mess up his attention. He takes a deep breath, sighs. He notices that the plane is crossing the border from South Carolina to North Carolina.

Wavering's mind wanders off again, he hazily wonders what the president does at his white houses. The president says he works as hard at the Largo white house as he does at the DC white house. He says he works hard. He works very hard, and everyone better believe it. But Wavering reminds himself his job is to fly and he shouldn't speculate on what the president does at either white house. But he does believe the president works hard, very hard. That's what the president told him, and people better believe it.

Wavering recalls from watching TV how at white house press conferences press secretaries tell all the wonderful things the president does. By wonderful, they mean they are the most ever in the history of the planet. The best national economy, the best relations with other countries—Wavering assumes that means countries where the US isn't waging war or threatening to attack. He's done more since he came into office than any president before him. From his evangelical background, Wavering wonders if he's able to do more than God. Who knows? Maybe he does. After all, it's written that God takes a rest. At least a TV evangelist said he did after the six days of creation. But the president never says anything about taking a rest. Maybe he does. Maybe he doesn't. Wavering just doesn't know about that.

Wavering tries to still the swirling in his brain by staring out the window. At forty-three thousand feet, the sky is clear, the sun brilliant. He sighs to himself, this is my world. The sky, the sun, the dials, the screens, the controls that surround him, Air Force One turning, descending, ascending from his movements of the control yoke and powering up or down with the throttle handles. He relaxes his muscles, shakes his head to make himself more alert. The flight is so routine and with the autopilot he worries that if he had an emergency he might not respond the way he should. That would upset the president and his aides, and the press would be unhappy. He surely wouldn't want that.

"Well, not the button exactly," Colonel Revere continues. "You know, it's the briefcase I carry." Yes, Wavering knows it's the briefcase, it's fluttering around in his head. Yes, it's the transmitter called 'the football.' And there are the codes on 'the biscuit.' Colonel Revere doesn't need to repeat it as he is now droning into Wavering's ear. But Wavering still doesn't feel any connection with what Colonel Revere is telling him. The president pushed the button and launched an attack. It's out there somewhere, it's other people, it's another world. There was no word there was a threat from anywhere.

Colonel Revere says, "I saw him read the codes on the biscuit. At least I think he read them. Then he typed in the code to order an all-out attack. Whether he meant to order an all-out attack, I'm not sure. You know he can be impulsive."

Can be impulsive. Wavering feels guilty even thinking it. It's as if he's criticizing the president, and he would never want to do that. Can be impulsive joins he pushed the button and the other bats flitting around inside Wavering's head. He's overheard the president's aides complain they never know what he's going to do. Every morning, they announce the president's schedule for the day. It gets printed in The Hill so everyone in the government will know what to expect. Consultations, conferences, lunches, more lunches, summits with foreign leaders, meetings with Congress—he does a lot of that. Meetings, that is.

The aides don't announce decisions. Decisions come at any time of the president's choosing, and he communicates them himself with tweeted messages. He orders the arrest and immediate trial of anyone leaking information out of the White House. He says there will be a purge of leakers. Or he announces he will sign a treaty. Usually it's a treaty with another country that will add billions of dollars to the United States treasury.

When journalists ask him later in the day about the purge or the treaty, he stares at the journalists and says, what purge? What treaty? They tell him the one he tweeted about earlier in the day. He shakes his head, waves the journalists off with a brush of his hand, says, "What're you yammering about? You're making up fake news." They tell him he tweeted about the purge and the treaty that morning. He tells them they're all fake and they should go get real jobs.

Wavering thinks of how the president likes and then doesn't like journalists. So when he doesn't like them, why does the he keep them? If he doesn't like them and says they're all fake, why does he take them on board? Wavering ponders the question, but has no answer. He thinks, well he's the president and whatever he wants to do is his right. He can do anything he wants.

Wavering reminds himself that the televangelists said the president has divine right. Something about "be subject to the powers that be." That power is is the president. And if God says everyone should be subject to that power, then we should not argue with what the president says or does.

He pushed the button. It keeps echoing in Wavering's head like a musical tune he can't shut off. It's big to press the button. It's a big deal. But Wavering hasn't heard anything from the president or his staff that warned there was a threat. An imminent threat, that is. It would have to be an imminent threat for the president to order an all out attack. Wavering thinks that's the right word. Imminent. There's always a threat, from somewhere. Sometimes he feels like it's everywhere. But imminent?

The president's critics accuse him of fueling flames of fear. There are so many somewheres to fear that Wavering loses track— China, North Korea, Iraq, Iran, all of the --stans, at least a dozen more. The threats keep the country perched on the edge of peril. Maybe that's what the president wants. Although he's brought everyone to the edge of peril so many times it's possible that for some people it's become old hat, as they say. Wavering speculates that's maybe why he pressed the button isn't causing more of a stir in his head than if he were told the president pushed the button of a doorbell, or the president pushed the button of an elevator. Wavering chides himself, why doesn't he feel anything. Shouldn't he when he hears, 'he pressed the button?'

Wavering recalls tuning in to Fox News, Fox NBC News, Fox ABC News, Fox CBS News, Fox CNN News, Fox MSNBC News, Fox CNBC News or one of the other Fox News—they're all Fox now—where the president frequently reminds everyone that the country is facing an emergency. Of course, declaring emergencies reinforces the president's absolute power, something he seems to enjoy. When he's on TV declaring an emergency, he wears a smiling smirk which conveys he knows something no one else does. Of course that's his job.

On different days, the emergencies are different, but it seems there's always one in play. It keeps everyone on edge and counting on the president to protect them. Wavering doesn't know if that's what the president wants, but when he describes the threats as 'catastrophic,' 'horrific,' 'totally destructive,' 'the worst ever in history,' everyone tries to take him seriously. They don't want to be blindsided by the worst catastrophe the world has ever known. Who would want to miss out on that?

Wavering takes his headphones off and twists around so he can see Colonel Revere. He's younger than Wavering, about 30, wearing a black suit, white shirt, with a military service tie. Lines crease the forehead of his face drained of color. His eyes blink. "He grabbed the case from me." Colonel Revere pauses, Wavering hears quick gasps, he might be hyperventilating—Wavering hopes not, hopes he'll be okay.

"You don't believe me?" Colonel Revere says, eyeing Wavering closely. Wavering doesn't know if he believes him or not. He pushed the button just rattles around in his head. Does he believe it? He knows he should. After all, Colonel Revere is the president's aide. But might he be acting, Colonel Revere an actor on a stage? He could be performing according to some script. Yet he could be real. Maybe the president did actually push the button. That would be really bad. So does he trust Colonel Revere or not? Wavering wishes he could make up his mind.

Colonel Revere continues, "We were in the Communications Center. He and his cabinet were watching the big screen. It showed images transmitted from the radar station on Guam. I could see the images over the president's shoulder."

"What did they tell you?" Wavering asks. But he wonders, does he care? The president and his elves—Wavering knows he's disrespectful when he calls members of the staff and cabinet 'elves' because they follow the president around like the elves followed Snow White--watching a radar screen? He's seen them do it, but most of the time they're watching some version of Fox News.

"There were spots," Colonel Revere says. "The president said the spots were over Indonesia."

"Bright spots?" Wavering asks. He's not sure if he cares whether they were bright or dull, but he feels a need to keep the conversation going. Colonel Revere's gasping is not diminishing.

"Well, he said they were bright spots. I thought they were fuzzy.

They looked like cottonwood seeds."

Cottonwood seeds? Like the phrases blowing around inside Wavering's head. "Many?" Wavering asks.

"It was hard to tell. Maybe half a dozen. They faded in and out. The president stood up, pointed at the screen and shouted, 'It's a full-scale attack.'"

"The others in the center?" Wavering asks. "What did they say?"

"They didn't say anything. You know they never do." How true, Wavering recalls. He's never seen staff or cabinet members question the president. Colonel Revere continues, "An intelligence agent in the room said it might be a happenstance alignment of orbiting satellites coming over the western horizon. It's happened before."

"Did the president listen to him?" Wavering asks. Although as soon as the question wedged itself into his mind, he recalled he'd never seen the president listen to anyone. Even in an interview, when someone he's talking to starts a question, the president cuts him off and declares another success he's accomplished. Did the president listen? Probably not. He isn't alone, of course. Like now, Wavering thinks. He may not be listening to Colonel Revere. Colonel Revere's words keep blowing around inside his skull like those cottonweed seeds. It could be that the part of his brain that was designed to listen has shut down.

"The president didn't reply," Colonel Revere says. That makes sense. If you don't listen when someone says something, you don't reply. So the intelligence agent spoke, but the president didn't listen to what he had to say. Colonel Revere continues, "He looked at the biscuit. He typed a code into the transmitter. His hands were shaking."

From Indonesia? That's what Colonel Revere said. Wavering reminds himself he doesn't know much about Indonesia. He knows it has mosques, that alone qualifies it for the president's target list. But he's heard no warning from the president or his other aides that the US would be attacked by nuclear missiles launched from Indonesia. At least Wavering doesn't think so, although with so many phrases and ideas swirling in his head he could have heard a warning, but it went past him. If he gets what Colonel Revere is saying even partly right, the president sent the signal to launch an all-out nuclear attack because he saw fuzzy dots on a radar screen and believed they were missiles launched by Indonesia. Yes, that would be something big. Wouldn't it? That is, if he actually sent the signal.

Since latitude and longitude coordinates are part of Wavering's world, he does some quick calculations. Jakarta to San Francisco, say? It's over eight thousand miles. He's not sure even the US has missiles that can reach that far. And to San Francisco? You don't wipe out the United States with an attack on San Francisco. Or Los Angeles.

You'd knock out some creative thinking. At least what's left of the country's creative thinking after the Fluke succession of presidents labeled creativity a threat to national security and fired all the researchers and creative artists that could be found. Wavering doesn't know if creativity was a threat to national security, but when President Augustus Fluke III grumbled that creative people only pretended to regard him as president, Wavering believed him. The president claimed creative people whispered behind his back that he was full of phony blah blah. Because they did that, he termed them 'handicapped.' Wavering doesn't know much about people who are handicapped that way. The president said they were handicapped in their brains. After that, there was no more word about creative people. Wavering didn't see them on TV anymore either. It was as if they'd all gone off to an island and never returned.

Wavering isn't sure he can make sense of what Colonel Revere says. He's trying. He can fly the airplane with throttle handles, oil pressure gauges, navigation scopes, fuel tank levels, and myriad switches and warning lights. Everything there makes sense. But trying to understand the world President Augustus Fluke III lives in is exhausting. No matter how hard he tries, he can't fully connect. He remembers he had the same problem with Augustus Fluke II. At least Fluke II didn't grab the football and punch in the chain of command codes to launch an all-out nuclear attack. That is, if Colonel Revere is to be trusted and Fluke III did launch an attack.

Wavering fixes on the dials and scopes and switches in front of him and his hands ready to grasp the control yoke. He glances at the brilliant blue sky he sees through the windshield. That is the real world. Isn't it, he wonders?

"The president orders you to head out over the Atlantic," Colonel Revere says. His jaw muscles are so tight he's squeezing out words between clenched teeth. Wavering thinks he doesn't appear to be doing well. He hopes Colonel Revere isn't plunging into some kind of seizure. Maybe Colonel Revere wishes he'd grabbed the football back from the president before he could use it. Although the president would have him court-martialed if he did.

"Over the Atlantic?" Wavering asks. "Where 'over the Atlantic?'" Over the Atlantic isn't much of a destination, although Wavering realizes the president isn't usually strong on detail.

"Anywhere, just not over land," Colonel Revere replies.

Anywhere? Air Force One's navigation equipment is designed to put the plane on a heading toward a specific designation, a target that has latitude and longitude coordinates. Anywhere doesn't have coordinates. It isn't a destination.

But still, he pushed the button. The phrase is driving Wavering crazy, he can't get it out of his head. He feels he's like an actor who can't find his role and doesn't know what his lines are, but he keeps obsessing over one ludicrous phrase. Other actors, like Colonel Revere, are in character and talking, but he's so far away from them he can't grasp what he's supposed to do. "It's a drill? It's got to be a drill?" he ventures. "The president wants to see how everyone reacts?"

Colonel Revere stands mute. He could be delusional. His empty stare tells Wavering he might have words flitting around inside his head, just like he does. Colonel Revere must be wrong. He saw wrong, he heard wrong, he's talking wrong. But his order seems real.

Wavering switches off the autopilot, grasps the yoke, banks into a right turn, and levels off when the compass points due east and the nose has nothing in front of it but blue water. He could turn his head and look out his window to the left. Would he see flashes? Mushroom clouds billowing up over Richmond and DC and Philadelphia? He doesn't turn. He doesn't look. He has a sinking feeling that the retirement house with grass and trees and flowers he dreamed of, and the pretty wife who would always find him at home, are going to be delayed.

***

President Augustus Fluke III lies on his Air Force One king bed with his head propped up on pillows so he can monitor the dozen TV screens on the far wall. There's a smug look on his face, the look of a man bursting at the seams with pride at what he's done. His eyes gleam, he guzzles another diet Coke as if he's been dragging across the Sahara on a hot day. He holds in his small hand a walkie talkie to talk to a technician on the floor below who controls what is shown on the monitors.

"Jakarta," III barks into the walkie talkie.

"Where's that?" asks the technician.

"Indonesia, you idiot," III replies. He wonders how in the world he gets staff members who know so little.

"Yes, Sir." The image on one of the monitors changes. The scene is a main street teeming with cars, motorcycles, motor scooters, bicycles.

"You're sure that's Jakarta?" III asks.

"Positive, Mr. President. The satellites confirm."

"Then why is it there?"

"There?" the technician replies. "Where?"

"There," III shouts. "There. Not gone. Can't you understand?"

"I'm trying, Mr. President. All I can say is it's there because it's there."

"It's there because it's there? What kind of nonsense is that?"

Long pause, then the technician replies, "We don't have a confirm that it's nonsense, Mr. President."

"What does that mean?"

"I apologize that I have to inform you, but it means that it's there. Jakarta, Indonesia, is there."

"So it's not gone?" III asks.

"Mr. President, if it's there, it most likely isn't gone. Am I making sense?"

"No, you're not. It's there, so it isn't gone. That's nonsense. It's supposed to be gone. That's what I did. Gone."

"Yes, Mr. President."

"What does that mean?"

Long pause. "It means that it's supposed to be gone. Because of what you did."

"Then why isn't it gone?" the president barks.

Long pause. "We don't have an update on that, Mr. President."

"Then get one. I want that screen to turn blank. Do you know what I mean?"

"Blank?" the technician replies. "Yes, Mr. President, I know what blank screen means. Do you want me to make it blank?"

"You? You make it blank? No, I want our missiles to make it blank. I launched missiles to strike Indonesia because they're attacking us. I targeted a few other places as well, I guess. I've never been able to figure out how to use that football and biscuit. You know what I'm talking about?"

"I know the football and the biscuit, but I've never been trained on how they work. It must be difficult."

"Damn right it's difficult. A list of a bunch of targets and then codes I can hardly read that I'm supposed to type into the football. Well, I did that. But I'm not sure what I did." III scans the other monitors. "Hey, what's going on? Moscow. St. Petersburg. Vladivostok. Beijing. Now London, Paris, Rome, Berlin. Monitors are going blank all over. Are you doing something funny with the feeds?"

"No, Mr. President," the technician replies. "We're not touching anything. All those feeds have been interrupted. There are no signals coming from any of them."

"Then what's going on?"

"I'll check, Mr. President." Long pause. "I'm back. Satellite imaging shows all of those cities covered with clouds. They look like clouds rising into the stratosphere from large explosions."

"Large explosions?" the president repeats.

"Large Explosions," says the technician.

"From what?" The president scans the other monitors. "More are going blank," he says.

"Yes, Mr. President. More feeds are cut off."

"New York? Philadelphia? DC? Chicago? Boston? What's going on?"

"Satellites show large clouds there, too."

"Large clouds? I didn't target our own cities. You're an idiot. You've got to be wrong. You are wrong."

"Yes, Mr. President."

"What does that mean? Are you admitting you are wrong?"

"Negative on that, Mr. President."

"Negative? What does that mean?"

"It means not in agreement."

"You mean 'No?'"

"In so many words," Mr. President.

"Then why don't you just say it? Why can't you say what you mean?"

Long pause. III guzzles his diet Coke, presses the send button on the walkie talkie. "Are you there? Why are you taking so long?"

"Yes, Mr. President, I'm here."

"Then why can't you say what you mean?"

"Sometimes it's difficult, Mr. President."

"Difficult?" III barks. "I never find it difficult to say what I mean."

"Yes, Mr. President."

III scans the monitors. Most are blank. He fixes his glare on one. "That Jakarta. It still isn't blank. Do you see that?"

"Yes, Mr. President."

"Not blank," III shouts. "I want Jakarta blank. I want Jakarta out. Do you hear me. I want it out. I targeted Indonesia. Someone has messed up so that Jakarta is still there. Send me that aide with the football. Jakarta. This is ridiculous. Can't I ever get anything done right?"

2

Regardless of whether III destroyed Jakarta with a missile, it, like the rest of planet earth, did not take to his pressing the button very well. Clouds of radioactive dust floated up through the atmosphere to the stratosphere where they spread over the globe and blocked sunlight from reaching the ground. Global warming that had been going on for a hundred years or so and was accelerating the extinction of live creatures well before Fluke III— although there were always those, including Fluke, Fluke Jr, Fluke II, and Fluke III who denied human beings had anything to do with the warming—suddenly stopped, the warming that is.

For a few years the global climate stabilized, but under clouds. With those clouds, crops slowed their growth, there wasn't enough food for cattle, pigs, sheep, and goats and the like, and malnutrition set in. For those who weren't incinerated by III's pushing the button, life became grim. Radiation and malnutrition shortened lifespans, people stopped having children, but Americans didn't blame Fluke III. They blamed the planet. The planet had turned against them. By 'planet' they meant the weather as well.

Although they weren't allowed to say it, they also wondered why God allowed the planet to become the way it was. The evangelists said it was sin. God was angry with the human race because of sin. But when Wavering tried to understand what sin the evangelists were talking about, he could not get a clear idea. They preached about homosexuality and abortion, but both had been outlawed. The evangelists said both were still going on, and God was angry, and God brought judgment on the human race. Well, thought

Wavering, if the evangelists said they were going on, they must be right. Who knew more than they did?

III not only agreed that the enemy was the planet, he became one of the main proponents of the accusation. He and the Fox News networks, at least the ones that still had studios and transmission towers and satellites carrying their signals. That may sound like a lot, but when III wiped out all the major cities on the planet, he also wiped out most of the Fox news stations. Whether he had thought about that beforehand, nobody asked. Perhaps because those most likely to ask had been incinerated in their studios.

But President Augustus Fluke III charged on as if his pushing the button caused only a slight glitch in the onward march of human history. Although Wavering noticed that whenever the president boarded Air Force One, he wore a curious expression. His face was the mask of a bulldog. His eyes looked through Wavering and the other crew members as if they were empty air. Wavering did brisk salutes and received in return dull waves of the arm, a reminder that he is the president's aerial chauffeur, a servant, next to nothing and highly expendable.

When they board Air Force One for a flight, the president climbs the stairs followed by his staff and cabinet of puppets quick-stepping like a line of wooden pull toys. III enters his palatial cabin, the puppets file into theirs. Doors close. Wavering settles into his seat and starts the engines. Routine, he says to himself. Always the same routine. As if the planet was still the way it was.

Wavering doesn't know if III notices, but most of the time they are flying through clouds. All the president has to do is look out of his window, and he will see. When Air Force One lands at destinations—all small towns—III tries to button his sports jacket, then mumbles to an aide to get his coat. The coat started in Montana and North Dakota. Then Colorado, then New Mexico.

Finally he donned it at Key Largo. Did he notice?

Having been told by his cabinet of puppets and hand-picked scientific advisors that nuclear war would do no serious damage to planet earth, he plunged ahead on what was left of TV saying, "I'm the greatest commander-in-chief ever. The greatest ever. I've rid the world of the evil Muslims." He made no mention of the billions of non-Muslims he also got rid of. And he never acknowledged that all the world's major cities were gone. Nor did he admit that in Florida, he and others were shivering with cold. Wavering attributed the president's optimism to his strength, strength to see through things that weren't so good in a way that made them good or else irrelevant. Nothing got him down. What a leader.

Evangelical preachers never stopped waxing hysterical. On Fox Christian Network they waved their arms, lifted them toward the ceilings of their giant coliseums and shouted, "Glory hallelujah, the Millennium predicted in the Bible has come. And The Great Tribulation. We are not living in the last times. This is the last time. Glory be to God Almighty." When asked why Jesus did not return in the air before the Great Tribulation or after, the preachers said the timing was a mystery. They declared that Jesus would come after the Millennium. There was just a scheduling slipup. Nothing major. Although to Wavering, when he thought too much about it, a thousand years didn't have the feel of nothing major. But what did he know? The preachers were the experts about tribulations and millenniums and those kinds of things.

Before the clouds became too dense for satellite cameras to see the ground, images of earth showed a white layer of ice growing out over dark water from the North Pole, creeping down over Canada and the northern half of the United States. At times, flying was dicey. Wavering took off in snow, climbed in snow, landed in snow. Including the airport that served Key Largo. When the crew opened the plane door for III to exit and snow blew in, Augustus said, "Don't worry. It won't last long." Of course with the heat on in Air Force One and in the winter White House and in his armored SUVs, he could easily convince himself there was no need to worry. Except for the coat, which Wavering didn't think he realized he wore.

Then one day on the Largo to DC run, Wavering receives a radio message from air traffic control that the White House and Congressional bunkers—all that is left of the capital building and the white house from what the preachers called the Great Tribulation--are no longer reachable. When he tells Augustus III this, Augustus looks at him as if he is an animated fossil from pre-Fox CNN. "Fake news," he grunts.

Wavering is about to reply but stops. Then he summons a modicum of courage. "Not news," he says. He knows that by countering the president he is imperiling his position and himself. It makes him feel uncomfortable. "Air Traffic Control, Mr. President. They don't do news." Wavering thinks the president might give control a mite of credibility. He doesn't. He sits at his eight-foot-wide teak desk in the cavernous ironwood-paneled Air Force One office and stares at Wavering as if he's a homeless panhandler.

"Have you seen the size of the crowds that are coming to my victory rallies?" he asks. Wavering has seen them. But maybe he hasn't seen them. He's heard from security police that Augustus's prep teams and promoters have been known to bribe and threaten people to attend his events. Since the major cities have been incinerated by nuclear blasts, all the rallies are in small cities. When the presidential entourage enters a town, Wavering notices the streets are empty, shops closed. Nothing moves but a stray dog or two. Near the rally stadiums there are buses—Greyhounds, black and white charters, lines of yellow school buses, white and gray vans. Have the promoters rounded up every living soul in the county and beyond?

But Wavering tells himself that isn't a question he has the right to ask. Yet he could see that the grandstands had a lot of empty seats. But Augustus III, upon returning to the plane, always says, "Another sellout. Another full house. Thousands outside who couldn't get in. Thousands. Did you see them? They love me. They love me." His cheeks puff, his eyes glow as if he beholds the whole world bowing at his feet. Wavering obediently nods with enthusiasm. The president's world is his world. If the president says there were thousands, there were thousands. If the president says he is the greatest ever, he is the greatest ever. Who would question that? Who would question President Augustus Fluke III?

The DC shutdown that air traffic control announced poses no problem for Fluke III. "Land as we always do," he orders. "Near the helicopter. I don't feel like walking far." As the Andrews runways come into view, Wavering does a fly-over and notes how snow is obscuring visibility. He strains to see a waiting helicopter, but near the snow-drifted hangers there appears to be none. No backup entourage of SUVs either. The runways are cross-streaked with ridges of snow. Runway marker lights and runway approach strobes are off. Wavering cannot see a single soul anywhere.

His job is to fly and do as he is ordered by the commander in chief. So he descends toward the longest runway, touches down, blasts through snow drifts and slews to a stop just short of the far end of the runway. It is then that Wavering realizes his face is beaded with sweat. He doesn't acknowledge it, but the real world of flight is meeting the other world of the president.

"Open the door," the president demands. "I'm in a hurry." Wavering glances out the main door window. No one is approaching the plane.

"Sir," he says.

The president cuts him off. "Open the damn door. I don't want to waste time."

"But the stairs?" Wavering says.

"Do you hear me? Open the damn door."

Wavering feels his chest tightening but stands his ground. "There are no stairs, Sir," he says.

The president looks at him as if he might be a sidewalk huckster blowing soap bubbles. He grows red in the face. "Do as I say," he shouts.

Wavering tries to find words, but anything he can say would be heard as defiant. He nods to the cabin crew. They swing the door open. The wind howls. Sheets of snow blast horizontally through dim light, concealing whatever lies in the shadows. Snow flakes drift into the cabin and settle on the floor. The president should have donned a hazmat suit to protect against radiation, but he denies there is radiation. His scientific advisors and cabinet members again.

He fills his ample chest, looks down to make sure his four-foot tie is ready for the TV cameras, checks that his open jacket is somewhat straight. He looks into his stylist's hand-held mirror to make sure his hair is combed and coiffured to his liking. He marches to the door ready to raise his arm to greet the cheering crowd and steps out——into nothing. Suddenly realizing it, the nothing that is, he grabs the side of the door and shouts, "Help."

He hangs there, his right hand bloodless from gripping the edge of the doorway, his ample belly bowed out over the tarmac. For a few seconds, those standing behind him freeze. Wavering doesn't know if it's the abruptness with which the president got himself into such an awkward posture. Or some subliminal undercurrent of doubt that suggests if he falls twenty feet to the snow-laced concrete and doesn't get up, the world might be better off. III quickly squelches that thought. It's the stylist who gets to him first. But the stylist is a ninety-pound woman who, if III's grip fails, will be jerked off the plane like a bait minnow on a hook. Another pilot and a cabin crewmember grab III's arm and with loud grunts haul him back into the plane.

"Where the hell are the stairs?" III bellows. The crew members look at each other. Bearers of bad news never fare well with the Flukes. Not that they'd be thrown off a cliff like Emperor Tiberius's cooks when they served up a meal that wasn't five star. But there was usually a period of non-appearance. Absent at meetings. Never spoken about. Phone calls not answered. Name removed from parking space, office cleaned out. When someone asked how to find the bad news messenger, office staff looked back puzzled and said, "Never heard of him."

3

With Fluke III and his cabinet of followers stymied in DC, their only alternative is the bunkers tunneled under the mountains of West Virginia. After the Air Force One crew convinced Fluke III there were no stairs and there were no bunkers he could occupy in DC, he shouted an angry "All right," marched into his luxury office and slammed the door.

Wavering starts Air Force One's engines, turns the plane around, taxies downwind, turns for takeoff. Clouds of snow blow across the beams of his landing lights. The drifts loom higher than when he landed. He spools up the engines to the red zone, throws on the afterburners—only AF One has afterburners—releases the brakes and crashes through drift after drift until they lift off, just before the runway runs out. Again, sweat drips from Wavering's face. He reminds himself he's experienced, but this kind of flying is closer to the edge than he likes.

With the ground-based Omni navigation system down and few signals transmitted from anywhere, Wavering relies on his onboard inertial navigation system to find the airport near the West Virginia bunkers. But he wouldn't want anybody to think landing there was like JFK with lights and runway markers and a manned control tower. No, when the INS shows they are at the field, they descend until Wavering can see flashing strobes at the approach end of the runway. It is hit and miss. Luckily, they hit.

The ground crew has plowed snow off the runway so Wavering has enough traction to bring the plane to a halt. He shuts down the main engines, and everyone waits while a line of black sports utility vehicles snakes up to the plane and the ground crew erects stairs for everyone to disembark. The ground crew thoughtfully brings hazmat suits so the passengers won't Hail Mary in the contaminated air as they leave the plane.

Augustus III looks at his hazmat suit with disgust. But he makes no comment and puts it on anyway. It stretches over his corpulent body like skin on a sausage. He huffs and puffs and sucks in with a grimace on his orange face while a ground crew member stuffs his oversize dark blue suit jacket and four foot red necktie inside the zipper that looks as if it is about to tear itself out of the suit.

As he is about to pass through the door to the frozen landscape, Augustus III turns to Wavering with a querulous look wrinkling his face. That look appears often, because frequently he seems to have little idea what he's doing or what he will do next. "You'll wait?" he asks.

"Wait?" Wavering replies a little too sharply to the president. That isn't what he anticipated. With snow piling up, if he waits, will he be able to get out? He's an airman, not bunker meat. "Why?" he adds. He was sure that once he got the president to the bunkers he would be released.

"I might need you."

"For what?" Wavering asks, his voice still too sharp for his liking, but he can't help himself. If the president thinks Wavering would leave the plane and join him underground, he has little idea who Wavering is. He doesn't go into bunkers or tunnels, any place that cuts him off from air and sky. Even though he feels the tug of loyalty to his commander-in-chief, he's just that way.

III's eyes float as if detached from his brain. Not unusual, Wavering notes, when III's moving into unknown territory. That unknown territory has come because III pushed the button, but Wavering assumes that to remind the president of that would not be well received. III's heading deep into a mountain to bunkers he's never seen that were prepared and supplied for him and his puppets in order to survive. He has shown Wavering the tall buildings he lived in, buildings with walls of glass. Some had vistas of beaches and golf courses, from some Wavering viewed other signature glass-walled buildings.

Gazing at the latter, III drifted into a trance as if gripped by a beatific vision. Devout religious believers in a trance said they saw the Virgin Mary. III had his epiphany staring at gold colored steel and bronzed glass and his name in bold capital letters. "Fluke West." "Fluke South." "Fluke Grand." "The Royal Fluke." "The Fluke." Apparently there were never enough Flukes to discourage him from building another.

Fluke's gaze narrows on Wavering. "In case I change my mind."

Wavering pauses. He glances out at the snow drifting on the tarmac Mind? In spite of Wavering's admiration for III, he has no history of seeing the president's mind focus on anything for more than a few seconds. It's as if he'd been born a mosquito. He seemed to live on and govern the country with nanosecond decisions written in etch-a-sketch. Thoughts, if you can call them that, were so quickly forgotten that Wavering concluded he lost many of them before they were uttered. But there was that mind ensconced in the orange skull of the man who bestowed upon himself the rare honor of destroying the world. Sure he would have made the biggest hit ever in the Guinness Book of World Records—if Guinness and its books and website hadn't been incinerated to ashes like everything else. But Wavering chides himself. What right does he have to question? III is the president and the greatest president ever. Everyone better believe it.

"What might your mind change to?" Wavering asks. He feels he's growing a mosquito mind himself. He is more than slightly uncomfortable commanding a large aircraft with snow swirling past the windshield and a sheen of ice building up on the wings.

Augustus's eyes float. It occurs to Wavering that the president might have developed a habit of number-painting himself through life. Now he has no spaces to fill in, no numbers to tell him what color to use, nothing to show him what is coming next. "In case I don't like it down there." He's referring to that inside-the-mountain bunker from which he and his cabinet of minions would govern what's left of the United States of America.

Wavering wonders what's the use of housing the cabinet in the bunker. As part of the Republican plan to reduce the size of government, cabinet departments were eliminated. Everything was consolidated under Augustus III, leaving the cabinet a vacuous cheering section to praise his accomplishments: "great, fabulous, tremendous, awesome, huge," whatever. Even for Wavering they got a bit boring after a while.

When the flow of adulation diminishes, III sinks into a sagging-jowls-sad-eyes funk, his face turns red, his voice rises, and he lashes out at whomever has the misfortune to be within range. When Wavering is flying him, he usually locks the cockpit door so that he doesn't have to deal with inclement weather up front and a possible Vesuvian eruption behind.

Shouldn't III know that unloading cosmic anger at your pilot while in flight is not a good idea? If he were a normal person, Wavering would assume so. But he doesn't seem to have any ability to put himself in Wavering's shoes. Does he put himself in anyone's shoes? Sometimes when they are landing, III will insist Wavering open the cockpit door to allow him to squeeze his bulging flesh into the narrow door frame and spout claims about the losers that make up his staff and how great the Russians are.

Wavering has not been to Russia, so he doesn't know how the great Russians are. Pilots who have been to Russia describe it as a wreck. Under Putin IV, the rich own ninety percent of the land, are building forty-thousand square foot Versailles mansions with gold trim, while in the countryside, the middle-class-now-become peasants till the ground and herd what cows and sheep and goats are left for milk and slaughter. They wield hoes and shovels so ancient they should be consigned to historical museums. The grain and vegetables and lambs and cattle and hogs they raise, the absentee landlords sell outside Russia, and leave the peasants with that immortal diet found under every delusional dictator: cabbage soup.

Wavering has not admitted it to anyone, but he has read books by Fyodor Dostoyevsky and Alexander Solzhenitsyn which immortalized that five star dish with their descriptions of life in the archipelago of prisons dotting the frozen frontiers of Siberia, prisons where thousands of prisoners died from malnutrition, exhaustion, and disease. Yes, the Russians are great, Augustus III, you've got that right. At least Wavering knows enough to be sarcastic, although he feels guilty about it.

So, if Augustus III isn't sure he'll like it down there in the bunker, how long will it take for his flitting mind to figure that out? And if it does, how long will the decision last? There have been countless times Wavering has flown him, and all through the flight he changed his mind about where he wanted to go. They were heading for Fluke Gold in Palm Beach. He got on the intercom: "New York. I want to go to New York. Fluke Taj Mahal."

"Copy that," Wavering said. He would bank Air Force One into a 180 degree turn.

Ten minutes later, the intercom again: "Fluke Monaco?" he says. "When were we last at Fluke Monaco?" Wavering holds off replying, because he can't remember. And flying to Monaco from over Virginia isn't a short hop. "It's revenues are down, did you know that?" III asks.

"No," Wavering says. Although he has heard III trashing his

cabinet as if they masterminded the decline. They just sat as still as wax figures and gazed at him. They didn't speak. Why, Wavering wondered? Why were they so speechless that they no longer seemed to know who they were or what they were supposed to do?

As Wavering looked at their sullen faces, he didn't know whether to be angry because they were so spineless or to feel sorry for them because Augustus III had beaten their brains into oatmeal. Didn't they have just a little self-respect that would prompt them not to hunch their backs with their eyes tracing the floor? Wavering saw no sign of it. They stooped silently until III's mind flitted off to something else.

Then Wavering wondered about himself. How would the cabinet members describe him? Yes, III's word was his command. But III is the president. Wavering worked for him. So you did what the boss said. Was there anything wrong with that?

To Monaco they went. Thank goodness the Air Force radioed there was a refueling plane offshore. They rendezvoused, tucked the flying boom into the receptacle in Air Force One's nose, and drank until the gauges said the tanks were full. The copilot and Wavering were bleary-eyed and not prepared to cross the Atlantic to the Mediterranean, but that bothered Augustus III not at all. He had his king bed and valet and the TVs on which he ran videos showing himself speaking to large rallies or marching what he deemed presidentially around the oval office. There was also one of Putin IV with his gray Ban-Lon shirt stretched so tightly over his torso you couldn't miss his muscles flexing as he met Augustus with fist thumping, arm-in-arm greetings.

III stands in the open doorway in his hazmat suit as if he's developed rigor mortis. "There's that rocket, isn't there?" he asks. He's thinking about the Genesis rocket located in North Dakota. He authorized it to be built and got it funded as a Noah's ark in case the planet was threatened. To Wavering, with Air Force

One's wings icing up, snow blasting past the plane's lights, and the smell of smoke drifting through the door because much of the air is smoke, he doesn't feel just threatened. As one interviewed expert said on an unauthorized TV channel, "We are doomed. The whole planet is doomed." Whether Wavering should believe what he said or not, he doesn't know, but he's having a hard time mustering optimism.

Wavering answers, "Yes, the rocket is there." The rocket is such an unknown he hopes III will get off the subject quickly. Piloting a rocket is like piloting an airplane. It takes reality. As Wavering looks at the face peering at him through the hazmat helmet, he wonders if he is seeing reality. What would Wavering do with III on board a spacecraft for a long period of time? An idle thought. But a thought, nevertheless.

III casts Wavering a pained look, the orange color of his face fades. "I've never flown in a rocket."

"There's a lot of risk, Sir," Wavering says. "A lot of risk. That rocket has never been tested." Wavering knows 'risk' is not III's cup of tea.

A flight attendant pushes the plane door partially closed to keep out the wind and snow and smoke. Wavering can see III's mind churning between life in a concrete bunker under a frozen mountain and life in a rocket hurtling through space to some place that doesn't have his name on it. If Wavering told him the destination was Galaxy Fluke and a planet named Fluke, he would jump at it. But Wavering is not going to flatter him with a galaxy or anything else out there because if he has to pilot the rocket, he would prefer to leave earth and forget there was a Fluke or buildings that bore his name in bold capital letters.

Wavering isn't sure what prompts III to open the door of Air Force One and depart, but he does. Probably just an impulse. Hasta la vista, Señor Presidente. Or something like that.

4

Wavering sits in the pilot's seat of Air Force One, drinking a cup of coffee made by a member of the cabin crew. But he doesn't sit well. He's kept the plane where it stopped to let III go to the bunker, but he hasn't fully shut it down. He runs the generator giving the plane light and heat and power to start the main engines.

Looking down from his side window, he sees one black SUV—the ground crew waiting for some word from August III. They might rush off with siren blaring and lights flashing to retrieve the president. Why they need the siren and lights when there's nobody on any road, Wavering doesn't know. Or other vehicles will bring III back to the plane. Or the ground crew will use what deicer they have left to make Air Force One airworthy, and Wavering will take off for North Dakota, sans III. He looks at his watch, shakes it. Has it stopped? The longer Air Force One delays, the more likely III will return. And the harder it will be for Air Force One to take off.

Even though Wavering knows the risks Genesis poses, he would give it a try. There's no plan B if the rocket fails, he knows that. But a concrete bunker underground in which he would live for how many years, he cannot imagine. The air everywhere is so radioactive no one has been able to calculate how long it will take for conditions to clear enough to allow life above ground to resume.

And to be in that bunker with Augustus III? Wavering tells himself he should feel gratitude to be in the presence of one of the greatest men ever. But there's a voice somewhere in his head, it's

III's voice accusing others of plotting against him. Wavering envisions III's bulging eyes glaring at those around him, eyes searching out a suspect for leaking news, for criticizing III, or for not adoring the great man. Wavering tries to muster hope that life in the bunker would be uplifting, but something nefarious warns him that it wouldn't be. But he also wonders, if you're imprisoned in an underground warren for who knows how long, is there any more 'down' that you would have to absorb? Could things be worse than they are?

A line of three SUVs, sirens screaming and emergency lights blazing, materializes out of the fog and snow and slides to a stop at the foot of the embarkation stairs. Wavering looks down holding his breath. The doors open, nine animated hazmat suits emerge from the vehicles and stumble toward the stairs. Wavering continues to hold his breath hoping Augustus III isn't one of them. Why does he feel that way? He should be ready to plunge into despair if III denies Wavering his company. Two of the passengers fill and stretch their suits the way III does, Wavering's out-of-control apprehension grows. He's gripped by an inexplicable urge to start the main engines and escape.

When the passengers finally board the plane and slide off their suits, Wavering is breathing again. Five men, four women and no III. Is Wavering done with him? He looks in the direction from which the SUVs came. Will another burst out of the frozen dark and III squeeze out of it and head for the plane? Wavering gets on the radio and orders the ground crew to deice as quickly as possible.

They mount the truck, turn on the nozzles, and splash Air Force One with deicer. But they move in slow motion. Streams of spray crawl out a wing, pause as if the crew doesn't know what to do next. Are they hoping Augustus III will be driven up and head for the plane so they won't have to put up with him in the bunker? If only III could realize how those who adore him have these uncontrollable, creeping doubts, but not a chance. In his mind, The whole world loves me. Loves me. Of course that was when there was a whole world. Now that he has reduced it to radioactive dust and ice and a handful of admirers, Wavering wonders if he realizes the adoration has diminished.

As soon as the deicing finishes and the trucks pull off the tarmac, Wavering starts the engines and taxis to the leeward end of the runway. He sees in the landing lights that snow has drifted across the runway, but he's not about to wait for it to be plowed. He locks the brakes, spools up the engines, fires the afterburners—the noise is deafening—suddenly releases the brakes and blasts the big plane into the air. As a former flight instructor, he knows he's broken a few cautions. So what.

As the plane lifts off and landing lights dim in the black fog, Wavering realizes he didn't say goodbye to Augustus III. Nor him to Wavering. Wavering wonders what his last words would have been. Auf Wiedersehen? Until we meet again? Sorry, no. Bon voyage? To a bunker? Oh well.

5

Piloting Air Force One over several years, Wavering frequently overheard those counseling Augustus Fluke III on nuclear war. They would rattle into his ear as if their advice was the final word: "Nuclear war won't be too bad. A few cities bombed. Mushroom clouds here and there. A few days of cloudy weather. Call it collateral damage. Bad but necessary. It'll blow over. Life will resume where it left off. A dose of radiation might help make people more resistant if there's another nuclear exchange." Cheery stuff. But since Wavering didn't know whether to believe it or not, he dismissed the advice as idle chatter. But now, well into a nuclear winter that shows no signs of easing, he bristles a bit at III's advisors and at III himself. How could they have been so misinformed? But does he have the right to ask?

To stave off depression, he strives to paint a more cheerful picture of his North Dakota residence——Motel Aurora Borealis. Shangri La, it is not. Brown faux pine board and pink faux limestone exterior, outside room doors peeling brown paint. It has an interior swimming pool, but they drained the pool. With the world a smoking ruin and most people dead, nobody felt like splashing about as if they were having fun. Plus they didn't trust that the water wasn't contaminated.

So they turned the pool room into their sitting room. White plastic chairs at two plastic tables on the concrete apron. Scattered chaise lounges reminding them there was once a time when the sun shone and people baked themselves under it. What they have now is only what they need. As are the cartons and cans, some stacked

34

in the swimming pool, others stored in the missile control bunker five hundred feet below them——cans and cartons that contain the only food they can find to keep themselves alive.

The plastic windows that arch over the pool give them their view of out there. Out there, the sun doesn't rise. It hasn't for so many days they've lost track. Lost track, even, of what a rising sun looks like. At least the sun as a ball of fire climbing off a green horizon into a blue sky. The sky now is a pall of gray haze, the sun a ghost of brighter haze that crawls from east to west and withers to the west leaving the sky coal-mine black. There's no moon, there are no stars. They blinked out when everyone stopped seeing the sunrise.

Wavering sits in the pool room memorizing the charts and manuals for the space journey he looks forward to, yet dreads. He's spread them out on one of the plastic tables. The air is warm from heat they are able to draw from the electrical grid. Wavering glances out the windows at the frozen tundra lying beneath the haze. Is it real? Does he have the ability to pretend the haze isn't ice particles, the frost that crawls in from the edges of the windows at night isn't frost? Maybe he can work himself into a disembodied state and not notice the snow he has to thrash through when he walks from the motel to the missile bunker entrance.

Sarcasm returns and overpowers him. He's angry, he knows he shouldn't be, but he can't help it. Thank you Emperor Augustus Fluke III, he voices to himself. Thank you for whatever the hell you did to grab the football and launch what you later called a 'prudent warning strike.' Did you really believe your explanation of what followed? No damage done? Don't worry? It's just the fake media? You yourself, Mr. President, you blamed your intelligence agencies because they didn't inform you that just one warhead would wipe out a radius of five miles and kill a million people. Multiply that times the hundreds of bombs and missiles you and the countries that retaliated set off, and what do you get? Are the neurons in your skull so torpid you couldn't begin to understand?

Then Wavering sinks into humiliation. That mind of his. Why can't he control it? He needs help. He needs to get into the world of August III and stay there. But III is more than a thousand miles away in a bunker in West Virginia.

6

The rooms at Motel Aurora Borealis are not up to Ritz Carlton standards. The nightstand next to Wavering's bed is veneered in peeling faux maple, pockmarked with circles made by drink-glasses. The phone rings. It's antique beige plastic with buttons that stick. Push down 9, and you get 99999. He picks up the handset and puts it to the earpiece in his hazmat helmet. The handset is wired to its base. Waves of remodeling have washed over Borealis as if they never happened. He and the others wear hazmat suits most of the time because they are wary of radiation. On the phone, an ominous computer robot: "A reminder from the office: check-out time is 11 AM."

Does he thank the robot? Is that important information? If he doesn't check out by eleven, what will happen? Who or what would know when or if he checked out? He hears his own voice of complaint and winces. He needs to get a grip. On what?

The phone rings again. He hesitates to pick it up. Maybe robo has an in-room camera or a hidden microphone and is upset because he's not leaving. The phone persists. All right. "Berwick here," the voice at the other end announces pontifically. Berwick? Ah yes. The trillionaire Fluke selected for Genesis to transport to another planet. A trillionaire?

"Wavering here," he replies. He doesn't know why he says 'here,' unless it's a useless echo he's picked up from Berwick. He means he wouldn't likely say 'there,' although he'd like to. Because then he wouldn't have to answer calls from Berwick. He thinks he's becoming what some might call 'antisocial.' Is that bad? He doesn't

37

know.

"Good," Berwick says. "I want you to meet me in the sunroom." The sunroom? The sunroom with no sun? Is his imagination so overstimulated he actually thinks there's sun in the sunroom? Wavering could tell him, Berwick, there's no sun. Haven't you noticed? Then again, Berwick is like Fluke III. No one can tell him anything.

When Wavering arrives, Berwick occupies a white plastic picnic chair, leaning forward in anticipation. A large belly from too many five-star dinners and too little exercise, white hair glued back on his round head as if combed by a wind tunnel, staccato motions to his hands and arms as if he's chopping wood or bone. When he speaks, Wavering knows he wants a gleam of admiration in his eyes to assure Berwick that he's a superior human being and Wavering subservient. Since Wavering is one of Augustus Fluke III's pilots, he knows he has the same status as one of Berwick's chauffeurs, butlers, valets, cooks, gardeners, and all the rest.

Berwick eyes Wavering hopefully. "So," he challenges, "Is this the day?"

"The day?" Wavering replies.

"For the launch. What else would I be waiting for?"

"Oh. The launch." Wavering knows Berwick is not a man who's used to waiting—for anything. "Same answer as before. I don't know."

Berwick shifts about in the chair flexing under his weight as if he cannot get comfortable. Wavering knows he can't. How he must miss the horsehide easy chair at his gentlemen's club. "Don't know?"

"Rocket launches are always 'don't know,'" Wavering replies. "Until she's fueled and all systems check out on 'Go,' she's 'don't know.' There's the weather, too."

"I can't stand these delays," Berwick grumbles. "I'm tired of being trapped in this dump of a motel clowning around in this damned suit. It makes me feel like I'm in a circus. I'm ready to go to the stars." His eyes glow as if he sees the upcoming space journey as a jaunt to the Riviera, or to some exotic tropical island with grass houses on stilts and scantly clad native girls serving him piña coladas.

Wavering doesn't want to say anything to tarnish Berwick's disillusions. Even though he knows that when they are in flight and empty space envelops them, the experience will be about as luxurious as diving 60 fathoms into a lightless ocean abyss protected by nothing but a bikini bathing suit.

Wavering has already gone through all of Berwick's anxieties with him. Space debris, yes, everywhere. Asteroids? Them, too. Big, how big? As small as a piece of gravel, although Wavering guesses that's debris. Or as big as Berwick's Bentley. Bigger? Berwick asks. How big? The biggest? Wavering really doesn't know, so he makes it up. Manhattan Island, he says. Or maybe Great Britain. Enough to put a dent in the rocket. That is understatement. If they get hit by a two pound rock at galactic velocities, they'll be blown into millions of pieces the size of fleas.

Berwick turns away with a sour look on his face, his shoulders drawn in a huff. He seems averse to not knowing something. Worse yet perhaps, knowing there is something, but he cannot control it. He had to have control to amass his trillion dollars. He owned or was fronted by a thousand private companies, corporations, LLP's, LLC's, you name it. Plus a staff of hundreds to keep track of them all, especially to make sure they made profits that flowed into Berwick's pockets.

But Wavering doesn't pull Berwick back from whatever looking glass he's entered. President Augustus Fluke III chose Berwick to be one of the survivors of earth to travel to another planet—perhaps to begin life by setting up a stock market and trading in imaginary commodities? Commodities? On another planet? Oh well. Wavering chides himself because his mind is wandering again.

Berwick accosts Wavering. "What the hell is this planet we're going to?" he asks.

Wavering can tell Berwick wants him to answer as if he's reading text from a four-color brochure. Or Wavering can show him an infomercial extolling the highlights: sandy beaches, coral atolls, breeze-rustled coconut palm trees rich with fruit, those bronzed girls who twirl in happy dancing.

'Course now, on earth, coral has turned to stone the color of dead bones with no living creatures darting about its fissures. Palm trees are blackened telephone poles with no leaves and no branches. And the girls, well they're like the rest of the population of planet earth, composting somewhere in preparation for the rise of a new creation and the coming of another race of upright-standing-big-brained creatures who will develop an 'advanced' civilization.

"The planet is Proxima b," Wavering says.

"Another earth?" Berwick asks.

"No," Wavering replies.

"Mars? Mercury? Not Jupiter, I hope?"

The real answer is that Wavering doesn't know. But he does know that kind of answer does not satisfy trillionaire Berwick. "I've never been there," Wavering says.

Berwick's face reddens. "Well hell, I know you haven't been there. Nobody's been there. But you must know something." He pauses to catch his breath. His belly and lungs exaggerate his exertions.

"It looks rocky. But it's not like planets we know. It's year is eleven days, that's how long it takes for one orbit of its sun."

"Wow," Berwick replies. "Eleven days. Think of the killing you could make on Wall Street with eleven day years." Berwick's eyes grow big, but Wavering can't tell what his mind sees. He has no idea why short years would bring Berwick more cabbage than he harvested from Wall Street on earth. Does he really need it? Isn't a trillion dollars enough? But Wavering doesn't say anything. For Berwick, it seems only natural to believe there is more loot to reel in. And reel in.

"Then it must rotate like a top," Berwick observes.

Wavering pauses.

"Well, does it? How long is it's day?" Berwick asks.

"It's day is a bit different," Wavering replies.

"Different? What the hell does that mean?"

"Its day is forever." Wavering pauses to let it sink in, if it will sink in. "So is its night."

Berwick scrutinizes Wavering's face as if he's lost his mind. Wavering knows he sounds like he has. "Forever? What the hell does that mean?" Berwick asks.

"It doesn't spin. The same half always faces its sun, the other half is always dark."

"You're sure?"

"That's what the astrophysicists told me."

Berwick sinks deeper into his plastic chair. "Then how will we get any sleep? If we're on that dark side, how do we wake up? That's the damnedest thing I ever heard." He breathes deeply to control his rising frustration. "Who decided we'd go there in the first place?"

"You did, Sir," Wavering replies.

"Never," Berwick barks. "I would never agree to a place like that."

"You did when you were told that the next nearest possibly habitable planet was thirteen light years instead of four. You said you couldn't wait thirteen years."

Berwick pauses. His jowls sag, his eyes lose focus and wander about. "Yeah, I guess I did say that."

Wavering looks at Berwick's sagging frame. Amazing what the memory will do—sometimes.

7

"This place is a dump," says Jimmy Jones, his nose elevated high in the air. He's referring to Motel Aurora Borealis. He calls himself The Reverend Doctor Jimmy Jones, his position——head minister of The Only Gospel Church. Before The Great Tribulation, it had been one of those multi-mega churches in Dallas, Texas. It claimed it reached fifty million people every Sunday. Of course there were over a dozen of those churches scattered about the country, and all claimed to reach 50 million people. Yes, the United States truly became a religious nation.

Actually, the United States became so religious that in 2045 Fluke Junior, or was it Fluke II, established the evangelical form of Christianity as the official national religion. It along with Roman Catholicism was established. Everything else was dis-established, which meant banned.

Jewish temples, Muslim temples, Sikh temples, Hindu temples, Buddhist temples, they were converted into restaurants: India House, Thai Satay, Olive Garden, Super Szechwan. Or shopping malls featuring flagship stores such as Nordstrom, Amazon, Niemen Marcus, and Apple. Some became 30-room French chateau mansions for billionaires, or Going Home Funeral parlors. Mormons, transmogrified into Latter Day Saints, had to trash their Joseph Smith myths and swear to the evangelical creed. They were allowed to keep their temple in Salt Lake City, but it was converted into a mega church with a TV ministry.

When Wavering watched TV broadcasts from the mega churches' worship services——with heavy-drum rock bands and leisure-suited preachers, he couldn't tell whether the larger priority was getting him saved, or his sending in money so he would receive God's blessing and the evangelist fund his Leer jet, six-place Sikorsky helicopter, and one-thousand-waterfront-foot sandy-beach villa in the Cayman islands that might have been less modest than what Jesus would have. Those accoutrements bothered Wavering, but he was assured God's messengers needed to look successful in order to be taken seriously.

Years before, there had been hysteria over the threat that Islam would take over the United States with propaganda and terrorist attacks, and Muslims would set up sharia law as they had in the Middle East. Fox News, Fox Business News, Fox Entertainment, Fox Kids World, everything Fox had their talking heads jabbering so loudly about the threat of Mosques with 5 AM public calls to prayer and women wrapped in burkas that Muslims were rounded up—usually by Gestapo-like strongmen—and thrown into internment camps. As were Japanese citizens during World War II. Actually, some of the camps were built in the very locations used for those Japanese citizens.

So, instead of Islamic sharia law, the United States had evangelical sharia law. Punishable crimes: being accused by anyone of being gay—not practicing, but being, no evidence needed other than an accusation. Being accused of being bisexual or transgender. Preachers and the Flukes and their chorus said sexual orientation was a choice—if you could choose to be gay, then you could choose to be not gay. It was as simple as being for or against the New York Yankees.

Those who were found 'being?' The camps. Camps that started with a few summer-type huts expanded to high rise apartments that kept popping up until they spread over thousands of acres. Most of them were dispersed in desolate deserts in Nevada, California, Arizona, and New Mexico. Since they were run by private companies which were doing so well running prisons, nobody was willing to admit what they suspected: once people made the wrong choice about their sexual orientation, they were incarcerated in the camps indefinitely. Where they were put to work writing anti-gay leaflets and newspapers, printing banners, billboards, bus stop placards, bus placards, and making TV commercials warning people against making the wrong choice.

City and state governments and the federal government paid handsomely for these placards and commercials, so the for-profit camp corporations made a nice profit. Everybody was happy, especially the investors who held stock in the sexual reorientation camps. Although gay, transgender, and bisexual people were not happy. Which delighted the rest of the people, because they were convinced that people who commit the sin of being something they should not be should not be happy.

Wavering quietly accommodated himself to his evangelical faith. He feels no embarrassment, he's doing what everyone else does. Being evangelical is just part of being an American, or a member of the white race. To get him his faith, his mother marched him to a huge evangelical church every Sunday where he was reminded that he had to be born again, washed in the blood of Jesus, and filled with the Holy Spirit—although he had difficulty understanding 'spirit' or 'holy'—or he would be cast into an unpleasant country with worms that never died and fires that never burned out. And live there forever. Worms eating and fires burning. He couldn't wait to hit the aisle that led to the front of the church where he could cry, which he did, and say, "Yes, Yes. I believe." Although he had no clear idea what he believed. He just didn't want to spend a lot of time with worms and fire that did not die. Worms weren't too bad, but he didn't even like hot days.

Like all evangelicals who also were the core backers of the Fluke regimes and eventually imposed their sharia law, he believed the whole nine yards, the whole package, whatever you want to call it. The core was evangelical interpretation of the Bible: Every word in every book of the Bible is the Word of God.

When the Bible said creation took six days, six sunrises and six sundowns it was. Monday through Saturday with God resting on Sunday. Wavering didn't know what God did on Sunday. But for him and his family, his mother cancelled his father's Sunday subscription to the newspaper, Wavering was not allowed to watch TV. She told him he was to think holy thoughts and rest. To him, Sunday seemed six sunrises and six sundowns long. Mysteriously they ignored the likely fact that God started on a Sunday, worked through Friday, and took Saturday off. That went out the window with banned Judaism, Seventh Day Adventist-ism, and a few other -isms. But that was OK. What difference does one day make six thousand years later?

As the Word of God, the Bible's sixty-six individual books were fused into one infallible tome so that every word and every part had equal weight as 'The Word of God.' So cutting off the offensive hand in Leviticus was equal to Jesus' 'Love your neighbor.' And Old Testament patriarchs with concubines were equal to Jesus' prohibition of divorce. How, someone other than Wavering might ask? Only they didn't ask, and neither did Wavering. To do so was to unmask yourself as a 'doubter.'

Not that evangelicals avoided having concubines or did not divorce. When Wavering in a paroxysm of doubt went to his minister to ask about these things, he said, "The Bible only sets standards. They're so high nobody can keep them." He paused and his liquid gaze sized up Wavering's soul. "That's why everyone needs to be saved from sin. You've got to be washed in the blood and made pure for the flight to meet Jesus in the air."

That washing of the soul for the aerial meeting was what Wavering's mega church and the other mega churches were about.

Preachers ever reiterated, "You've got to get closer to Jesus. Oh Jesus, we love you. But we are mortal. We struggle. Help us get close to you. Oh Jesus. My savior. My friend." They would cue the choir, and it would break into 'What a Friend We Have in Jesus.' Members of the congregation wept and wailed.

No matter how much Wavering threw himself into the prayers and songs, he never felt he quite arrived at knowing Jesus. He wasn't sure he knew what knowing Jesus was. How wondered how he would he know when he got there? So he got more dependent on his mega church, and his mother kept putting monetary offerings into the collection plate. In attacks of weakness, Wavering's mind wandered. Was she helping people know Jesus, or was she providing welfare for the preacher's Learjet, his helicopter, and the Cayman 'spiritual retreat' that advertised as a training camp for up and coming mega church preachers? He never revealed to her his blasphemous thoughts. She would label him a 'doubter,' and his name would be added to the prayer list at the mega church.

Every person who was saved had a life plan God had worked out in advance, in eternity actually. The preacher thundered, "Everything that happens to you is God's will. Everything. All worked out in advance before you were born." Somewhere those assurances stuck in the craw of Wavering's soul. He knew families where the mother died. A husband ran off with a concubine. A mountain exploded in the Caribbean and killed 30,000 inhabitants. Wars in the Mideast displaced millions of refugees. Well, he didn't feel for them because they were Muslims. God had nothing to do with Muslims. But if you were a Christian, no matter what happened to you or what you did, God's will. Wavering told himself to stop asking, to stop questioning. As the preachers said, these are matters of faith. You don't reason them, you believe them.

He also finally convinced himself to believe that doing nothing for anybody else could be God's will. In a convulsion of enthusiasm after he was converted, he read the Gospel accounts of the life of Jesus. The lepers, those called 'sinners,' a tax collector—he had to be especially bad, people sick from bleeding, some so lame they couldn't walk, that crazy-acting guy where the pigs ran into the Sea of Galilee and drowned themselves, Jesus helped them all. He said, "Love your neighbor and do good to those who hate you."

Wavering understood that Jesus had enemies who sought to do him in. But they weren't the Muslims or gays or immigrants or liberals that had been such a scourge before the evangelical faith and the Fluke succession of presidents came along. They were the holy men who hung around synagogues and the temple in Jerusalem. Religious people. What a shock that was. Wavering couldn't resist raising a question about that, but instead of an answer, he was quickly branded as a doubter. Or a backslider— church officials didn't specify, and he didn't know which was worse. Being ignored by leaders in the church, he learned that he was more reprobate than an atheist. Oh well, he thought. But he still hung on to the only faith he knew. To do so was to be a good American. And the Flukes only wanted good Americans to be on their staffs, in their cabinet, and flying their planes.

8

The launch team is taking a long time to ready Genesis for flight, so there's a lot of down time for Wavering and his flight crew. When Wavering isn't below ground in the launch center, all he sees when he's outside or looking out a widow in Aurora Borealis is the relentless gray, blowing snow, frost creating random patterns on windows. Occasionally he reminds himself that III said the conditions are temporary. Soon planet earth will return to what it was. But in the relentless snow and frost, Wavering can see no sign of that.

He's having a quiet reading time in the swimming pool room when Berwick shoves his bulk through the door with new worry wrinkles lining his forehead. Wavering can tell Proxima b is eating a hole in his brain. They'll be hurtling toward a planet that Wavering can't guarantee will work out for them. Since Berwick is, or was, worth over a trillion dollars, he might be wondering if the money will do him any good. Flying through space to a planet he can't know anything about might be a risk beyond his normal portfolio.

Berwick sits down and impales him. "Tell me about that planet's sun," he says.

That's another one of the many questions Wavering has been dreading. Wavering wishes Berwick would get off their destination and just take what will come. "Proxima Centauri?" he replies. "Is that what you're referring to?"

"Centauri? That's what it's called? Sounds like a brand of car," Berwick replies. "Although that 'proxima' makes it sound like it doesn't know what it is."

"Proxima Centauri is a red dwarf," Wavering blurts. Might as well get the bad news out there.

Berwick's face twists into a scowl. "A red dwarf? I don't like the sound of that. Can you imagine what investors will do when I try to sell them something called a 'red dwarf?'" He shifts about and rolls his head as if his neck muscles are seizing up. He casts Wavering a hard look. "What the hell is a red dwarf?"

Wavering runs several combinations of words through his mind to see what might prevent the conversation from digging a deeper hole, but all he's left with is to describe it for what it is. "It's a dying star."

"A dying star?" Berwick shouts, his face burning redder than telescope pictures Wavering's seen of red dwarfs. His cheeks quiver. "We're going to a planet with a dying star? A planet with no sunrise or sunset, eternal day on one side, eternal night on the other? It flies around its dying sun every eleven days? This is absolutely the best those astro boys could come up with?"

"At a near-enough distance to reach on your timeline," Wavering replies.

"Well," Berwick scoffs. He pauses. "Maybe I could sink in a hundred billion and get that damned planet to spin." He looks at Wavering as if he has divine insight. "Can that be done?"

Wavering thinks of all he knows about Proxima b, and the prospects don't look good. "If we could get it hit by an asteroid, maybe," he replies. "But the asteroid could also destroy the planet, so that might not be a good idea."

Berwick shrinks three inches and blows out air like a punctured blimp. Wavering says, "I'd like to be more encouraging, but when we get there, I don't want to cause you disappointment."

Berwick glares at him. "Disappointment? You already have caused disappointment. Total disappointment. This trip may be the worst investment I ever made in my life." His glare turns to accusation, as if Wavering created a planet that doesn't spin and has an eleven-day year and is orbiting a dying star that is unmarketably called 'red dwarf.'

Wavering thinks about how this whole journey will be proxima, approximate, the chances being slim that they will arrive at Proxima b and the women on board will have babies and they will start a new human race. As Wavering thinks about a 'new human race,' his mind clouds up with fog. Really?

9

The Reverend Doctor Jimmy Jones and Wavering sit next to the empty swimming pool. Why they sit next to the pool when there is no sun, and the pool empty, Wavering doesn't know. Except there's no other place in Borealis that offers any space with a modicum of comfort. They have to shout loudly through the helmets in their hazmat suits, so Jones's words reverberate with a muffled echo.

To many comments Wavering makes or questions he raises, Jones pontifically pronounces, "You are entirely wrong."

"On what basis?" Wavering asks. He knows Jones has already pigeonholed his asking questions as a clear sign he is lost. But Jones doesn't shun him as many other preachers would because maybe he thinks Wavering can be retrieved into his gospel.

"On the basis that you don't know your Bible. The Bible says it is infallible, the Bible says it is the Word of God. You are speaking against the Bible." Jones inflates his generous chest beneath the hazmat suit, revealing the collar of the baby blue suit he was wearing when the world ended. Baby blue suit jacket with pink tie. Wavering assumes everyone has their tastes.

Wavering sighs. "Where does the Bible say it is infallible?" he asks.

"Paul to Timothy, every word inspired by God."

Wavering pauses waiting for more, but it does not come. He knows that verse from his reading. "Inspired doesn't mean infallible," he says. " I can be inspired to write something, but that doesn't mean it's infallible. Inspiration is quickening the creative juices. Yes, God inspired, as God inspired Pascal and Augustine and Beethoven and Bach and others. There's no connection between inspiration and perfection."

Wavering might as well be talking to the motel's frozen flagpole dangling American and Christian flags encased in ice. Jones shuts his eyes as if he's drifting off to another planet, which they all will do in a few days with their eyes open. Has Jones mastered the trick of psychological dissociation so that he doesn't hear the question? He makes no response.

"You know," Wavering says, "the Bible was written in a pre-scientific age, so its science isn't science. You can't make millions-of-years-old rocks in six days, six thousand years ago. You can't make billions of galaxies and stars and planets and all the rest in one earthly week." Even as he speaks, Wavering cringes inside himself. He can't rid himself of the tendency to break down the wall that separates what his mind tells him and what he's supposed to believe. He just should never have taken science courses. And his penchant to read scientific articles is polluting his mind against the faith.

Jones casts him a look that he must reserve for a yellow jacket threatening to sting him. By the way, those yellow jackets survived the human-caused apocalypse and still enjoy themselves by stinging whatever they can find that is left of the human race. "It's the word of God, boy," he says. He likes to call Wavering 'boy' so he won't miss his condescension. Wavering knows it's the word Jones still uses for what he calls 'colored' people. Jones puts his chaise lounge back, stretches out, perches sunglasses over his hazmat suit visor to protect his eyes from the sun that isn't there, and breaks into loud snores.

Wavering looks at God's slumbering whale and wonders— does Jones really bend his mind to affirm what he says, as he would if he were a sociopath? Or is he a con man who discovered years ago that his version of the Bible produces so many adoring followers and such a solid budget for his Learjet and red Lamborghini that he keeps fueling his gospel that Wavering believes was mutated from the Jesus of the gospels because it benefits him? Wavering could ask him, but he knows the answer. He would be labeled a son of perdition, and only someone from the devil would ask such a question.

10

Wavering sees through the glass door of the pool room a shadow approaching. He quickly slides his e-reader into the pack of manuals and charts for spacecraft navigation lying on the table before him. He's reading Victor Hugo's "The Hunchback of Notre dame." It's not on the evangelical sharia list of approved books and thus banned.

The door opens, and Berwick rolls in with a gleam in his eyes. Wavering hopes he's been drinking, not thinking. But it's early. Wavering knows Berwick's hoarding a decent supply of Scotch, but his gait is steady, his eyes crosshair on Wavering. "I've been thinking," Berwick says. He sits down in a plastic chair, which bends under his weight. "This planet, what is it, proximate something?"

"Proxima b," Wavering says with a sigh that he has to go through this ritual every time Berwick raises the subject.

"Proxima b. Right. I've been thinking. You said it's made of rock. Is that right?"

"I said it's rock because the astrophysicists said they think it's rock. I don't know what it is. They launched a flyby years ago, but it's slower than we will be. It has over twenty years before it reaches the planet. We have nothing to go on but telescope images, light pulses, reflected light. They suggest some gases and rock, but they're not guaranteed."

Berwick cocks his head. Wavering guesses that means he's still thinking. "Well, let's say it is rock. Rock? Do you know what that means?"

All Wavering can think is that it means rock. Rock is rock. "No," he replies softly.

"Minerals," Berwick almost shouts. "Do you realize Proximate b might be loaded with minerals? And it has never been mined? We may be headed for a thousand mother lodes that will make the California gold rush look like an Easter egg hunt. Do you realize that?" His eyes bulge as if they might explode from the voltage of expectation.

Wavering hears Berwick's voice, but nothing in him stirs. Minerals? A gold rush? All Wavering sees are the challenges of survival: is the planet habitable? Can he land Genesis safely? Is there water? Is there air? Might the place be so toxic they all die instantly? And if the planet is rock, how do they plant seeds to sustain life? The crucial question is whether they will live or die. Rushing off to dig into Proxima b's rocks or whatever is there and starting a gold rush? He can't take such an idea with any seriousness.

Berwick looks at Wavering as if he's reading his mind. "Gold," Berwick repeats with puffed oversize chest. "Do you realize what that would mean? Tons of it?" He pauses. "Platinum, too. Diamonds. This may be the greatest strike in human history." He pauses as if blinded by a flash of transcendent light. "Ours. All ours."

Wavering looks at him sitting there and feels he's watching one of those old movies of aliens from another planet landing on earth. Aliens who can't connect in look or language or anything else. Gold, platinum, diamonds? How do they help the Genesis crew land and survive on Proxima b?

Berwick can see on Wavering's face that he's under-impressed with what excites Berwick. "Do you know what a trove like that would bring on the world market?"

"World market?" Wavering remarks. "What market? What

world?"

Berwick shrinks like a deflating blimp, his cheeks sag, his chest collapses. He casts Wavering a strange stare. "You're not very upbeat about this, are you?"

Wavering knows Berwick would love to convert him to his mineral religion. He's that type. "I have a lot on my mind," Wavering says evasively.

Berwick isn't listening. He gets up, rotates slowly in his black patent leather shoes and heads for the door. He pauses. "That preacher guy. Now he's upbeat. He says the streets of heaven are paved with gold. Maybe heaven is our Proximate b? Did you ever think of that?"

"No, I can't say that I have," Wavering says. Even in his days as an unquestioning evangelical believer, streets paved with gold seemed like too much gold. Better than blacktop or concrete, he'll grant, but he likes bricks and those pavers that Europe had and America took on. Although he can see Berwick happily driving down streets paved with gold in his gold Bentley. "But," Wavering adds hopefully, "If you think the preacher's got something, go for it."

Berwick looks at Wavering as if he's an alien. He scoffs, bangs open the door and is gone. Wavering's body becomes lighter, stress eases, the muscles in his neck release their tension, the headache that was creeping across his cranium recedes.

But then Wavering thinks. Sixteen years of Berwick on Genesis? The headache clamps again onto his forehead.

11

Dr. Drone saunters to poolside in his hazmat suit with a red cross emblazoned across his chest. Dr. Drone is a wiry man with premature gray hair whose medical credentials are still hazy to Wavering. But he is Berwick's personal physician, so he is the one anointed to accompany the crew on its journey to Proxima b.

Berwick is obsessed with staying in good health, quite a feat when he weighs in at 300 pounds and eats twice as much as everyone else. Every day, Dr. Drone pulls out his instruments and checks Berwick's blood pressure, oxygen level, temperature, thumps his chest and back to make sure he's breathing properly, and takes an eeg to assure that electrical charges are flashing across his neurons. When Berwick drones on about stock markets and hedge funds and gold streets and the like, Wavering wonders what signals his brain sends to Dr. Drone. Or are there any signals at all?

Berwick is generous in offering the rest of the crew the same tests, but they decline, at least to take them daily. Once a month is good enough, at least for Wavering. His Holiness the Reverend Doctor Jones waves off any tests saying, "The will of the Lord be done."

Dr. Drone also holds up a meter to check the toxicity of the air around them. He was doing that daily, but Berwick put a stop to it. He didn't want to start the day with bad news. Although when they wake up in the morning and look out a window of Motel Aurora Borealis at the ice-covered landscape, how can they avoid bad news?

Since the rocket trip is going to take a long time, Proxima b being four light years away from earth, Dr. Drone is responsible for putting all of the crew, including himself, in a hibernation state. He will inject them with serum which includes bear blood so their metabolisms will slow to the point where the sixteen year journey will age them only a few months. At least that's what Dr. Drone says.

It has not gone down well with the crew. "Do you have to do that?" Berwick barked at the diminutive doctor.

"Yes," Dr. Drone replied. "If I don't, you'll age sixteen years, and with your age being what it is now, you'd be too decrepit to get out of the lander. You'd be a burden, a drag on the rest of us."

Berwick glanced away in frustration. "I wish there was another way," he huffed.

"We'll all be hibernating," Dr. Drone continued. "Nobody is going to do anything to you during that time. We're just a capsule flying through space with no need for anyone to do anything. Everything is programmed to get us to Proxima b and then wake us up for the landing."

Berwick breathed heavily like he was climbing a steep slope in the terrible condition he's in. "Couldn't we rotate? At least one of us stay awake to make sure everything is OK?"

"What Dr. Drone has planned is fine," Wavering says. "The space capsule doesn't need us. It's robotic. But if you'd like to get there as a lurching old man and be the first funeral service held on Proxima b, you're welcome to it."

Berwick glares at Wavering with contempt. He's so used to shouting into a phone, "Buy." "Sell." "Hold." Assured someone at the other end will do exactly what he said. But a rocket isn't like that. He has no idea how it's controlled. Wavering thinks it makes him feel helpless. Maybe looking over Wavering's shoulder in flight would give him some satisfaction, but Wavering doesn't need it.

12

"If only we could have the sun." The plea emanates from a teary face attached to a thin body. Olga Carlyle's mascara is running——again. She's perched horizontally on a poolside chaise lounge next to her daughter, Eva. They spend part of every day beside the empty pool waiting for the rocket to be ready, or for the sun to shine, or some weather-braving messenger to bring news that earth was not destroyed and the Federal Emergency Management Agency——although it was phased out years ago because Augustus III needed more money to wage his wars against Muslims——was sending aid.

Olga is sixty years of age, give or take a few years, she never said exactly. One thing the crew does know about her exactly is that she has had seven husbands. "I'm not a serial divorcer," she assured them. She teared up, "My husbands, bless them all, met with untimely deaths. It was heart attacks. Heart attacks," she repeated as if repetition would convince everyone she was truthful and genuinely grieved at each loss.

"Well, Mom, you came out of it pretty well," Eva says.

Olga squints in hurt at her daughter. "Pretty well? Seven dead husbands?"

"And every one of them rich," Eva adds. "You and Mr. Berwick could almost buy planet earth." Wavering knows what Eva means, but anyone could buy what's left of planet earth. So Olga's a billionaire. So what?

She's a friend, or maybe a concubine, of Berwick's, and, since he and she were close to Augustus III, Augustus insisted she be on

60

the flight. She and Berwick have rooms 11 and 12 at Motel Borealis, but whether the door connecting the two stays shut, no one knows or cares. Neither she nor Berwick comment.

Apart from her mascara that runs because the human race pulled the nuclear trigger and pushed the earth's ecosystem over the edge and blotted out the sun so that she cannot baste herself in expensive lotions and turn brown like a roasting turkey next to the Motel Aurora Borealis swimming pool, she has nice skin. The high cheekbones and blue eyes are enthralling. Having had at her call a flock of physical trainers, masseuse, nutrition counselors, hairdressers, pedicurists, manicurists, and skin specialists, her body has shriveled and shrunk more slowly than give or take sixty years would suggest.

Only now, with her support staff having gone the way of the rest of the human race, she's sliding into her seventh decade with her body going solo. "Eva, you're so good to me," she sobs.

Eva sighs. She knows what's coming next. "Tell me something to make me feel better," Olga says. "I know you can do it."

"Oh Mother," Eva says with clenched jaw. She stares at the rivulets rutting down Olga's cheeks and dripping off her jaw. "Tears won't bring back the sun. And they're making your face a mess."

Olga looks at Eva as if her shapely brunette daughter has turned into a female ogre. "I just don't feel good," she says.

"All right," Eva hisses with exasperation. This is an exchange that occurs almost daily. "At least you're alive while seven billion people are dead. We think seven billion people are dead? Is that right?" she asks, turning to the Reverend Doctor Jones.

Jones is in his usual supine position on the chaise lounge with his eyes closed.

"Is that right?" Eva shouts at him.

Jones stirs, his hazmat-hooded head pops up so that he can see who is accosting him. "Is what right?" he asks.

"Seven billion people are dead. Everyone but us. Is that correct?"

Jones's chest heaves, his eyes roll. He is not a man to be found bereft of an answer. "Unless the Lord raptured some of them," he says.

"Well, that's your thing. Rapture. Did some get raptured?" Eva sits upright and spits the questions at him as if he must know what happened because he knows everything.

Wavering feels the heat radiating from Eva, because that is the kind of young woman she is. In her eyes, Jones has certified himself as omniscient. Wavering has to admit that now Jones looks as if he wishes he could duck inside his hazmat suit like a turtle withdrawing into his shell and pretend he doesn't hear her questions or see her burning eyes.

"The rapture, that's your thing," Eva says. "When my mother and I attended The Only Gospel Church, you were always talking about the rapture. You said there would be a great tribulation, but before the great tribulation, or maybe it was after the great tribulation, or was it during the great tribulation, all those people who were saved would be snatched into the air to meet Jesus somewhere in the atmosphere or stratosphere or ionosphere, somewhere up there. Right?"

The question hangs in the toxic air for a few seconds while Jones wrinkles his brow as if he's rifling the file cabinets of his brain for an answer.

"Well," Eva fires, "were they or weren't they? And if they were, why are you still here? And my mother and me? We went through all your hoops to be certified by the federal Department of Religious Affairs as bona fide believers."

Wavering recalls the Department of Religious Affairs popped up in the middle of the century when Augustus II officially pronounced that the First Amendment prohibiting the establishment of religion only protected religions from being controlled by the government. The Supreme Court, popularly known as the Republican Kangaroo Court, in 2049 ruled that nothing prevented religion from controlling the government. Thus evangelicals, fronted by the Republican Party, did take control, and that's what produced what Wavering calls the evangelical sharia law.

The gears in Jones's brain seem to be grinding, his mouth moves. "Maybe the great tribulation hasn't come yet." He pauses, his eyes search the leaden clouds for enlightenment. "If it hasn't, then the rapture won't have happened."

"The tribulation hasn't come?" Eva asks incredulously. "The planet is trashed, the air poisoned, water turned into frozen swamps of sludge, most likely seven billion souls liberated from their bodies, and the tribulation hasn't come? May I ask, what is there left for the great tribulation to tribulate? With seven billion people croaked, who is going to meet Jesus in the clouds?"

Jones pulls himself upright and casts Eva a self-righteous sneer. "God moves in mysterious ways," he says. "Even Jesus did not know every detail of how the end would come."

"But you do," Eva says sharply. "You stood up there like you were the word of God yourself. You preached as if you could see saints popping out of the windows of cars and houses, stores, office buildings, and drifting into the sky from their jobs. With of course trains and airplanes and boats running out of control because their saved pilots and drivers were drawn like a magnet into the sky." Wavering wonders if that was fair to the clods who were left, because airplanes and trains and boats without drivers would not have much chance of arriving safely at their destinations.

Jones shrinks into his hazmat suit at Eva's machinegun bursts of questions. "God moves in mysterious ways," he says.

"He may move in mysterious ways," she says. "But a bunch of people flying off the earth into the sky ought to be noticeable. That would be no mystery. Don't you think?"

Jones sighs, a pontifical far-off look glows in his eyes. "You have to have faith," he says. "We are mortal creatures. We are not the ones to question the ways of the Almighty."

"I'm not questioning the ways of the Almighty," Eva says. "You stood up there and said a bunch of things in behalf of God. I want to know where they are. Is that too much to ask?"

Olga sneers at Eva. "You're so hard on Reverend Jones, dear" she says. "You can't expect him to know everything."

"Not everything," she replies. "But he should know something about what he talks about. Otherwise he should not talk. Or he should admit that the timeline he cobbled together from his reading of the Bible is wrong."

"Well," Olga huffs. "That's a mouthful."

"Mother, I'm just trying to understand. I have my right." Eva's voice rises. "Like this," she says. "The Apostle Paul said that 'to be absent from the body is to be present with the Lord.' Jesus said the repentant thief on the cross would be with him in paradise that day. But Jones here teaches that neither the dead nor the living will be present with the Lord until the rapture. Don't you see a timing conflict?"

Wavering looks at Olga and Jones, but they are stretched out on their chaises as if the sun has come out to baste them. Eva continues, "So if I die now and I'm present with the Lord, why do I have to wait for the rapture to be present with the Lord?"

She might as well be speaking Svengali for the response she gets from those two faces. Are Olga and Jones asleep? Or are they running for cover? Either way, they don't answer. Eva sighs. "Maybe I'm too practical," she says. She looks at Wavering. "But why not?"

13

Berwick and Holiness Jones complain that Motel Aurora Borealis is ramshackle. They're right, of course. Wavering knows they're used to The Five Seasons and Fluke Taj-ma-Tower and the like, so to them Borealis is a dump, a slum. Wavering doesn't mind Borealis though, because when you're an Air Force pilot, you take what you're assigned or what you can get and figure that if you grab a decent night's sleep, you're fine. A cot in a base barracks, a mat and sleeping bag on the floor of a tent in the Afghan desert.

But Borealis is a notch above the bunker five hundred feet below the motel where the launch team prepares Genesis for its journey. And where the travelers, if you would call them that, sometimes eat and sometimes struggle to relax. It's a tunnel. About two hundred feet long and forty feet wide. It was built a century ago for Minuteman missiles stationed there. But now, water seeps through cracks in the arch ceiling and dribbles down the concrete walls to the floor where the crew keeps it at bay with sandbags.

The long wooden table the flight crew eats at was retrieved from Motel Aurora Borealis and lowered on the elevator. At least it isn't gritty and gray concrete like the bunker. It's more luxurious than the slab of plywood supported by saw horses at which the launch crew eats. The chairs for the flight crew are wood while the launch crew's are folding metal. The seat pads are worn through and the metal covered with rust.

The launch crew is used to it. They were all recruited from missile launch complexes, they're accustomed to living underground like rabbits in a warren. Wavering wonders if the concrete and the dampness and voices echoing off the hard ceiling ever bother them. Like submariners, Wavering guesses they get used to glaring lights and no sun. Well, sun, they don't have it at the motel either, so the flight crew isn't much better off.

The motel relieves the claustrophobia Wavering feels when he's in the bunker. The flight crew calls the bunker 'Houston.' Not to be confused with the Houston that once was the control center for NASA rocket flights. That Houston was obliterated by the incoming response to President Augustus Fluke III's preemptive strike.

Wavering flew the president over it, just so he could make sure it was gone. He leaned toward the window and looked down, but Wavering wasn't certain he saw the piles of broken concrete and porcupine spikes of rebar, twisted girders, cracked streets and roads. Or the blackened bodies of the dead incinerated by a nuclear blast. III's eyes looked down, but out of his mouth came, "The world can thank me. Thank me that I got rid of those Muslims. Got rid of those Muslims. They would have taken over the whole world. They would have put us all under their sharia law. Under their sharia law. Yes, that's what they would have done. And I stopped it. The greatest threat to the world ever, and I stopped it. I stopped it."

III pulled his head up and looked about. His bobblehead cabinet members mumbled. "Yes, Mr. President, you stopped it." "The greatest act of courage in history, Sir." "You, President Augustus Fluke the Third, will go down as the greatest leader who ever lived."

President Fluke smiled in appreciation. Wavering watched and his head nodded in agreement. If III said he was the greatest, and the cabinet affirmed him, who could doubt?

14

Houston's elevator door flies open, in pops an animated hazmat suit containing the flight crew's young Adam named Buck. He must have a last name, he must be Buck something or other, but when he introduced himself, he said, "Just call me Buck. Everyone calls me Buck. It's enough." His name is as lean as his thirty-year-old body which he hammers into shape every day. As he strips off his hazmat suit, sweat glistens on his pale face, wets his long blond hair, stains his white running shorts and tank top.

"Wow," Buck shouts. He does this every time he comes in from a workout, as if he wants everyone to be alerted that he has arrived. "What a run. Ten miles. Without stopping." He grabs a towel and blots the sweat from his trunks and top and wipes his face and hair. He bounces over to what he calls his 'weight room'——a pile of barbells, dumbbells, and a jump rope. Groaning, glistening with rivulets of perspiration, he lifts weights, jumps up and down through his daily routine.

Berwick watches this prodigy pummeling his body and nods in satisfaction. "He'll be a great Adam," he says for the hundredth time. The idea is that Buck and Eva will mate. There's also the idea that Buck will mate with Eva's friend Sarah, but the crew has seen so little of Sarah, and so has Buck, that everyone wonders where that non-relationship will go.

Having had the Bible drilled into his head as a youngster, whenever Berwick talks about Buck and Eva mating, Wavering thinks not just of Adam and Eve, but of Cain and Abel, and here we go again. Has that occurred to Augustus or Berwick? Or even to the most holy reverend Jones? When they set off to another planet and start another human race, will they think about the history they left behind? They never mention it.

Wavering expresses his concern of déjà vu occurring on Proxima b to His Holiness Jones, but Holiness just scoffs. "Well that's easy to take care of," he says "We'll warn Buck that when Eva, or Eve if she's called that, offers him the apple, he's not to eat it."

Jones is referring to the apple the first Adam ate in the Garden of Eden. Wavering knows Jones believes the gestation of that apple plunged the human race into multiple races, gay, bisexual, and transgender sexuality, abortion, alcohol, drugs, and demon possession——mental illness in Wavering's book, but Wavering knows Jones is strong on demon possession. That apple also brought on the scourges of liberalism, socialism, communism, the Democratic Party, hurricanes, floods, droughts, tornadoes, tsunamis, volcanic eruptions, earthquakes, and all the medical illnesses, including ingrown toenails.

Buck finishes with his muscle toning and lopes to the dining table. "Hi everybody," he says as if he has just realized they are there. He takes a chair next to Eva and scans the bowls on the table. "Beans?" he asks as if he has not seen them before.

"What else?" Berwick replies angrily. "You expect crab cake Benedict? A rasher of bacon? Hot biscuits? Beans are all you and Drone could find. I still say you didn't look far enough."

"We went as far as we could," Buck replies. "There's nothing but frozen wheat fields up there, in case you haven't noticed. Crab, bread, bacon, and biscuits don't flourish in ice. That abandoned Sysco truck was all we could find."

Wavering thought that after they ate through the beans at the back end of the trailer they'd get to something tasty. They'd been eating beans ever since they gathered at Motel Aurora Borealis.

Wavering had to admit he was beginning to have nightmares where beans rise out of a bowl and attack him. Like a swarm of flying beetles he can't swat away.

"Well, we haven't found anything else," Berwick says. "I'm as tired of these beans as the rest of you. But Drone here assures me they contain protein and some other vital nutrients that will keep us alive."

Evangelist Jones stirs. "The Lord has provided," he says in a sanctimonious tone.

"Well," says Olga. She's sitting with her pink bathrobe tightly wrapped around her nightgown. "You'd think the Lord would provide a diet he would like to eat himself. I know I'm to have faith and be thankful and all that, but beans ream out your insides like Roto Rooter scours pipes."

"It's called 'cleansing,' Mother," Eva puts in. "We need to be purged to maintain good health. I gave you those books that touted the virtues of scrubbing our insides."

"Yeah, but every day?" Buck says. "I feel these damn beans are scrubbing the flesh out of my gut. Someday there'll be nothing left. I'll implode."

"You won't implode, Buck," Dr. Drone says. "Take my word for it."

Buck nods as if he might understand. He has a hard time assimilating information. Just a quirk. "This Adam thing gnaws at me," he says. "What if these beans make me sterile? There we are living on Proxima b and Eva and I, and maybe Sarah, if there is a Sarah, are supposed to start hatching kids like rabbits so we can populate the planet. What if I can't do it?"

Silence falls the length of the table. Wavering expects His Holiness Jones to spout his usual "God will provide," but Wavering guesses an infertile Adam is something he doesn't quite know how God would deal with. Jones shoves out a shambling word that sounds like "faith," but that's all.

Dr. Drone puts his hand on Buck's shoulder. "Buck up," he says. "You're as healthy an Adam as we could get. You take care of yourself. You'll do fine."

Buck glances at Eva. "What do you think?"

"What do I think?" she replies. "What difference does it make what I think?"

"Well, it does make a difference. We're in this together. You need to be attracted to me."

Eva runs her eyes over him. She squints. "Look, we've got sixteen years to get acquainted. No need to rush."

"So it's not love at first sight?" Buck scans the faces at the table looking for reassurance. But he is looking at stone heads on Easter Island. "Don't you find me attractive?"

Eva looks at him and shrugs. "In some ways," she replies. "But we can get the job done. That's all that counts. If you're talking about romance, it doesn't mean anything. Even if I found you repulsive, we can get the job done."

"Job?" Buck asks with wrinkled brow. "Job? Is that all it is to you?"

"Well, isn't it?" Eva replies. "You and I were chosen for an assignment, a job. Bear children and populate another planet. We're like laboratory mice. Reproduce and reproduce. Do you think mice talk about romance?"

Buck's eyes fall to the table. It doesn't appear he knows anything about mice. He has such a fragile ego that the slightest questioning throws him into a funk. Wavering admits to himself Eva is right, this probably isn't a marriage made in heaven, although he realizes there is a pun there because Eva and Buck's relationship is going to be made in the heavens.

15

The flight crew is finishing breakfast when Malcolm McLaughlin walks in and peels off his hazmat suit. They haven't seen much of Malcolm and know him even less, most know nothing at all. He's a tall slender African American with short curly hair who largely keeps to himself. When he emerges from the elevator, his eyes do not rise to meet theirs. He walks to the table, but does not acknowledge anyone. It's as if they aren't there.

As usual, nobody knows how to greet him. But, also as usual when he shows up, Eva is game. "Malcolm, how goes it?" she asks.

He nods slowly as he dips the ladle into the bean bowl and scoops beans onto his plate.

"That mean Okay?" Eva asks.

He looks at her without expression. "You might say that," he replies. His voice is gentle, quiet.

Although he came to the cockpit once in a while on Air Force One, Wavering still has trouble figuring out what Malcolm is about. He was one of Augustus's Secret Service agents, but Augustus released him so he could be one of the crew to come out of West Virginia. Getting rid of him, Wavering assumed. Augustus never treated people of color well. At least people of color who didn't look at him as if he were a beatific vision. He would take praise from anyone, but that didn't mean he respected them. If he saw a cockroach bowing to his greatness, he would love that cockroach. That's just the way he is.

When Wavering told Malcolm they intended to rocket to the distant planet Proxima b, he stared without expression for a few minutes, then said, "Got room for me?" Wavering wondered how the rest of the group would receive him, there had been so much racism before the apocalypse. But Eva was adamant, as was Wavering, that he should have a place on the journey. Buck frowned in disapproval. Olga's eyes glowed as if she were smitten with Malcolm's physical prowess, demeanor, and the mystery that came with him. Wavering wondered if she was concocting a plan to reel in husband number eight. If so, would Malcolm survive it? Just a thought, Wavering reminded himself.

"Malcolm, sometimes I think you don't like us," Eva blurts with childlike naiveté.

Malcolm pulls himself up, his eyes avoid all of them. He shrugs his shoulders.

"What does that mean?" Eva pleads. "You like us? Or you don't like us? Or you like some of us and dislike others? Maybe you think we're all racists." She pauses, glances at the faces at the table. "I would if I were you," she adds.

Wavering agrees with Eva, this is not an inclusive crew. You could never have one when the members were recruited by Augustus Fluke III. He declared how he loved African-Americans and Mexicans and Arabs and Jews, but he never put one in his cabinet of mental dwarfs. Although Wavering wonders if III asked people of color, but they refused to debase themselves to join such a brainless cabal.

Holiness Jones shifts about his overweight body and fixes his beady eyes on Eva. "I resent that," he says. "I was not a racist. I am not a racist. I have always had black friends." It's true that Holiness and other mega church evangelists welcomed everybody, but not because they weren't racists. They believed God kept score of how many souls they saved, and the more they bagged, the higher their position in heaven. Perhaps more importantly, the more suckers they roped in, the larger the pool of potential contributors to the Lear Jet, helicopter, and I. M. Pei-designed 'cottage' in the Cayman Islands.

Malcolm's brown eyes slowly shift to Jones and rest on his pallid face. Jones squirms ever so slightly. Wavering doesn't know if Malcolm is going to reply or not. He seldom defends himself, something Wavering admires in him.

Feeling the hackles on his neck rise, Wavering fixes on Jones. "I don't believe what you just said. I'm an evangelical. Most of us are as racist as they come. Not Jim Crow types who segregate restaurants and restrooms, but we want black people to know their place and keep it. We were missing in action in the struggles for civil rights, voting rights, and the rest. We voted for Republicans who never supported civil rights and did nothing about enforcement."

Jones glares at Wavering. "You're accusing me of being a racist because I'm evangelical?"

"I'm saying you are a racist. As was I. When segregated housing and segregated schools returned under Augustus's executive orders, and blacks were discriminated against in the job market and everyplace else, what did you and I do?"

Jones rears back his head and glances upward as if he beholds the face of God. "I preached the gospel, that's what I did. That gospel is the good news to save everyone."

"You're talking about your born-again-meet-Jesus-in-the sky gospel," Wavering says. "Since 'gospel' means good news, what good news did you bring to people living in hardship on earth?"

Jones's face burns red with resentment. "Why we helped black and brown people all the time."

"Helped?" Wavering asks. He can feel the heat rising at the back of his neck. He's aware that he has this problem of turning against what he is, perhaps too vehemently. What is that? he wonders.

"We had clothing drives. We had food drives. We welcomed them into the church so they could be saved. We did not discriminate."

Wavering says, "I'm not saying you did. Not explicitly. But the problem was white people who were better off than people of color, who sent their children to better schools, and who were not confronted with discrimination in the housing or job markets. It was those white people, myself included, who controlled how things went, and anything short of civil rights and enforcing civil rights meant a lot of minority people got the short end of the stick."

"Our church was a powerhouse for the poor," Jones blurts.

An awkward silence descends on the table. Not that there is full disagreement, because Berwick and Olga are in Jones's camp. But Wavering thinks 'powerhouse' is a bit more than anyone expects. Malcolm squints at Jones as if he were a rat that had just crawled out of a garbage can.

Wavering sighs deeply. "Powerhouse for the poor?" He repeats softly and without incrimination, but with a taint of incredulity. "In what way?"

Jones glances about at everyone, perhaps hoping Berwick or Olga will speak up in his defense. But their eyes are fixed on their bowls of tired beans. Buck is a candidate too for the defense, but Buck has already shown himself to be expert at avoiding controversy. He may be long on muscles and conditioning and ginning himself up to be the new Adam, he is obviously high on himself and his physique, but when it comes to stepping into disagreement, he's like Superman on kryptonite. Perhaps that is why Eva feels that as the new Adam, as the father of a new human race, he is only functional. Not the star of a romance drama.

When Jones finally realizes he's alone, he says, "I already told you."

"Clothing? Canned food?" Wavering says.

"We gave out tons," Jones replies.

Wavering says, "You know, Dr. Jones, the Bible says a lot about the responsibility to work for justice. The Old Testament prophets railed about it to their kings and rich people. People who got rich and glorified themselves on the backs of the poor. But they did nothing to change the system so the poor weren't poor."

Jones impales Wavering with a self-righteous stare. "God feeds the poor. That's what Jesus said. My obligation is to preach the gospel so the poor can get saved. Then God will make them rich. Yes, that's the way Jesus set things up. Jesus first, salvation, then as people get close to Jesus, God rewards them with riches and health…"

"And BMW's and Lamborghinis and mega-yachts and multiple houses and private jets and the like," Wavering adds. "Look, I was there. Not the BMW's and jets, but I know the game." Then Wavering chides himself because he truly is a hypocrite. Much as he hates to admit it.

As Malcolm fixes Jones in the crosshairs of his brown eyes, Wavering becomes aware that Jones is squirming in discomfort. As if the gears are turning in his ever repetitive mind looking for some response. But all that comes out is further deadening of the silence that has fallen. In that silence, Malcolm's lips move ever so imperceptibly. "Bullshit," he is heard to say in a soft voice.

That's a word Wavering doesn't think Jones has ever heard inside the hallowed walls and faux stained glass windows of his mega church with a sitting and TV congregation of 50 million enraptured souls. At least it isn't a normal part of the vocabulary he and his people used. They may have used the term under their breaths with regard to Democrats, liberals, socialists, scientists, gays, Lesbians, transgenders, bisexuals, Muslims, Mexicans, Chinese, Japanese, Koreans and who knows what countless others who had not bowed the knee to Jones and his like and come under the great American country that worshipped God purely and was a blessing to the entire world. Until III pressed the button, that is.

16

"She's a beauty, isn't she," Berwick says. He and Wavering stand side by side at the bottom of the silo looking up at the Genesis rocket. With the overhead blast covers temporarily open, she gleams in the leaden light leaking from the sky. The first stage at the base is the diameter of an oil storage tank. It narrows to the thinner but longer second stage. Above that stands the third stage which will accelerate to a velocity that will launch the flight crew on its 16-year journey.

On top of the third stage perches the spacecraft in which the nine crewmembers will live, if they survive the launch, if they survive slingshotting the sun, if they don't get hit by space debris or worse, and if they can land on a sphere of alleged rock a third larger than earth. When Wavering stands back and considers the flight, he wonders if he's gone through a mirror. Or is it down the rabbit hole? He gets confused. As if it matters.

The rocket is a beauty, the largest ever built. But looking at the nozzles in the first stage, their bell shapes widening to a diameter of twelve feet, Wavering wonders about their ignition. Twelve million pounds of thrust. That will either send them off on their blessed journey to the stars. Or twelve million pounds of thrust that will explode with such violent force they will be vaporized in a nanosecond. At least there would be no time for pain. Is that a consolation?

The three engineers working on the first stage engines stand out from the robots, which wear no protective suits, since they have nothing organic to protect. The robots do almost everything the men do, but they work 24 hours a day and need no food, no water, and no rest. Black boxes inside the robots are attached to cords that plug into black boxes in the rocket to make sure all the systems are powering up properly and there are no computer glitches.

What will happen to the launch crew after Genesis launches? you might ask. They are committed to go to the White House bunker embedded under that mountain in West Virginia. They and Augustus Fluke III will follow the advice of Dr. Strangelove in the movie of the same name, where Dr. Strangelove, restricted to a wheel chair, delivers a clenched-teeth-barely-restrained-Hitler-leather-covered-right-arm-salute forecast of how survivors of a nuclear holocaust will hole up underground for a hundred years and then emerge to begin life anew. Wavering thinks about it and wishes them luck. And thanks God he doesn't have to hole up in that bunker.

Projecting out from the wall of the silo are connecting walkways at different levels that give men and robots access to the rocket's systems and provide electricity for the black boxes and fuel for the engines. Very impressive. But Wavering does wonder about the possibility of vertigo when he steps onto the narrow walkway suspended from the wall of the silo to the space capsule five hundred feet above the floor. "That capsule is a long way off the ground," Wavering remarks to Berwick.

"Don't look down," he replies. He's a practical man in some ways. But Wavering wonders if it has crossed his mind that this five hundred billion dollar baby might turn into a five hundred billion dollar bomb that could end the flight crew and leave a smoking crater two-hundred feet wide. Goodbye Motel Aurora Borealis. Although to Wavering and the rest of them, that wouldn't be much of a loss.

<h1 style="text-align:center">17</h1>

The launch team has informed Wavering they're getting close to ready. Wavering doesn't know if he likes hearing it. Finally leaving earth will be a pleasure. That is, if they actually leave it. In one piece.

The flight crew has just finished breakfast. Beans—again. Oh well. The phone connected to the guard station at the silo entrance rings. Wavering answers. It's one of the guards. "Sorry to bother you, Colonel Wavering."

"What is it?" Wavering asks.

"It's the president. President Augustus Fluke the Third," the guard says.

Wavering's throat tightens, he suddenly finds it hard to breathe, he can't find words to reply. He wants to shout to the guard that he's wrong. It isn't President Augustus Fluke the Third, it's someone who looks like him. It's an imposter. Wavering wants to say, Tell him he can't come in. Tell him to go back to West Virginia.

"What should I do with him?" the guard asks. Wavering's mind churns. Tell him we're gone? No, the blast covers over Genesis are still in place. He won't believe it, any more than he believes anything he doesn't make up. Tell him it's too late? No, when Augustus is blocked, it only makes him more determined to get what he wants. Wavering can't do that to the bunker guards. Then Wavering wonders why he can't make up his mind. He should welcome his president.

"He's on his way," the guard says. "I couldn't stop him."

Wavering knows what happened. Augustus bulldozed through the guards on his way to the elevator. No one is going to tell him what to do.

The elevator door opens, and there stands His Majesty. He doesn't look majestic clad in his hazmat suit, but when he pops the helmet off, he radiates that smirk he puts on like a mask whenever he needs to assert that he is in control. Admire me, because I am the greatest.

Although as Wavering looks at the rest of the flight crew, he doesn't see the smiles of admiration he anticipates. Except for Olga. She still thinks Augustus walks on water. Berwick and Jones as well. Olga smiles at Augustus in that desperate way that suggests he is the messiah who will deliver her from the glaciating earth, Motel Aurora Borealis, the bunker, Genesis, and the prole crew, including Wavering.

"It's so good to see you, Mister President," Olga blurts. Having shucked off the shell of his hazmat suit, he strides to her, arms outstretched and gives her a hug. Nausea ripples across Wavering's stomach. Partly from Olga's overplayed affection. More so because Wavering nurses a growing apprehension that Augustus has decided he wants on Genesis. A sixteen year rocket trip to Proxima b and every waking moment Augustus is floating around the spacecraft cabin spouting praise of himself and acting like he's in command of the journey? Wavering chides himself for the way he feels. He needs to get hold of himself.

18

The countdown has started. The flight crew is all in the 'white' room—just a name, the room is not white in color, just bare metal walls and floor—where they don their spacesuits. On the side of the room beyond which Genesis stands ready, there is the door that opens to the crew access arm leading to the spacecraft. Wavering isn't ready for this—he's conflicted between not launching and launching with the possibility of being instantly vaporized—but flight conditions improved quickly, there's no excuse for waiting.

Wavering realizes he has a problem he has to solve. To raise it he might risk throwing a match into a bucket of gasoline, but he has no choice. "Look," he tells everyone, "We cannot take Augustus, Berwick, and Jones on the flight. Too much weight. Two others would have to stay. I won't do that."

To a person, they all say, "I'm not giving up my place." They don't seem to have the apprehension about Genesis that Wavering does. Of course they're not pilots and haven't had simulator training with rockets swerving off course or blowing up. Most of those scenarios end up on the ground with smoke rising from a black crater. Mercifully the simulators don't simulate the deaths of the pilot and crew.

"All right," Wavering says desperately. They quiet down. "I'll ask for a vote."

"No," Augustus shouts. He plants himself in front of Wavering, facing the crew. "I am the commander-in-chief of the United States of America. I am the one decides who goes. I. I make the decisions. You better believe it."

Wavering finds himself caught. He isn't a confrontational type of person. Not by nature, not by training. He prefers blending into the background. But there comes a time. "Commander-in-chief of what?" he barks. Augustus's neck grows redder than usual. Wavering adds, "Commander-in-chief of a country that no longer exists?"

"The United States does exist," he says. "Who are you to say it doesn't? Who are you?"

Wavering lets III's words echo off the ceiling and walls. When quiet falls, he says, "Who am I? I am the commander of a rocket that I know exists. As commander, I choose my crew. You better believe it." Wavering looks past Augustus and eyes everyone. "We vote. That's final." Augustus turns and glares at him. III is famous for long stare downs against people he doesn't like.

In a quiet voice Wavering says, "You know that without me, Genesis goes nowhere. Mr. President. Unless you can pilot it, I suggest you move out of the way."

III glares at Wavering, searching for words that don't come. Finally, he moves aside.

Wavering calls off the three names and asks for a vote. Nothing unanimous, but there is a decision. Wavering announces, "President Fluke and Jones are on. Mr. Berwick is not."

Berwick steps toward Wavering. "I won't have it," he shouts. The echo of his voice reverberates and dies. He stomps about with his lips trembling. He fixes on Augustus. "You, you were the one who assigned me here. Are you a traitor? Are you a liar? Are you a hypocrite?" Berwick gestures toward Wavering. "How can you let him get away with this?"

Berwick stalks toward Augustus and leans in his face. "What will you do on 'Proximate' b? What you did on earth? Destroy it? You are of no value to the mission. You're a drone——pardon me, Dr.

Drone, don't mean to be down on you. You have absolutely nothing to contribute. Unless you think you're going to be the new Adam, in which case you'll spawn a population of self-centered, ego-centric, lying, greedy, brutal, and planet-destroying human beings. You've done enough. You've disbarred yourself from ever being in charge of anything."

Augustus smirks at Berwick as if he's a petulant child screaming at him for not buying him an ice cream cone. That smirk is his trademark for everything. He assumes it firewalls him against reproach. He has never responded to his critics with other than derision. "I didn't destroy the world," he announces.

Berwick pounces. "You didn't? If you didn't, who did?"

"The Democrats," Augustus says.

"The Democrats?"

"They hacked the launch codes. I never initiated the attack. It was them. They are at fault. The Democrats. The Democrats. That's what everyone says."

Berwick sighs heavily. "Everyone? After everything that's happened? You're still lying?"

"I don't lie. But you, Berwick, let me ask you, when you profited from my presidency, did you ever complain?"

"I gave you millions to keep you in power," Berwick says. "When the Democrats challenged you, I was the one who funded your propaganda campaigns to mislead everyone. It was I who stood at your back to tell you to stay the course."

Augustus glares at Berwick. "And your hand was always out for government contracts and for deals with the Russians and everyone else who could add to your fortune."

"T minus 30 and counting." Wavering has almost forgotten they are in the countdown. He checks scopes and dials on the portable monitor, throws switches. The fuel tanks are filling on schedule. The guidance program is loading into the computers, the automatic checkout will be completed with time to spare.

Berwick turns and levels his gaze at Reverend Jones, casts a pleading gesture toward Wavering. "What does he have to contribute?" Berwick's tone suggests Jones has no more to offer than a horse fly.

Wavering ducks the question. "Everyone voted," he says. "I did not choose. Apparently there's a feeling that Jones has more to contribute than you do." Of course Wavering can't think what it is. With Jones having lived in his religious bubble for most of his life, the challenges of establishing life on a new planet will be far beyond his capabilities. And his, 'The Lord will provide' and 'It's the Lord's will' will do nothing to get life started. Wavering can find no reason for not concluding Jones is superfluous. Or maybe a hinderance.

Berwick is just getting warmed up on Jones. "You're nothing but a religious con man. A fraud. You sell hope and Jesus and the second coming and meeting Jesus in the air, but where are they? Of what use is all that on a new planet? If we don't screw it up like Adam did, we won't need preachers at all."

Wavering thinks, of course that's assuming eating an apple produced every ill in human beings and on the planet. A pretty large order for one apple. He could suggest to them the scientists' view that humans inherited their DNA from the animal world, and that world never was perfect. God helps people live, flawed though they are, with what they've got, not escape to a wonderland that has nothing to do with reality. But he's not there to preach.

"How dare you," Jones shouts at Berwick. Jones glares at Berwick and Augustus. "I am the one who kept your government and your business worlds cobbled together. The people were restless. They wanted to know where decent wages were. They questioned why they didn't have health insurance. They believed their government had abandoned them. So I assured them you were chosen by God to rule the nation. You were a modern Moses leading the way to the Promised Land."

Promised Land? Wavering's mind flips through images of the ravaged planet. He's seen promises fail, but that one is beyond the record books. Snow, ice, radiation, dust, freezing temperatures? Moses? Promised land? But Jones is right to say he influenced a lot of people. In TV interviews, people echoed Jones's assurance. "The president will restore the world." "The president just needs time. He will solve all our problems."

Wavering has to admit, even though he was one of them, many religious people drove him crazy. He was once in that tunnel of shallow principles and prayer and books and teaching, and he did not put his head outside. Religion blinded him to the larger world. Oh well.

"Promised Land?" Berwick shouts with contempt. He's thinking Wavering's thoughts. He gestures toward the surface above them. "Promised Land up there? Ice and snow and frozen fog and no sun and seven billion people dead? That's the Promised Land?"

Wavering knows what's coming. He cringes. Jones is like a gumball machine. Put the coin in the slot, and out comes: "God moves in mysterious ways."

Berwick stares at Jones as if he's an imbecile. He asks, "Is that what you're going to say on Proximate b? Is that what you're going to contribute? That and, 'It's God's will.' You talk gibberish. You preach to fill your coffers. Who cares if God ever does what you promise?"

Jones juts his chin forward. "And you don't think you were filling your coffers? We did it in different ways. Who are you to accuse me of anything?"

"T minus 25 and counting." Wavering checks the fuel levels in the tanks. Three are full, five others nearing the fill mark. As countdowns go, this is optimal. Which is good, because they don't have much of a window for the launch.

Wavering doesn't have more time to listen to these three argue with one another about who is the most worthless. "All right," he says. "Berwick, back to the motel. The launch crew will take you to West Virginia."

Berwick casts Wavering a defiant look. "I'm not going." He makes no move toward the door. Wavering nods to Malcolm and the launch crew. They rush Berwick, pin his arms behind his back, and frog march him to the door. "No," he shouts. "You can't do this to me. Fluke, you've stabbed me in the back. Jones, you're a fraud."

Malcolm and the launch crew shove Berwick through the door. The door clicks shut, and Berwick is gone. Although his voice echoes down from the elevator shaft leading to the silo entrance above. Wavering sighs in relief. But it's short lived. There stands Augustus with his face drawn up in that smirk. Good grief, sixteen years of this?

"Launch aborted," Wavering hears. "Wind speed is above the limit." He sighs in relief. Getting rid of Berwick has reamed him out. And he doesn't mind the delay to determine whether Genesis will explode on liftoff. But this crew nattering? It doesn't make his day. And it will be several days before another launch window. Oh well.

19

Augustus III stumbles in to breakfast, his face scrunched like a sour pumpkin. Without a word, without a glance at the rest of the flight crew sitting at the table with their beans, he wrenches off his hazmat suit and throws it down in a pile. So much for the pegs the rest of them hang their hazmat suits on.

The crew keeps chattering away in conversation, aware of the demonstration but ignoring it, it happens so often you might call it routine. III does it to monopolize everyone's attention, which it did at first, but by now the material is old. Surprising, because with no computers or smartphones or pads or anything else that connects to the outside world, because there is no outside world, the crew has a lot of time on its hands.

At first, the withdrawal from electronic communication was like delirium tremens, the symptoms of withdrawal from consuming too much alcohol. The crew developed nervous tics, hyperactivity sent them through motions of working or exercising, but they accomplished nothing. There was just them and their large brains with nothing in them but what had been put there before the world ended. Without steady sluicing from Facebook and Twitter and texting and the Fox channels assuring them the Fluke presidents were the greatest ever, their brains were drying up.

Augustus stalks to the table as if he's going to smash it to pieces. His face, usually red-orange, is so red it almost blinks. "She's at it again," he shouts. He scans the crew like the searchlight beam of a prison watchtower, his glaring eyes defying them to counter him.

They ignore him, although they all know who he's talking

about, and apart from rare sightings, they know nothing about her. It's Sarah, Eva's friend, who has taken reclusiveness to a level not achieved by Howard Hughes in his latter years or the novelist J. D. Salinger, who published "The Catcher in the Rye" and then became the man who was but isn't.

Augustus keeps search-lighting them, but they keep their heads down, spooning their beans as if they might even enjoy them. They also know that for whomever does respond to III, the ride will be less than pleasant. Finally Augustus's puffed up eyes stop swiveling and fix on Wavering. He cringes, knowing they would. One of the advantages of being commander of Genesis. "I want it stopped," III shouts.

Wavering slows his eating, his hand holding a spoonful of beans suspended in the air. He knows Augustus hates pauses. He wants instant responses. He assumes whomever he's talking to knows what he's going to say before he utters the words. Or else he wants to prevent thinking, perhaps because thinking has so successfully eluded him. Finally, Wavering asks, "Stop what?"

"That girl. That woman. What's her name?" Augustus is so angry that the minuscule part of his brain devoted to memory is shorting out. Wavering waits for him to answer his own question. But the more the gears grind in that empty space between his red ears, the less comes forth.

"Are you talking about Sarah?" Eva asks quietly.

Augustus spins and impales Eva with his glare. "Sarah. That's the one. She's a spy. She's spying on me." He swivels back to Wavering and thrusts his head forward. "You. You're in charge. I want you to stop that woman from spying on me."

This scare of Sarah spying on him is the next chapter in Augustus's saga of being spied on all his life. Even when he was president of a country that existed and had Malcolm and dozens of other Secret Service agents protecting him, he kept accusing others of spying on him. Russia. Germany. And always, Muslims.

Wavering glances up at III's corpulent body swaying over him. He really is scary to look at, bulging eyes, veins in his neck standing out like mole runs on a golf green, puffed cheeks quivering. Wavering's muscles tighten, it occurs to him that III might be close to taking a swing at him. He senses Malcolm tensing slightly, he's wired like that when he feels there may be violence. His sixth sense, Wavering calls it.

"Why do you say she's spying on you?" Wavering asks. His voice is cool. He knows Augustus goes apoplectic when others don't share his panic.

"I hear her at night," Augustus says.

"How do you know it's her?" Wavering asks.

"Who else?"

"To be honest, it could be any one of us. Even me." Wavering pauses. "Or it's no one. It's a figment of your imagination."

"No," he shouts. "It's her. She's at my door. Spying. I know it's her."

Eva has been watching the exchange without expression. "It could be her," Eva says nonchalantly. "If it is, so what?" She pauses. "You lock your door, don't you?"

"Of course I do," Augustus snarls. "Do you think I'm an idiot?"

Wavering's mind jerks to a halt. Augustus really shouldn't ask a question like that. Many people did say he was an idiot. Or a moron. Or an imbecile. Take your pick. As for Wavering, he'd say when it came to smarts III is an idiot because he never read literature or history or psychology—he never read anything. And he doesn't seem to know anything other than what's blowing through his brain at the moment. Or he repeats what he heard from the cabal of his staff and cabinet. Boldly stated nonsense.

"When she's at the door, who knows what she can get?" Augustus asks.

Wavering would like to let Eva, brave soul that she is, continue to respond, but the buck stops with him. "What can she get?" he asks. "That is if it is she who is at the door and you're not hallucinating?"

If anger can cause rigor mortis, Augustus has it. When he can unclench his jaw, he hisses, "How dare you. How dare you."

"Look," Wavering says calmly. "You're making an accusation against a young woman we hardly know and you have no evidence whatsoever. Do you think that's fair?" He knows 'fair' is not a word III uses or respects. 'Justice' either. The only standard is what suits him, what fits his mood or whim at the moment. When he's crossed, his only response is revenge. But what can he do against Genesis's pilot when he needs that pilot to get him to Proxima b? Besides, Wavering would rather have this struggle before they launch instead of in the space capsule. Does it occur to Wavering that he should leave III on earth? Not only does it occur, it shouts at him that he's a damn fool if he doesn't.

Augustus sinks into a sulk with his eyes on the floor. His arsenal of defeat skills is limited. In his mind, he has never been beaten. Even though fair minds would consider his ending the world a defeat, he would never see it that way or ever admit he was the cause.

20

With Sarah living among them but not appearing, she exists in the crew's minds as a ghost. As the commander of Genesis, if Wavering takes the job seriously——a bit of a stretch because part of his mind suggests the whole venture is a fool's errand—he should know his crew well. When they reach Proxima b, if they do reach Proxima b, then he needs to have an idea what Sarah can do. If they land and she disappears, she isn't likely to contribute much to the new earth.

Eva takes Sarah bowls of nutritious beans. Sarah has been sighted wandering the hallways of Motel Aurora Borealis at different times of the night. Dressed in a white gown, she appears not to walk, but to float like a vapor. She's a close friend of Eva's, there are rumors Sarah left her parents when a teenager and Olga took her in. Eva and Sarah became close, almost like sisters.

One day, without any prior sign, Sarah arrives at dinner. They are all at the table staring at those damnable beans that are becoming more and more difficult to eat. Beans, beans, beans. "They're good for us," Dr. Drone drones from time to time with no response from anyone. Yet when he eats his own beans, he has the look of a sommelier forced to down a decanter of corked wine.

The elevator door opens, and there stands a thin figure in a white hazmat suit. The figure does not stir, the others just see two eyes peering out from the helmet with some curiosity. Will she get off the elevator? Will she shut the door and vanish? A hush falls.

Finally she steps forward, well not quite steps, but carefully puts one foot ahead of the other and glides her almost no weight toward them. She seems so frail, Wavering wonders if she could fall.

Eva gets up and strides to her, grasps her helmet and removes it. Sarah has short blond hair, a narrow, pale face, and bloodless lips. Her eyes? Green maybe, some brown, rich looking, but sad. She and Eva talk, but the others can't hear what they say.

Eva helps Sarah strip off her hazmat suit. She's wearing a white jumpsuit that is so tight it fits like skin. The white gives the impression she's not fully there, or she's fading into the distance. It's not the uniform of someone who wants to be noticed. With her blond hair and pale face, she's monochromatic. Wavering thinks she's got to be anorexic. Or maybe she doesn't relish the beans Eva takes her. He can understand that.

The two of them, pole thin Sarah and hourglass Eva, approach the rest of the crew. They could not look more different from each other. Eva leans toward Sarah and whispers in her ear. Could be she's prepping Sarah for what she thinks will happen next. And it does.

Augustus shoves his chair back, hauls his corpulent self to full height, and thrusts his head forward. His crotch-length necktie, open blue sports jacket and white shirt make him look larger than he is, although he is a big man. But Wavering reminds himself he is in charge now, and if Augustus is going to launch into a paranoid spy investigation, it's his job to cut him off.

Wavering rises out of his chair and steps toward the approaching young women. "Sarah," he says cheerfully. "How good it is to see you." He approaches her, but the look on her face is disarming. No smile, no twinkle in the eyes, just a slight nod to indicate that Wavering is standing in front of her. She's going to be a tough nut to crack. But he must admit he doesn't mind the challenge of fathoming someone who casts a pall of mystery. With nothing to watch or read or listen to, except mindless comments by the crew, a little sleuthing is welcome.

"She's the spy," Wavering hears roared from behind him. It's Augustus, of course, redness amped up in his face, veins rippling across his forehead and in his fleshy neck. Looking at him, you'd think his chasing delusions might lead to a heart attack. Sarah's eyes don't flicker. She makes no response, just lets Eva glide her toward an empty chair and help her sit down. Once in place, Sarah looks at no one, says nothing.

Augustus glares at her, but his under-developed prefrontal lobe can't seem to locate words. He angles his head from side to side nervously. He looks like a cat who has been playing with a mouse he intends to eat, but it lies inert in front of him. He can't determine whether the mouse is playing possum and will jump up and run away, or if the mouse is dead.

Wavering hasn't been watching Eva, so her attack is unexpected. "Leave her alone," she says icily, glaring at Augustus.

Augustus glances at the rest of the crew, they're all glaring. It occurs to Wavering that this conflict is not the chemistry he wants for a sixteen year journey to Proxima b. Eva refuses to take her eyes off Augustus. When he realizes she will out-stare him, he turns away and heads for his hazmat suit. Wavering recalls he has a reputation for not knowing how to deal with strong women. It might be true.

21

Getting to know Sarah is like peeling the proverbial onion. In her case, an onion that is so toughened against being peeled that she offers no assistance at all. When she's with other crewmembers, she connects with no one but Eva. The two are very close, as if Eva is a part of her that Sarah does not have.

But Eva makes no attempt to speak for Sarah or to offer any explanation of why she is so guarded. Meal after meal, Sarah sits as she did the first time she appeared, looking at no one, speaking to no one, showing no response to anything anyone says.

It casts a chill on the rest of the crew. As if the chill killing off the earth isn't enough. Or the chill of the concrete control room in which they eat and congregate to talk about the nothing lives they are leading. Every so often one of them reminisces about some incident, or some journey they took when they still had a world, but they always end up sadder because those stories reinforce the certainty that the world where they had all those experiences is gone. Gone forever.

Wavering tries not to let it get him down, but sometimes he has to admit to himself that they are in a hell of a mess. He can't help but wonder whether Genesis will be a new beginning or the flaming fireball of the final end. He tries to rein in his mind and think about nothing. It isn't easy.

Occasionally the crew speculates about Proxima b, and directs questions at Wavering. But how many times can they ask, Will there be water? Will there be oxygen? Will there be anything living? Plant? Animal? Perhaps a kind of life they know nothing

94

about? Like monsters or green men or octopus-shaped creatures depicted in old movies?

All Wavering can reply is, "Look, the astrophysicists had various theories based on telescopic images and spectrographs. They indicated their might be various elements and possibly water and oxygen, but nothing is certain." He'd like to think they'll land in a green Shangri-La. But they might find themselves in Death Valley. Or eek out death in the Kalahari. Perhaps they land in an ocean miles from land. Or a swamp where they sink into quicksand and disappear. He wishes he could throw a switch and turn off his imagination. Maybe it isn't that the brain is too big, it's that the damn thing never rests.

They're talking about the options when Sarah finally speaks. "Who cares where we land?" She looks at no one. Her dry, brittle voice conveys she certainly doesn't care.

Her words launch a heated discussion with each member of the group trying to outdo the other in generating optimism. Wavering understands. What have they to lose if the landing is a bust and they all die? Earth is frozen death. If they were to go up on the elevator without their hazmat suits and trek across the frozen tundra, within an hour, they would be lumps lying in the snow buried by the never-ending flurries. Wavering doesn't say anything about that. It's better that they delude themselves that there is still some down-side left. That if Genesis misfires and they don't get off the planet, there is still an option. Although Wavering has no idea what it us. Oh well.

22

Wavering sits alone at the launch bunker dining table poring over the manuals the launch crew and their gurus have prepared for the flight. The elevator door opens, and in walks Sarah. As usual, she makes no eye contact. She silently doffs her hazmat suit. She glides in Wavering's direction and sits down two chairs away. He nods to acknowledge her, but he's learned that if they're to converse, she must begin.

He continues poring over the manuals when she says, "May I see them?"

He looks at her for a moment, wondering if he's hearing right. "They're a slow read," he says. "They're filled with charts and graphs and mathematical calculations which I find difficult to grasp."

"I know," she says. "Trajectories, thrust, burn times, solar wind, gravitational slingshots, maybe space time-warp, and the rest." Her eyes fix on the manuals like she's reading section titles.

Wavering squints at her as if she's a space alien who just emerged from proverbial Hanger 51 at Roswell, New Mexico. He recalls that's where, in the last century, space nuts declared that aliens had landed and either lived in the hanger or were imprisoned there, and the whole affair was hushed up by the United States government. It made for good science fiction, but as far as he's concerned, that's all. Unless some of the escapees became politicians.

"Maybe not such a slow read," he says to her. He hands her the manuals he's gone over. She reaches for them with small hands and fingers so slender they're just skin stretched over bone. She stacks them, puts them under her arm and heads for her hazmat suit.

"You're taking them away?" he asks.

She pauses. "I'll guard them," she says. "I know how valuable they are."

Wavering pauses. At seeing them get out of his hands his nerves are shaking with anxiety. If any one of them were lost, or if she's so unstable she destroys them, they would have no manuals on how to pull off the flight. "Not just valuable," he says. "They're our lifeline. Without them, we don't have a chance."

She nods almost imperceptibly. "I know," she says. She turns and pulls on her suit, lowers the helmet in place, secures it, picks up the manuals and heads for the elevator.

Wavering wants to stop her. He has a sinking feeling that he's crazy to let her do this. If she does destroy them and the others find out, they will cook him to add flavor to their diet of beans. But she's so fragile. She seems to have so little confidence in herself. If he challenges her, what damage would he do to her?

23

"This isn't going to work," Sarah says. She's sitting at the dining table pointing at the flight manuals in front of her. Wavering has just doffed his hazmat suit. Miss fragile and delicate speaks with such authority he wonders if she's more than one person, of if she's one person with more than one personality.

He approaches her. "What isn't going to work?" Whatever she's talking about isn't something Wavering had any idea they would get into. He thought she would struggle to make sense of the numbers and charts and graphs and then give up. After all, rocket science is rocket science.

She opens to the graphic showing the trajectory from the moon to the sun, points to the entry point for the sun slingshot. "It's too far off the surface," she says.

Wavering looks at the drawing and the distances indicated. "Good grief," he says, "even at the altitude on that drawing, if there's a large solar flare, we're toast." He recalls the discussion he had with the programmers about that very thing. He wanted the distance far enough to assure they'd get through no matter what the sun did, but the programmers were adamant. Now Sarah wants them even closer.

"I know we're toast," she says. Her tone suggests that becoming toast is just a part of life. They shouldn't worry about it. In a way, she's probably right. If a flare did burn them up, death would come so quickly there would be little suffering, maybe none. Wavering wonders how desperate he is for small consolations.

He looks at her. The same thin face and green-brown eyes,

shallow furrows in her forehead. "Do you mind if I ask?" he says. "I don't mean to be abrupt. But who are you?" He halts awkwardly. "I don't mean it quite that way. I mean, what qualifies you to review the work of experts and judge it incorrect?" His voice sounds to him a tad accusatory, but it's late in the game to revise the flight plan.

She rests her eyes on him. "Caltech, JPL. I was on the programming team for interplanetary probes." She searches his face. "Those probes were low-powered. We had to use slingshots to get the velocities we needed."

Wavering acknowledges she knows what she's talking about. It's a given in space travel. Gravitational slingshots increase vehicle speed with little expenditure of fuel. Insert the vehicle to reach a certain distance off the surface of a planet or moon or sun. The gravitational field will accelerate the vehicle. Then exit the arc in the direction in which the planet or otherwise is moving. Add the planet's velocity to the approach velocity of the vehicle. Complicated, but it works.

Wavering looks at the drawing. "Where did we go wrong?" he asks. He's still not sure how much of an expert Sarah is on this, but if she's right and the charts wrong, Genesis will hurl through space forever and arrive nowhere. There's lot of nowhere out there.

"The exit point," she says, putting her finger on the line of flight as it moves away from the sun. "It's too soon, too high. It won't put us on a trajectory to Proxima b." She turns to another graphic which shows the flight path from the sun to Proxima b. She says, "In order to achieve it, we have to arc closer to the sun, go in at a steeper angle."

Wavering thinks of mythical Icarus flying so close to the sun the wax on his wings melts. A metaphor for human beings who try so hard to achieve something that they destroy themselves. If Icarus were to follow Sarah's trajectory, concern about wax would be minor. Icarus's wings would burn off. Icarus would be roast god.

"I don't think we can survive it," Wavering says. But if she's right and they end up on a trajectory to nowhere, there isn't much survival there either.

"We have to try," she says. "We'll need to keep the capsule as cool as possible."

"Of course. But I don't think the air conditioning is adequate to handle that much heat."

"You'll rotate the spacecraft?"

"That's the plan." Rotating the craft will be like roasting a chicken on a spit. Evens out the heat and prevents burning on one side. But, like an over-roasted chicken, the whole craft might get so hot the air conditioning won't cope, and they'll suffocate. This line of thought suggests to Wavering they might be living in theater of the absurd. Chicken on a spit, burning up. And the sun is only the beginning of their journey?

"Good," she says sharply, as if she is the commander of the mission.

"Good?" Wavering replies. "Good what? If we don't survive?"

"You know," she says. "Just as the sun has flares, it also has lulls. If we cross the surface during a lull, we'll do fine."

Wavering hates to ask the question that has popped into his mind. But Sarah's far more into spacecraft trajectories than he is and assuredly has sent probes through solar slingshots. "What are the odds?" he asks.

She wrinkles her nose. That seems to be something she does when she's thinking hard. "Fifty-fifty, I'd say," she replies with a lilt in her voice, as if the flip of a coin can't help but produce a positive outcome. "We only lost one probe to a sun flare. Temperature shot up to ten thousand degrees. Nothing is assured."

Wavering thinks of the odds makers at Vegas before they got incinerated. That Genesis thing going to Proxima b? Don't go near it. Dead on arrival.

24

Augustus Fluke III's presence among the crew is not going well. At meals, if they can call gagging on beans a meal, and other times when they are together and Augustus is there, discussion about who finished off earth rises to the point where arguments break out.

Most of the time Malcolm is silent. Not sullen, just not unengaged. Wavering senses he's watching and listening and tuned in to what others are saying. But he prefers being quiet. It gives him an aura of mystery. Something Wavering believes he enjoys.

Until once, when Augustus Fluke III repeats what he's said many times. "I did not order the launch. The Russians hacked into the signal codes. Hacked. Can you believe it? I thought they were our friends. Good God, we let them hold onto the Ukraine. We looked the other way when they took back the east European block that was part of the Soviet Union. We forced Germany to give back former East Germany. They divided Berlin as it had been during the Cold War. And they hacked into our launch codes? Can you believe it?" Augustus casts about that smirk of self-confidence that defies anyone to argue with him.

After a few moments of silence, Malcolm raises his head and levels his gaze at Augustus. "You did initiate the launch."

Augustus presses his head toward Malcolm. "Who are you to counter what I say?"

"Who am I?" Malcolm replies. "You know who I am, and you know I was in the Communications Center when you grabbed the football and sent the codes."

Augustus sputters. "You were in? You were not in."

"I was in," Malcolm asserts strongly. "You never noticed your Secret Service detail. You took us for granted. But we were there, and I was there when you entered the codes from the biscuit."

"Bullshit," Augustus roars. "You're lying. You're a liar. A liar." He glances about for support, but everyone stares with cold detachment. He turns back to Malcolm. "If you were there, then you can testify that I did not do it." Augustus's voice rises to the threat level they heard so often from him. It's a wonder he hasn't killed someone who opposed him. Maybe he has, through surrogates.

Malcolm doesn't flinch. "I was there. I saw you grab the football. You fumbled with it, swore a couple of times, pulled out the biscuit card you carried and entered the code. You said, 'There, that ought to fix those godless Muslims once and for all.'"

Augustus's face turns purple. "Lies. Lies. Lies. Why should anyone believe someone like you?"

"Me? Because I'm black?" Malcolm replies. "Because I'm the same color as Barack Obama, whom your great grandfather accused of spying and lying and declared him a fraudulent and failed president?"

Malcolm is flying into the maelstrom on this one. The whole Fluke line has done nothing for people of color. Wavering has no doubt they're white supremacists. Fascists, with their tyrannical dictatorships. But few ever called them out the way Malcolm is.

Augustus trembles with anger. "But the Russians...," he shouts.

Malcolm cuts him off. "The Russians fooled you. I saw the Guam radar images. Yes, there were objects rising from the direction of Indonesia. But they weren't missiles. The Russians assumed you and your advisors were smart enough to know that Indonesia had no missiles. They hacked into the radar computers and planted false images to challenge US defenses and see how they would respond to a real attack. But you and your advisors were so dumb you didn't listen to the intelligence chiefs about Indonesia. You just grabbed the football, and here we are."

Augustus hyperventilates. "I could have you court-martialed. I could have you sent to Guantanamo. I could have you executed."

Malcolm looks at the rest of them. "Court-martialed? Guantanamo? Executed? Really?" He lets silence fall. "You still don't realize it's over, do you? That there is no court-martial, there is no Guantanamo, there are no executions—unless you're going to pull one off right now."

Augustus gives all of them one more look. Not seeing any support, and with no one speaking up, not even Holiness Jones, he pushes to his feet, stomps to his hazmat suit, stuffs himself into it, stalks to the elevator and disappears.

The crew turns to Malcolm. "Really, Malcolm?" Eva asks. "You're on the level?"

"Every word," Malcolm replies. "Just as I saw it."

"Then why are we taking him with us?" Eva asks.

"We voted," Olga says. "We got rid of Berwick and kept him."

Wavering groans inwardly at the mention of Berwick. He planned to go to Proxima b and mine gold and get rich on the world market. Delusional. But Wavering knows delusion is becoming common. Is it getting worse? Or is it that more delusional people gained power and prominence? Fake news. False news. Alternative facts. Fake facts. False facts. Alternative truths. They were creating their own facts and news and world. Was it a disease, or was it the next step in evolution whereby the human brain detaches itself from reality? People were willing to believe anything, no matter how preposterous, how ridiculous. They believed promises alone would lead to education and jobs and peace and greatness, but of course they didn't.

Wavering sighs and his body chills. I bought into it too, he admits to himself. He couldn't be with Augustus as much as he was and not get infected. A part of him knew III never stopped talking nonsense. But Wavering was paid to serve him, and serving him meant he had to support him. He could not do that without cramming his mind with a false responsibility to support whatever III said and did. Yes, I am guilty, Wavering acknowledges. I suspected he spouted nonsense, but I did not speak up. Was I so obsessed with piloting Air Force One? Yes, I was intoxicated.

So now, Augustus is going on their mission? They did vote, as Olga says. But what if they were to un-vote? Especially now that they know for certain what he did to end the world? Can Wavering be a responsible person if he takes to another planet the individual who ended life on earth?

25

It's like two jugglers tossing hand grenades. The contest is between Holiness Jones and the crew's PhD biologist, Gretchen. That they would eventually detonate the grenades all were aware. The only question was what would ignite the inferno and when.

Gretchen is one of the brainiest people Wavering has met, although maybe Sarah outdoes her. He did not know her before she was chosen for the flight. He guesses someone in Augustus's entourage decided that if life were to be started on another planet, there'd better be on board someone who knew about life. A someone who was not living in an alternative reality. So they chose Gretchen. Summa cum laude from Harvard, PhD from Johns Hopkins, she wrote dozens of articles and several books and was considered an expert in her field.

About 35 years of age, her hair a mixture of black and premature gray, which she tries to tame with the quick swish of a brush——Wavering doesn't think she has a care in the world how she looks. Blue, piercing eyes that pinch slightly when she's making a point she deeply believes. Thin almost to the point of bony, cheeks slightly sunken. If she has lipstick, it never appears.

They don't see a great deal of her, because she has turned the lobby at Motel Aurora Borealis into her green house. Not a real green house, which is impossible because there is so little natural light.

She has dozens of small seedlings growing under multicolored lamps. She hopes they'll grow large enough to seed and add to the cache of seeds she already has. Her plan is to take those seeds to

106

Proxima b, plant them in something that will sustain growth——a huge gamble——and have them grow to the point where they are blessed with corn and tomatoes and potatoes and beans——green, Wavering hopes, and not those pasty white beans they're gagging on at their meals. Grains, too, so they can make froot loops and over-sweet cereals like those that used to rot the teeth out of children's mouths.

But meat? Wavering recalls the Bible's account of Noah's ark, but they are not Noah's ark. Two by two from every species coming on board is not in the cards for a spacecraft. But DNA from various domestic animals, even dogs and cats, she has that. Hearing her describe the DNA, he wonders what she would inject to create a cow, or a goat, or a pig.

"Mice," she said. She took him to the back of her lab and showed him cages of mice, cages that she will put on Genesis. He wondered, if Dr. Drone doesn't put the mice in hibernation, won't Genesis be overrun with them? But he figures Gretchen is smart. She'll work that out her own way.

"After we arrive and get settled, I'll inject the mice with large animal DNA," she said. "There's not much background on doing that, but it's our only hope."

"And if it doesn't work?" he asked her.

She shrugged her shoulders. "A cow-sized mouse?" she said with a laugh. "Whether it would produce milk or not, I have no idea."

Wavering doesn't know much about biology, but he thought he should at least show interest. "Mice reproduce fast," he said. "If they're as big as cows?"

She laughed again. "We'll have to eat beef every night," she said. "We could do worse, you know."

26

The explosion occurs after dinner, and beans are not the cause. "So you say I'm descended from an ape?" Jones says to Gretchen. Wavering looks at Jones. With his enormous belly and round head and his I'm-superior-to-you look, he does have some resemblance to the great apes that Augustus scrubbed from the face of the earth. To mock evolution, on TV Jones did his ape dance where he gestured ape-like with his arms and went "hugh-hugh-hugh-hugh."

He wasn't smart to do that. Most people had seen videos of real apes, and Jones is much closer to those jungle characters than he realizes. If you're going to make a point, reverend, please have the smarts not to turn yourself into a caricature.

Gretchen smiles at him as if she's conversing with a homeless man pushing a stolen grocery cart loaded with a dozen plastic bags of recycled bottles, cans, paper, and soiled clothing retrieved from dumpsters. She sighs. "Mr. Jones, you must have heard this before. Five million years ago, there were creatures that were neither apes nor humans."

"How can you have that?" he fires at her.

"How?" she replies. "I don't know how. I only know what fossil records show. It was an animal that had structural elements that could be described as both human and primate. That line split. From one line came primates, from the other human beings."

"Five million years ago, you say?"

"Yes, because that's what dozens of anthropologists and archaeologists report. No one person could do all that research."

Jones pitches his body forward. "There was no five million years ago. The earth is six thousand years old. Your scientists have no regard for the word of God."

"You mean no regard for your version of the word of God. Which I would say is the word of Jimmy Jones."

"It's the word of God as verified by over two thousand years of the history of the church and countless theologians."

"I'll grant you that," Gretchen says. "Along with the earth being flat and the sun orbiting the earth and the stars and moon being dots of light stuck to a dome that covers a flat earth. A dome like the cover on a high-priced dinner delivered by a uniformed server at a top-end restaurant. Or a planetarium or a domed football stadium. You must admit the church didn't get everything right."

Wavering braces himself, knowing Jones is a fanatic for infallibility. Even though Wavering once believed the way Jones does, he realizes that for Jones the very thought that the church fathers, and fathers they were, ecclesiastical fathers who believed women's wombs were priceless and their brains worthless, could have been wrong threatens the towering cathedral of cards that constitutes his understanding of life and the universe. If one card slips, the whole structure comes crashing down.

"Well, flat earth and sun and moon," Jones mumbles under his breath. "The church reversed on that."

Gretchen sits up straight. "And why did it reverse? Because scientists told church leaders they were ignorant and foolish in the face of scientific facts."

Jones's face drains of color. "So how does that prove I'm descended from apes?" he snorts.

"I didn't say you're descended from apes," Gretchen says. "I said apes and humans have a common ancestry five million or so years ago, but they split. So you are not descended from apes. It's complicated, and the science is incomplete. I'm just giving you what we've learned."

"You put your flimsy theory against the word of God? Who's to say God did not create everything six thousand years ago and man as a special creature made after God's image?"

Gretchen rolls her eyes. "Look, if you want to believe that, it doesn't bother me. But I don't. The universe is roughly fifteen billion years old. Our best telescopes detected galaxies that are over thirteen billion light years away. That means light traveling at 186,000 miles per second takes over thirteen billion years to reach the earth. And you compress that into six thousand years? Well, as I say, if you want to believe it, it makes no difference to me."

"It makes a difference to me," Jones retorts with accusation. "Because you belittle the word of God. You mock God. You are a blasphemer. You are part of the anti-God, anti-Christian movement that brought the world to an end. You and all those who supported gays and abortion. You are all of the devil."

Gheesh, Wavering thinks, here we go. Chilling reminders of his evangelical upbringing. Can't religious fanatics just leave people alone? They start with a collection of the sixty-six—more if you're Catholic—books of the Bible, transform them with some ecclesiastical fusion into one book, and designate every word in that fusion the word of God.

Wavering minored in English literature in college, and to him, a book is a book. That's the way he reads the Bible, and he does read it, at least the parts that he finds relevant. Of course he's biased, but weren't those early church fathers biased to protect their version of truth and their ecclesiastical and political power? He wonders, where do you find one single human being who isn't biased? And when they're all in the same profession and under the same pope and unity at any cost is the price they're willing to pay to protect the church from atheism and Islam and Hinduism and Buddhism and bogey-man religions that never existed, how could they not avoid bias?

"Look, Reverend Jones," Gretchen says. "If you read Jesus' life and teachings, he never condemned gays or abortion. He never condemned anyone based on the prejudices of the time or any prejudices at all. He allowed women to be part of his entourage, he allowed them to touch him, he spoke to that Samaritan woman at the well, and when the religious fanatics in Jerusalem heard about it, it must have made them as virulent in their condemnation of him as you are of me and the rest of us who don't cotton to your views."

Jones's face shades red. Wavering thinks he loves the heat of the battle where he believes he is defending God against outrageous sinners. "You know nothing about the Old Testament or the apostle Paul."

Here they go again, Wavering thinks. Get out of the gospels of Jesus as quickly as possible and plunge into the thicket of the Old Testament and the letters of Paul. Pluck out eyes, cut off hands, stone to death——also handmaids employed to sire children of patriarchs when the wives were never ripe, genocides based on ethnic and religious stereotypes, and, yes, negative comments about gays.

Paul had those inferences too. Plus women are inferior to men and are bound to be obedient. They are to leave their hair long and not speak in synagogues or churches. If you take the cosmology of the Bible, heaven is up somewhere in an overarching dome, hell somewhere down below the level of King Solomon's mines, and the oceans connected beneath the continents. Wavering has to admit, even in the gospels there is reflection of ancient times. What they now know to be mental illness caused by physiological abnormalities in the brain was thought to be demon possession.

"Look," Gretchen says to Jones. "As I said, you're entitled to your beliefs. I don't condemn you for that. But I will not tolerate your contempt. Jesus said, 'judge not,' and I would like to leave all this stuff right there and not raise it again. Can you do that?"

"No," Jones shouts. "If I do, I deny my faith. I deny my savior. I deny my God."

"Look at it this way," Gretchen says. "'Do to others as you would have them do to you.' Do you want someone hammering at you until you give up your views and adopt theirs?"

Jones smirks smugly. "The golden rule doesn't apply."

"Doesn't apply?" Gretchen asks with astonishment. "What's that about?"

"It's for another age."

"Another age?"

"Yes. It's for the millennium. Not now."

"The millennium?"

"A thousand years of peace."

Gretchen's eyes pinch in disbelief. "A thousand years of peace? Well, we've got that now. Peace. Since your evangelically backed dictator wiped out human life on the planet. We must be in the millennium. So now we do unto others?"

Jones smiles beatifically. "I don't know the times or the seasons."

"You don't?" Gretchen says. "Then how do you know Jesus didn't mean for his sayings to apply in his time and now? How do you know they're for another age?"

Jones's beatific facade softens slightly. Then, "I just know."

Wavering realizes he's not the only one there with an evangelical past. Gretchen sounds like she was locked and loaded. Perhaps as a scientist she'd already had several rounds with religious science-deniers. She says, "It's because there were Bible teachers who taught it. And they had no more to go on than their own whims and imaginings. It was a violation of Jesus' prohibition against listening to the teachings of men rather than the teachings of God."

Wavering's mind is racing—Jones is coming with us on Genesis? The question pushes its way into Wavering's brain--Why? He had thought if Jones got physically fit he could help with the heavy work they will face. But if he's going to preach all the way to Proxima b and continue to do nothing but preach, it occurs to Wavering, why the hell are we taking him?

Jones continues, "I am called of God to convert every pagan I'm with."

"Well, thanks for the compliment," Gretchen replies with light sarcasm. "So unless I hold your—what I believe to be harebrained—views, I'm a pagan?"

"Absolutely. I believe the word of God."

"Yes, I heard you say that before."

"You think you believe in Jesus?" Jones taunts. "What kind of Jesus do you believe in?"

Gretchen pauses, scratches her chin. She looks at Jones. "Double Oh Seven with a license to love," she replies. Then adds, "Without the casual use of women."

Jones glares at Gretchen as if she is the reincarnation of Jezebel. Wavering is sure Jones believes he is the prototypical Jesus and she the prototypical devil. But to Wavering, the thought that heaven will be populated with creatures like him? Who would call that heaven?

"It's the vice president," the voice says. The voice is one of the two guards topside covering the entrance to the bunker. Wavering doesn't know why they call them 'guards' when there's nothing to guard for or against. Who is there left to wander across the frozen tundra through dense clouds of airborne frost to get to the shed? The guards mainly control who comes and goes. Which Wavering appreciates.

And he hopes they avoid being outside the shed long enough to suffer hypothermia. Although from his training, he knows it may not be the worst way to die. For fifteen minutes, you're functional and thinking right. The second fifteen minutes you're beginning to lose sense of what's happening and what to do. In the last fifteen minutes, you're off your head. You may get buggy enough to believe that death is a wonderful idea.

The flight crew is sitting at the dining table five hundred feet below the shed having their afternoon, at least they believe it's afternoon, coffee. Wavering stands at the intercom, which is on speaker. Everyone has heard the guard. But what is Wavering to do? Does the vice president want to be onboard Genesis? Him and Augustus III?

Wavering eyes Augustus. "What's going on?" Wavering asks. "Why is he here?" Wavering thinks if the VP wants on board Genesis, they'll have to go through another election. Then who gets bounced? When Wavering took on commanding Genesis, he never dreamed he'd inherit a major human relations job. He'd like to keep the VP topside long enough for him to decide to go back to the White House bunker.

"Send him down," Augustus barks. "Ask him what he wants. After all, you're in charge."

"So when it comes to the vice president, I'm in charge?" Wavering says. "I thought he was your man."

"Send him down. That's an order," Augustus says.

Wavering hesitates. An order. Augustus still doesn't get it. Oh well.

The vice president stumbles off the elevator wearing a hazmat suit, pops off the helmet, strips off the suit. Underneath, he's wearing a dark blue business suit with white shirt and tie. He looks as if he thought he's going to the Ritz for a formal dinner. He's a small man with white hair, pale face, and obsequious look. He eyes the crew for a moment, then focuses on Augustus. "Mr. President, we have a problem," he says.

A problem? Wavering thinks. There is a time for understatement. But holed up in the silo bunker with the entire planet sinking into a millennium of ice, it seems that to declare they have a problem is the ultimate in non-breaking news. Like the captain of the Titanic, with the stern of the ship disappearing into the Atlantic, acknowledging there are more passengers than there are places in the lifeboats. We have a problem?

"What problem?" Augustus asks.

"Those of us in the bunker," the VP replies hesitantly. "We're getting worried. If the weather doesn't change and it's always winter and the snow keeps falling and the temperatures are below freezing and there's no sun…"

Augustus cuts him off. "Get to the point, will you." Wavering heard enough on Air Force One to know Augustus's relationship with the VP is not a good one. Augustus has a way of saying what's on his mind with one phrase framed for instant TV consumption. His questions are the same. Long questions or answers make him squirm with frustration.

"We're afraid we're at the start of an ice age," the VP says. It sounds as if a bit of reality has seeped into the White House Bunker. What happened to the tone deafness to scientists warning a nuclear war would be catastrophic? Wavering knows the president and VP were convinced an all-out nuclear exchange would cause mild radiation for a few years, and then the human race could go back to clogging freeways, attending mega church services, and making gobs of money. On Wall Street, if they were blessed of the Lord.

Augustus stands and marches to the VP with rapid steps. "That's ridiculous," he says. "A hundred years at the most."

"No," the VP replies. Is his face turning red? Did he just disagree with the president? Wavering never saw that before. "The snow is piling up. If it keeps on for weeks, or months, or years, glaciers will cover everything. They could grow to a mile deep."

"So what?" Augustus taunts him. "You're underground. You're well supplied. What's the problem?" Wavering knows Augustus has no empathy for anybody, but does he need to showboat it?

The VP is animated more than Wavering has ever seen him. "We need leadership," he says. "We need someone who's smart enough to figure out what we should do."

Wavering thinks to himself. Smart is not a word that he thought was in the vocabulary of either the president or his vice. The cabinet members and staff III brought on the plane did not put forth smart ideas. Or any ideas, come to think of it. They just genuflected to Augustus III and said his ideas were the most brilliant they'd ever heard. Nuclear war? We'll get over it. Global warming, although it's hard to believe now that was ever a problem——a natural cycle the planet goes through from time to time. Human-caused smoke and dust and pollution have nothing to do with it. Just the planet. The planet makes the problem. The planet solves the problem. Or, as Holiness Jones would say, "God will provide."

Augustus glances at the crew. "Well, we have some smart people here. At least they say they're smart." He speaks with no conviction. They've taken enough of his smirking to know he respects none of them.

The VP hesitates for a moment, then, "We were thinking of you, Sir. You're the smartest person we know. If there's a way of getting past this ice problem, you'll find it."

Augustus settles his gaze on Wavering. "Well, commander, who should be chosen to help out in the bunker?"

Wavering scans the crew. There are only three they can get along without: Jones, Olga, and Augustus. So, Jones or Olga? Jones spouts religious gibberish and never demonstrates he's in touch with any real problems or solutions. Olga is somewhat well-read and smart, but Wavering hasn't been living with his eyes closed. Augustus's and the VP's administration did not demonstrate any belief that women were equal with men. No female cabinet officers, no females in any position of authority. They didn't need Jones harping 'Be submissive' to believe and act as they did. Olga would have no weight.

"Well, Sir," Wavering replies to Augustus in as convincing a voice as he can muster. "I think you're the best choice. You were smart enough to be the president. You're the man the vice is looking for." And, Wavering admits to himself, getting rid of you would be relief for the rest of us.

The VP nods. "We need real leadership. If there's anyone who can get us through this, respectfully, Sir, it's you."

Augustus's eyes grow blank with puzzlement. Wavering can see the two choices arguing inside his brain. On the one hand, he can be a messiah, a savior, the great hero of the only saga left on the planet. That is, if those in the bunker survive.

On the other hand, if they don't, because he found no solution, the bunker entrances will lie beneath miles of compacted snow and ice, and generations of humans, if they can make generations in the bunker, will succumb to hopelessness. Some day travelers coming from outer space will discover that deeply buried bunker with perfect sets of human bones scattered about. Some sitting in chairs, some lying down, some in heaps as if they collapsed standing up. Augustus is either going to be a hero or he's going to be a skeleton among skeletons. Wavering doubts that fits his ambition.

"We feel you bear some responsibility," the VP ventures. He's dancing close to the fire saying that.

"Responsibility for what?" Augustus retorts.

"Well, you are the president, the commander-in-chief," the VP replies. "So if we are to be saved, aren't you the one to do it?"

Augustus eyes the VP with a squint. His jumbled neurons aren't tossing up a clear picture of what he should make of the VP's statement.

"Think of it," the VP adds. "History will attest that you are our country's greatest president."

A gleam shines in Augustus's eyes. How he loves flattery, any flattery, all flattery. But his blank look suggests his mind has gone into gridlock. Risk with the rocket crew and possibly end up as compost on a North Dakota wheat field? Or risk in the bunker with your department heads and staff depending on you to get them through an ice age? What would nudge him in the direction Wavering wants him to take?

"They're your people," Wavering says to Augustus. "You chose them. They have been loyal to you. They need you. You are their leader." Wavering feels like shouting 'leader' to drive the point home. And to make III take seriously that on Genesis, he is not the leader. And he will not be. In the cave, he will be on top, as he always has been. But Wavering can't say it that way because he'd apply pressure, and he knows III has an animal instinct to resist anyone pushing him.

"We need you," the VP adds. "There's no one else who can do it." Augustus could suggest the VP do it, but no one would believe him. III selected the VP to do what he told him. He didn't want someone who might have ideas of his own. He wanted a derivative, the kind of person who lives off everyone else and has no inner life. The VP was a perfect choice. Not that he isn't friendly and amiable and all that. But leadership? Zero.

Whatever gears grind in Augustus's brain aren't producing a response. Wavering knows he's hell-bent on his own survival. But he understands that III can't figure out whether survival is more assured on the rocket to Proxima b or in the bunker. Wavering certainly can't answer it.

The VP isn't finished. "We need you to make America great again," he says.

No one has used that phrase coined by his great grandfather since Augustus III finished off the planet. III's eyes brighten. The VP has hit the right button. Of course there is no America to make great again. Any more than there is anything else to make great. But Augustus's eyes brighten as if he's having an epiphany.

Wavering can't imagine what he sees. How III can make a country he destroyed great when he's sitting in a concrete bunker complex in West Virginia with mega feet of snow and ice piling up on the ground above? Wavering's sure he doesn't see that. It's the phrase, "Make America great again," that exploded some memory bank in his brain.

III marches about and waves his arms as if possessed. "Yes, make America great again. Make America great again," he repeats in a loud voice. "My country, I will answer your call." He glances about with that smug grin that suggests he is obeying a command from God. He puffs out his chest like he's fulfilling his destiny. He is the new messiah. Go for it, Wavering says to himself. Go for it.

28

The departure of Sir Augustus went quickly. The VP couldn't settle himself. He squirmed when sitting down and paced nervously when standing. He was as nervous as an ant on a hot skillet to get Augustus Fluke III back to the bunker to shore up the sagging morale of the cave dwellers. Someone in the bunker must have convinced the VP that previous ice ages loaded the northern and the southern hemispheres with miles-thick ice that for many years slid toward the equator and carved out minor features such as the Great Lakes and Hudson Bay and took centuries to melt.

There was no send-off party. When all you've got is cans of beans, what do you do, place a candle in the middle of a bowl of cooked white beans and call it a celebration? When Augustus appeared in the underground dining room to say goodbye, there were no speeches, grand or otherwise.

Wavering thought that when Augustus was suited up and preparing to go, at least Olga would spring forth with a tearful goodbye and regrets that he was going and how wonderful he had been. But she just stood there statue-like and mumbled, "Augustus, it was wonderful to have you here. We wish you well. Good luck in the bunker. Say 'hi' to everyone for us."

Wavering thought she might throw her arms around III. He took a step forward as if he thought the same. But she cast him a little flick of her hand that said goodbye and that was all. Wavering wondered what kind of relationship there was between Augustus and Olga. The crew surmised they were conjugal without being conjugal. Easy to understand with Olga, since she'd been through seven husbands and maybe hadn't played out her hand. She certainly didn't need any of Augustus's wealth. A moot point since it didn't exist any more than did that of her seven deceased husbands.

Maybe Olga's mind was on Eva and Sarah. She didn't say much about them, but she often huddled with them in serious conversation. A mother hen watching, nervously concerned, but not pushing herself on them. Wavering thinks she's a good soul who might have had a lot of bad luck. She certainly didn't have a natural talent for selecting husbands. Although there are rumors that she contributed to their demises. Wavering never explored that. The journey to Proxima b, that is his business, and it is big. Thankfully, he's not Olga's eighth husband. Otherwise, in addition to anxiety about blowing up on launch, burning up in a solar flare, or finding himself on a misguided space capsule seriously off course, he'd have to be on guard for the mickey. How much can a man take? Oh well.

Wavering took Augustus aside before he left to tell him there was something on his mind. He knew III had no knowledge of ice or surviving in cold weather or glaciers, absolutely nothing. Another world, from III's point of view. Wavering sat down next to him and said, "That problem with ice building up over the bunker entrances. Are you open to an idea?"

III blinked at Wavering as if he had nothing to contribute beyond flying Air Force One. But III did pause as if he might give Wavering a few seconds. Wavering interpreted that as a sliver of openness.

"I was in Jackson Hole one winter," Wavering said. "The temperature never got above zero degrees Fahrenheit. There was a flock of ducks on a pond behind the house. The pond was freezing from the edges in. But in the center there was a hole with open water, through which the ducks dove for food. How did they keep that hole open? Every day, they paddled madly in circles along the encroaching slab of ice, and thus kept it from freezing over the entire pond."

III looked at Wavering as if he were a lunatic from the Audubon Society. Wavering knew him well enough that he thought any idea originating from someone other than himself, especially someone who served him, was not worth listening to. But still III cocked him an ear.

"The point is," Wavering continued, "you're going to have to have a crew go topside every day to shovel away the snow that's fallen. They're going to have to do that indefinitely, or you'll be iced in. As ice builds up around where they're clearing, you'll find the bunker entrances are at the bottom of an increasingly deep hole in the ice. That's the only way you'll have access to the surface and get air to keep you alive."

III stared at Wavering with a look he had seen often. Eyes open, brain seemingly engaged, but dull non-recognition in the eyes that told Wavering III had no idea what he was talking about. So, whether III will have a crew maintain a hole in the glacier to keep from suffocating, who knows? At least Wavering is satisfied he tried.

29

Berwick is back. That's all Wavering can think. It paralyzes his mind. It happened like this. The flight crew was lounging beside the empty swimming pool at Motel Aurora Borealis, reading, sleeping, pacing nervously because they couldn't get used to not having computers and smart phones and smart pads and headphones and the like.

The door from inside the motel opened and in stepped a rotund figure encapsulated in a hazmat suit. Wavering looked around to make sure he hadn't misplaced Holiness Jones and this was him. But Jones was stretched out on a chaise with his eyes closed. Doing what, Wavering couldn't surmise. Talking to God about what happened to the rapture and how did Jones get it wrong? Confessing that the earth deserved to be destroyed because of gay marriage and abortion? He would never confess to racism or sexism or greed or xenophobia or religious bigotry or waging genocidal wars to keep the U.S. on a war footing and thus perpetuate Augustus Fluke III's dictatorship. No, those were not sins. They were the product of liberal thinking that flirted with the demonic scourge of socialism. On the other hand, the way Jones rumbled like an agitated volcano, Wavering concluded he was sleeping.

Who then was the intruder? Off came the helmet, and oh no. Berwick. Everyone stared at him with looks ranging from surprise to face-lighting-up rage. Which Wavering surmised was probably the hue on his face. What on earth was he doing back? They got rid of him, got rid of him by vote. Goodbye Mr. Berwick, have a great time and don't call. But here he was.

The swimming pool room became quiet as a tomb. The crew might as well be figures in Madame Tussaud's Wax Museum in London. Except Madame Tussaud's Wax Museum in London is no more and the wax figures melted and burst into flame like candles under the incinerating power of countless nuclear bombs that exploded over the city. The city is no more either. Wavering guesses, when you think about it, Mount Rushmore was a better idea.

Even Olga, long-time friend of Berwick's, just sits in a plastic chair leaning slightly forward with a look reminiscent of those of the women who went to the tomb of Jesus that first Easter morning expecting to find a corpse to embalm and encountered instead Jesus walking around doing whatever a messiah does when he's awakened from the dead. At least Olga's look is what Wavering thinks those women would have had on their faces.

All Wavering can do is blurt, "Berwick." He can't disguise that his attempt to express surprise is smothered by disgust. Wavering should ask him why he is back, but he doesn't want to. He doesn't want to know. He doesn't want him back. And to ask him why is to acknowledge that he is back and probably burned up whatever capitol he thought he had in the West Virginia bunker. In Berwick's mind, he is here to stay.

Berwick smiles with that fake grin he cast at the Fox News cameras when Fox interviewed him on his latest monopolistic acquisition and the billions of dollars involved in the deal. That smile could not mask the internal machinery of his brain working on the next deal and the next, this man could not show genuine satisfaction or gratitude even if he bought the entire universe.

"Hi everyone," he says as if the crewmembers are good friends and glad to see him return and missed him while he was gone. It doesn't break the ice, it feels as cold in the swimming pool room as in that frozen mist that shoulders up to the windows and slumbers on the roof.

Someone has to say something to him, so Wavering guesses it's his turn. "This is a surprise," he announces lamely. What else is there to say? Welcome back? Wavering can be hypocritical at times, but he doesn't want to sound phony to the core. How nice to see you? As if Wavering can say 'nice' with anything other than the echo of a hollowed-out log.

"What happened?" Wavering asks him icily. He can hear his tone is accusatory, but so what. It was a nice day before the door opened and Berwick entered. Then the day descended to hell.

"I decided with President Fluke III returning to the bunker I'd be needed here," he replies "You lost one. I'm taking his place."

"You thought you'd be needed here?" Wavering asks. "Did Fluke III tell you you were needed?"

"In so many words," he says tentatively. Berwick may be a mastermind at making money and screwing the middle class and poor people, but he's not far up the learning curve on mendacity.

"Berwick, be real," Wavering says. "No one authorized a switch, and Augustus knows it. You know it. Stop blowing smoke and tell us truthfully why you're here." He throws in 'truthfully' even though he never connected truth with Berwick or Fluke III.

"I told you. I thought I would be needed," Berwick says. "With the president gone, you're one short." It's amazing how Berwick can count. One minus one equals zero, which is just fine with Wavering. Now they're back to plus one, and what a one it is.

Wavering stands and paces. His nerves crackle. He's amazed at how his brain tells him to stay cool and calm, don't get emotional, keep your feelings to yourself, but the nerves still jolt with electricity. He wants to shove Berwick out of Motel Aurora Borealis into the snow and ice and cold and shout at him never to come back.

"You thought you would be needed?" Wavering asks in a dubious tone. "Needed for what?" Berwick has demonstrated only one talent. To make money which he used to manipulate whomever he needed to make more money. Since Wall Street and all the banks and all the investment houses have been vaporized, there isn't much left in the way of paper assets to pass from others' coffers to Berwick's. Maybe locating Bank of America and Citibank and Wells Fargo and Credit Suisse and the others in large cities wasn't a good idea. They might have survived if they had been in Kansas wheat fields or Iowa cornfields or South Carolina pig farms, but Wavering deems that a moot point.

Berwick stands with his eyes glassed over. "Needed for what?" Wavering asks again. "Look, you say you came back because you were needed. Either you had something specific in mind. Or that isn't the reason you came back." Wavering admits to himself he takes demonic delight in making mister big man with big money squirm. If only he had to pay back the millions of people he bilked with his mergers and acquisitions and hostile takeovers, costing the raided companies millions of jobs. Wavering finds Berwick to be a man he has no way of respecting or liking.

"I want the real reason you came back," Wavering insists. "Or do you want me to guess?" That wouldn't be difficult to do, but he wants to see if Berwick will volunteer. He'd have to admit some kind of failure, and admission was something Wavering never heard from him or Augustus, even when the failures were monumental.

If there are any wheels turning in Berwick's head, Wavering can't detect them. "They didn't want you," Wavering blurts. "Did they? They kicked you out. They found out the truth, that you bilked them out of pension funds and retirement funds and life savings while you made billions for yourself?"

Berwick pulls himself up straight, raises his nose. "I don't know what..."

Wavering cuts him off. "Good grief, Berwick, let's not play innocent. You know what you did. They know what you did. They don't like it. So they don't like you. They drummed you out. And when the plane came with Augustus Fluke III, that was the perfect opportunity to get rid of you. That's what happened, isn't it?"

Everyone glares at Berwick the way they would glower at a rapist or a murderer. He deserves it. So would Wavering shove him out into the cold? Would Wavering do what Berwick would do in Wavering's shoes? Does he become like Berwick and like Augustus and all those male egos cut from the same cloth who twisted the country into a slot machine for their own benefit and the people be damned? Sometimes Wavering finds the Golden Rule a burden, but damn it, fly against it and how do you live with yourself?

30

Sarah approaches Wavering in that abrupt manner he's trying to get used to. Her brow is wrinkled in a querulous look. "I found something," she says.

"Something?" Wavering says. "What something?"

"There's a bank of files in the computers that's locked," she says.

Wavering doesn't answer. Even though he thought eventually she might ask the question. The locked computer bank? He knows what's in that bank, because he put it there. But does he divulge to her what's there and that he's responsible?

She stares at him for a moment, but doesn't comment. Wavering likes the way she senses when to back off. The opposite of Jones and Berwick with their blah blah and no realization that he's not interested in what they're saying and they're boring him to kingdom come. You'd think from the blank look on his face they'd get the message. They never do.

Wavering meets Sarah's inquiring gaze. But does he answer? With Berwick and Jones hanging around, something could go wrong. Everything in that computer bank is banned.

Wavering recalls how Fluke II and then Augustus Fluke III tightened their grip on the country. In order for their power to grow, the power of the people had to be weakened. Better said, the people's power had to be killed off. The Flukes found that their chief enemy was democracy. Democracy, that's what gave the people power. If people had power, that limited the power of the president.

How to break the power of the people? White supremacy and thought control. It started early in the century with the campaign against immigrants, the refusal to enforce civil and voting rights laws, discrimination by sex, and then oppression by religion.

It was oppression by religion that led Wavering to what is stored in the locked computer bank. Actually it was the third Fluke II amendment that prompted him to take the risk. The amendment that made the evangelical Protestant faith and conservative Catholicism the official religions of the United States. Most people thought it was a store window effort with no teeth in it. Would that it were.

The religion amendment had far-reaching consequences. As if both evangelicals and Catholics had been waiting for years to take over. The Flukes gave them the green light. Curriculums in all schools were converted to religion-based teaching: evolution was prohibited and replaced with creationism——the heavens and earth were created in six days six thousand years ago; boys were taught that men are superior to women and women are bound to obey them; offenses such as being a non-Christian or gay or associated with abortion were elevated to criminal status.

How to find the criminals? Politicians and religious leaders learned from Nazi Germany and the Soviet Union that the best policing is done by neighbors spying on neighbors, family members on family members, everyone spying on everyone else and turning over to the authorities those who did not conform to evangelical Sharia law. Wavering includes Catholics in that law, because the views of the Catholic church conformed to the evangelical agenda. The only difference was the organization of the Catholic Church and its hierarchy, which were outside constitutional restrictions and thus irrelevant.

Getting back to the locked computer bank Sarah found. Wavering thinks maybe she's too young to know, but the United

States has taken backward jolts into past history: books burned, art works and sheet music, tapes, and disks all consigned to the flames. In every city, in every town, people brought their banned books and the rest to the center of their town or neighborhood center. Self-appointed vigilantes splashed gasoline on the piles and lit them. Police and fire fighters stood by approvingly as wheelbarrows and bins and baskets of books, magazines, tapes, sheet music, paintings and even sculptures were hurled into the flames to be read or viewed or listened to no more.

Digital copies as well. Which is where Wavering is attached to those files Sarah found locked. Augustus II passed a law that digital copies of objectionable material were to be erased from all computers, all storage drives, all clouds and the like. With the open information act, government officials had access to everyone's computer and storage drives, and anyone not complying received a friendly visit from the security police who hauled them off for thoughtful reflection in the local jail.

What was Wavering to do? A lit major, a lover of books and art. What Fluke II authorized was sacrilege. But Wavering discovered he had an advantage. While piloting Air Force One and taking a break, he overheard Fluke II and Augustus talk about plans for the purge. There were evangelists and ministers and priests and archbishops and bishops on board. They drew up lists, not of what was banned, but what was approved. The approved list was short and thus made the task easier.

People would think it was just heretical religious works that were banned. Not by that band of holy thugs. Everything that did not buttress their teachings. Hardly any of the world's great literature or art or music passed their test. For paintings, they were left only with the Flemish and similar works depicting figures from the Bible and church saints. Impressionism, abstract art, expressionism, surrealism, everything other than religious representational art went to the flames.

Books? Even though many writers, especially the great ones, referenced biblical themes--the struggles of morality and life and faith and death, if the characters depicted were troubled, doubtful, unsuccessful in solving their problems, into the fire went the books. The standard was 'victorious faith. ' Any portrayal of people having doubts, not victoriously succeeding against every kind of struggle, those books were consigned to the flames. People who never had a doubt, never struggled, just believed, their works were preserved.

Wavering saw all this going on. He was upset. But what to do? The safest would have been to ignore the literary pogrom and do his job. But because he was a presidential pilot, he realized he had cover others did not. He could avoid suspicion. He knew that sometimes when you're close to a leader, you can get away with more. The way Nazi Germany resistors met at the Berlin restaurant run by Adolf Hitler's brother to plot against the Fuhrer.

Using a false ID and an altered password, Wavering loaded thousands of books and photographs of art works and written and digital copies of music into storage files. They are what he locked into the computer bank on Genesis that Sarah asked about. From time to time, he loads selected volumes into his e-book, but he only reads them when he's alone. If only they could get rid of Jones and Berwick, how much more freedom they would have.

31

The flight crew is gathered in Borealis's pool room. Wavering looks at each one, confirming to himself, yes, they will be part of my crew. They're far from a group the Air Force would have recruited for flight duty. Or space travel. But they are Fluke III's selection. What does he know?

Wavering knows that every commander, the title he bears on Genesis, needs a cohesive crew. Always. The more demanding, the more risky the mission, the greater the need for the crew to support each other. It's not a dream, it's not an unreachable ideal, it's an absolute necessity.

But as Wavering looks about, he fears he doesn't have it. Gretchen, maybe tired of bottling up her irritation, continues her inquisition of Berwick. When Wavering let Berwick back into the group, she and others sank into a funk. But they held their tongues. Until now. Gretchen speaks matter-of-factly to Berwick: "I can't believe Wavering let you back on."

Berwick neither looks at her nor replies. Wavering know he buys Holiness Jones's truth that women are inferior to men. Men don't have to respect women or listen to them. Strange that this billionaire with the swept back gray hair and stone-hewed face, with all the notoriety he got, succumbed to Jones's religious babble.

Of course Wavering knows he didn't succumb. Berwick and his billionaire club members funded Jones and his religious clone-heads so they could gaslight millions of people and keep the Flukes in power and support them as they staggered from a failing democracy to a failing fascist dictatorship. It was mutual: Jones gave divine license to Berwick's greed. Berwick funded Jones's religious propaganda that won over the masses. Amazing what strange bedfellows the lust for power can make. But it worked.

"If it weren't for you and your billionaire friends, Augustus Fluke III wouldn't have bumped off the planet," Gretchen says to Berwick.

Berwick refuses to look at her. Wavering has seen it before. Berwick was that way with him when he was on Air Force One. He has a way of looking through people as if they're not there. You only get his attention when you have the scent of money. A salaried researcher like Gretchen? Not a chance. Especially a salaried female researcher.

"I blame you for the planet's destruction," Gretchen says. She pauses for a reply, but there is none. "And the death of seven billion people."

Berwick looks away as if he's following the flight path of a fly buzzing on the far side of the room. The way he avoids eye contact, some might think he's autistic. Wavering knows that for Berwick to look at Gretchen would threaten him with the risk of having to respond to what she says. But Gretchen's accusation seems to be rankling the gray man. His face tinges pink, his look of avoidance develops a high blink rate. "I gave Cornell its new science building," he says.

Everyone is waiting for him to say more. Or to explain the relevance of a science building with Berwick's name on it that is now rubble. But Berwick's smug look says he's off somewhere else.

"We're in hell, do you know that?" Gretchen says. "The hell you and your billionaire friends and Augustus Fluke III and the Reverend Jones and his saintly cronies created."

"I funded five productions staged by the Metropolitan Opera in New York," Berwick replies.

Wavering can't figure out what is going on in Berwick's head.

A science building, five operas, but he funded the president who wrecked the world.

"I don't understand what you're saying," Gretchen says. "Are you suggesting that your charity makes up for your political philandering?"

Berwick's gaze suggests not only that he isn't listening to Gretchen, he's not in the room. Wavering has known men who have that ability. Usually politicians and retired millionaires. Their body is present, but they say nothing, look at nobody, all they do is fill a pocket of air and betray no interest in communicating with anyone.

"There's the Berwick chair supporting a professorship in economics at the Wharton Business School," he says.

Gretchen cocks her head as if she can't hear what she's hearing. Or does she wonder if Berwick is legally deaf? "You were one of the key climate change deniers," she says. "Ninety-nine percent of the world's scientists said climate change was caused by human beings. But you funded that shill Krautspoon who said global warming was a normal natural occurrence. Even though ice samples from thousands of years ago disproved it. Krautspoon was a hooker paid by oil companies that you made money from, a lot of money."

"Reverend Jones has a mission in Africa that distributes food to the needy. I supported that. Jones helped a lot of people."

"I'm sure he did," Gretchen replies without enthusiasm. Wavering knows Gretchen is more into systemic change than relief, as he is. But he lets it go.

She says, "You also told Augustus Fluke III that nuclear war would not end life on the planet. You said that a little radiation might be good for people. You had a shill scientist whom you quoted as an authority. That Hannibal, who was paid by the nuclear power and uranium interests. I have to hand it to you, you have an uncanny ability to find whoring scientists who will testify to anything as long as you put money in their pockets. You have to admit that."

"I supported the Billy Sunday Institute of Science," Berwick says.

Wavering almost chokes. "What an oxymoron that is," Gretchen says with a laugh. "Science and the evangelists have nothing in common. The evangelists were anti-science. They said scientists were liberal communists who were selling fake research."

"We had a chance to make America great again," Berwick says.

"Great?" Gretchen asks. "What do you mean by great?"

"We could have created a country with more self-reliance than any country in the world."

"Self-reliance? I hope you don't mind if I translate that: 'I got mine, you get yours.' There were people who were handicapped, some physically, some mentally. There were people who because of their birth never had a chance at a proper education or jobs. They needed help, but you supported Augustus Fluke III in providing nothing."

Berwick says, "We are a Christian nation, a shining city on a hill, as George W Bush said."

Gretchen cocks her head. She examines Berwick as if he is a mysterious biological specimen. Wavering is convinced she considers him to be delusional. "Mr. Berwick," Gretchen says, "Do you have any idea where 'city on a hill' really came from?"

"Bush," he mumbles.

"No, it wasn't Bush. Or Ronald Reagan who used it before Bush. It was originally coined by John Winthrop at the time of the founding of our nation. Do you know what it meant then?"

"It meant America is the greatest country in the world." Berwick glares with confidence.

Gretchen laughs. "The original thirteen colonies struggling to pull themselves together and exist were the greatest country in the world? You must be kidding."

Berwick's face shades toward red. "All right, then you tell me."

"I will. Winthrop envisioned an America that balanced justice and mercy. He coined the term as a religious principle. It had nothing, nothing to do with superiority. Or with America being more godly than any other nation. Recent politicians twisted it into this 'America First' slogan. Although America sure was first to end the world."

Berwick's gaze reaches out into empty space. "We could have given all our citizens a good life," he says. "But the Democrats, the socialists, the liberals undermined our efforts."

"Undermined what?" Gretchen asks. "They had no power to do anything. You and Augustus Fluke III and Jones and your clones controlled everything."

Berwick replies, "The country didn't listen to the evangelists. They said God would strike down the earth if we allowed abortions and gay marriages. We couldn't stop them."

"You did stop them. Only Fox News said you didn't. For what reason, I don't know. Anymore than I understood the rationale behind any of Fox's pronouncements. You funded Jones and the other evangelists to garner public support for Augustus Fluke III."

The red in Berwick's face drains away to deathlike gray. Wavering wonders if he's going catatonic? What is Berwick's problem? That he's listening to someone he believes so far beneath him that his brain is short-circuiting?

"It was all going so well," Berwick says. His eyes squint in strain as if he's trying to envision paradise rising before him.

"The lies, Mr. Berwick," Gretchen says. "You bought the lies of fake scientists. You applauded Augustus Fluke III's preposterous distortions and exaggerations. You funded Jones's holy temple, because Jones could marshal the support of people who not only believed your lies, but were convinced that because you had money you were blessed by God. And because Augustus Fluke III was a ruler, he was called of God. Prove to me that what I'm saying isn't true."

Wavering feels the determination radiating from Gretchen. She may be reserved, but she's got fight. Understandable for a biologist dedicated to the preservation of life seeing life extinguished and confronting the man she believes responsible.

"It was the Russians who brought on the attack," Berwick says. "We didn't know what they were doing with their hacking and disinformation."

"The Russians?" Gretchen says with a smile of incredulity. "The Russians. Always the Russians. You and Fluke III, you mean you can't see what you did? You still don't realize your talk about surviving nuclear war was idiotic? I know your only compass in life is money. But surely you can see what's happened to the planet and its people. Or do you pretend it didn't happen?"

Gretchen pauses. Berwick's teeth grind. His face retains its tomblike hue. Wavering isn't certain Berwick is able to speak. Finally Berwick scowls at Gretchen. "I admit to nothing. Even if I did, what do you expect me to do?"

"Do?" Gretchen asks. "Isn't it obvious? Take yourself off Genesis. This mission is for life. To have on board a major player who ended life is unthinkable." She pauses, her brow wrinkles. "Do you truly believe you have the right to live when you killed off the human race? Do you think you can escape to another world and begin new life? Over my dead body you'll do that."

Wavering looks at Berwick's gray skull, but it's hard to tell what is going on inside. He's sure Berwick's thinking he'll call security and have Gretchen dragged to the slammer. But security will only respond to Wavering, and there is no slammer. Berwick must realize that if life is to continue on another planet they have to have a biologist.

Gretchen turns to Wavering. "Commander, what are you going to do?" Wavering was afraid of that. It's one of his weak spots. Having pulled the trigger on missiles and bombs from his F-22 over Iraq, Syria, and Iran, weapons that killed many innocent civilians, Wavering vowed that he will take no more innocent lives. Save them if he can. Genesis gives him that chance.

But Berwick? Wavering knows Berwick is far from innocent. However he's not going to kill him. There is an out. For Jones as well. After Genesis launches, when the ground crew flies to the White House bunker to hibernate with Augustus and his court, Wavering can put both men on the flight. He has that authority. But perhaps there's a more tactful way to do it.

"Berwick, I want to make something clear," Wavering says. "If you are on the flight you will do as I say. No argument, no resistance. When we get to Proxima b, every one of us will have to work hard to establish life. That means building shelters, probably out of stone. Plowing and preparing soil for planting seeds. We may have to improvise to get enough oxygen and water. It will all be heavy labor. Do you understand that?"

Berwick has the look of a man who already resides on an alien planet. Manual labor is so foreign to him he may have no idea what it means. Butlers, chauffeurs, cooks, personal assistants, who knows how many he had on his staff? Housekeepers, gardeners and landscapers. His greatest physical effort was swinging a golf club.

Wavering feels he might as well put everything on the table. "You'll have to get physically fit to do the work."

Berwick stands and paces impatiently. "What's wrong with the way I am?"

Wavering takes in the balloon shape standing in front of him. He wants to be tactful, but how? "You're out of shape," he says. "Dr. Drone can help you with diet. Buck can put you on a routine that will make you stronger. Much stronger, I hope."

Berwick casts a quick glance at Drone and Buck, his nose raised as if they cast a foul odor. "And if I won't do it?" Berwick taunts. Through the time Wavering knew him on Air Force One, Berwick had this habit of taunting his opponents to get his way.

"You'll go to West Virginia," Wavering says. "You can decide right now that Genesis is too much for you and sign on for the plane ride to the bunker. There will be space."

Berwick looks like a balloon that's losing air. His head slumps forward, his shoulders sag. He's never had choices imposed on him. He's always decided what he wanted to do and then bulled and bullied his way to get it. Now perhaps he realizes the choices are not of his making.

Gretchen says, "If he's on the flight, he'll always carry the stigma as one of the murderers of the world. I will never forget." She pauses and looks at Wavering. "I'm sure you know, you will have to drive him to do physical work."

"What's your choice, Berwick?" Wavering asks, hoping Berwick will decide to leave. It's difficult to be merciful to the merciless. Yet he's supposed to forgive. Well, forgive if there's some apology. But he's not hearing that.

Before Berwick can answer, Wavering adds, "There's another condition. If you are to be on Genesis, I want you to confess that what you did was greedy and brutal and wrong and that you're sorry." Not that such a confession would change anything, including Wavering's distaste for this smug ball of greed. Or that any confession or penance could in any way make up for what he did.

Berwick stares at him without speaking. In years of hearing him blabbing around Air Force One, Wavering never heard regret. No admission of malfeasance. Augustus Fluke III did for Berwick what no one else could, pulled strings and voided regulations to allow him rise to the top of the billionaire pyramid.

Wavering thinks about this and feels sick. To realize that this one man was the one who egged Augustus on with his baloney about how benign nuclear war would be and how the United States would not just be great again, but be the greatest power ever in the history of the world.

Berwick could fawn all he wanted over Holiness Jones, but he knew that Jones would never realize that Berwick not only did not follow Jesus of Nazareth, he had no interest whatsoever in Jesus of Nazareth. Berwick knew that Jones's evangelical ditto-heads, with kneejerk obedience, fell behind Augustus's leadership. That's all that counted.

Berwick's brain is stuck. He doesn't speak. He looks away as if Wavering and Gretchen are children pestering him.

"All right," Wavering says. "We've several days before launch. The plane to the bunker won't leave until after we're gone. Plenty of time for you to be on it. As for right now, you've got a First Class seat. On the flight to the bunker, that is."

Berwick glares at Wavering as if he's a rodent with rabies. So what?

32

Wavering hears a plane. Or is it a dream? He wonders where he is. Then he realizes his head is resting on a pillow, he can feel a sheet over him. He moves his legs. The sheet scrapes like sandpaper. He recalls it's been a while since Motel Borealis replaced linen, and there's no housekeeping. Five blankets weigh him down—what it takes to keep him warm at night. He wishes he's having a nightmare. But he doesn't think he is. The world is really gone. He is lying on a worn-out bed in an end-of-the-world motel.

A plane? The drone gets louder, then wanes, only to grow loud again. They're circling, Wavering thinks. He holds up his watch, it is seven in the morning. His body stiffens. There can be no plane. Not at seven or any other time. Augustus III is gone. He cannot return. Wavering has nightmares where III is rambling about in the Genesis silo bunker, babbling about how great he is. He's the greatest leader the world has ever seen. Wavering pulls the blankets over his head and drifts off into oblivion.

Later that morning, the door to the swimming pool room opens, and Mike, one of the launch crew, walks in with a worried look. Augustus Fluke III, Wavering thinks? It must be Augustus Fluke III Mike has come to tell him about. Wavering braces himself. An impulse to dive headfirst into the empty pool grips him.

"It's the First Lady," Mike says. Wavering's brain grinds to a halt. How in the world did she get here? The last Wavering knew, she'd gone to St. Petersburg to visit her ailing mother. Augustus III never mentioned her after the apocalypse—and not much before.

He had a way of ignoring anyone who was not immediately relevant. It didn't surprise Wavering that she vanished like yesterday's newspaper and III gave her no thought.

She is his third wife. She's thirty-five and was a dancer in Cirque de Soleil. Augustus III and his entourage witnessed a private performance of the Cirque in the White House. He frequently was presented with private performances of shows——vetted of course to make sure they didn't tarnish his image. He also saw films that had been approved before production to make sure they did nothing to challenge Augustus's reign. Wavering saw some of those plays and films. They gave new depth to the definition of 'boring.'

At the Cirque performance, Augustus was smitten. Some of the proles like Wavering were allowed to attend. They watched Augustus fix his eyes on a dancer with black eyebrows and long black hair. She was dressed in a body-fitting gold gown. Stones like rhinestones twinkled on her slippers.

III sat watching next to his second wife of five years. She had been a clothing designer. Blond, with a full figure and brown eyes, she was beautiful. But during the performance he paid no attention to her. She and the chief of staff seated next to her whispered to each other from time to time. Since Augustus seldom appeared with his wife, regardless of who she was, Wavering didn't know if what he witnessed was unusual.

The dancer was Regina. She came from Russia and had joined Cirque in France. She'd been a gymnast, good, but not good enough for the Olympics. It was natural for her to join Cirque. Wavering had to admit as he watched her pirouette and flow around the stage with the other dancers that she was striking.

As soon as the show ended, Augustus jumped up from his seat and strode behind the stage. He was gone for a long time. His wife lingered talking to the chief of staff. The chief put his arm around her as they conversed. She looked into his eyes as if she were having a beatific vision. Then they slid out of the row of seats and sauntered to an exit.

Wavering did not see Augustus return. Although Wavering saw him frequently on Air Force One, III did not appear much in public. When he did, it was usually at a press conferences, where he was introduced by his press secretary, who had the look of a female wrestler. Tall, with broad shoulders, thick arms, she was someone you would not want to tangle with. Once introduced, Augustus would say, "I have breaking news." All his news was breaking. There was no other kind. He would announce, "Our troops have crushed the Muslim armies in Baghdad and Mosel. An amazing victory. Amazing. A victory." At other times, the crushing had occurred in Iran, Saudi Arabia, Syria, Jordan, Afghanistan, Pakistan, Kyrgyzstan, a bunch of other '-stans' and then India, Yemen, Somalia, and Indonesia, among others. Wavering marveled that the US had so many troops to do so much crushing.

Wavering concluded the point was that the US had victory after victory, nothing but victory, always. Sometimes his mind wandered, and he asked himself, how could the US have so many victories when they kept sending more troops to the fronts and none came home? None came home on their own, that is. He knew Air Force crew members who flew them back to the States. They flew in coffins, countless coffins, draped with the American flag and greeted with a fanfare of trumpets. The receiving dignitary, sometimes it was Augustus, always had the same line. "We are grateful to these loyal soldiers who gave their lives for their country. They will never be forgotten." Wavering was impressed that they would not be forgotten, especially by the president. Sometimes a small voice would caution Wavering that Augustus didn't have much of a memory. Oh well.

Wavering would have stopped viewing those press conferences, except that Augustus, when he saw him after one of his or his press secretary's appearances, would ask, "Did you see the press conference?" Wavering could have avoided them and lied. But III would ask questions like, "What do you think that woman from Fox Sports was asking about? War isn't a sport."

"No," Wavering would reply. "I think it was out of place."

"My thought exactly," III would say. "I'll ask the press secretary to ban her from future conferences."

Wavering nodded. He realized again with chagrin that he was one of III's obsequious bobbleheads. It made him proud, or it had for a time. But then that voice would push its way into his brain: Colonel, do you think it's a good idea that you always agree with the president? Wavering pushed back against the voice: Shut up. Go away. Stop bothering me. The voice did shut up, but what it said bounced around Wavering's neurons for a while after. It made him feel like a fake, even a traitor. That is if traitorous thoughts amounted to treason.

33

After the Cirque performance, Wavering never saw wife number two again. Nor did he see the chief of staff. During a press conference, the press secretary inserted between glowing reports of military victories against Muslims: "The chief of staff has resigned to spend more time with his family." That's all. It made Wavering wonder, though. When he had conversed with the chief of staff on Air Force One, he never mentioned that he had a family. And every time a staff member resigned, it was to be with family. Such devotion. Really?

Wavering expected the press secretary to announce there was a new First Lady. Maybe at least a line about a divorce, too. But there was nothing, ever. It was as if Fluke III had traded in a used car for a new one. Drove the old one in to the dealer, drove out with the new one. Off you go. Sayonara. Wavering was amazed at how quickly and easily III could make changes that took normal people months or years in the courts.

Regina slipped into her role as if she were a stand-in for a theater play. Wavering remembers when he went to the theater and there was a loose leaf insert in the program that listed the stand-ins. Regina filled the part well. When she appeared on TV, she stood in the background behind Fluke III as if she had always been there—her face a mask that would have spooked everyone at a poker table. Her lithe athletic body was an unmistakable replacement for number two's hour-glass figure, but no one commented. Sometimes Augustus III let Regina stand close enough behind him that on TV they looked together. But from

146

where Wavering watched at the door of the plane, they were not.

Sometimes when she slipped off her leash, at least that's what Wavering called her times when III was not near or watching, he got to know her a bit. They would be flying at forty thousand feet with the plane on autopilot, the instruments showing they were running optimally. In addition to officers behind Wavering monitoring the plane's defense systems, there was a security guard. He sat in a jump-seat behind the chief pilot. Always. Augustus's security advisors worried that a pilot bent on suicide could easily crash the plane and bring III's presidency to an unscheduled end of term. Pilots of some airliners had done that. So, Wavering and his flight crew were watched. Although most of the agents spent the time staring at their smartphones or dozing. It was a boring job.

Whenever Regina opened the cockpit door and slid in like a thief in the night, it was always Malcolm who was in the agent jump-seat. Wavering could see in a mirror that she poked her head into the cockpit, glanced about until convinced Malcolm was there, then slipped into the seat behind him. She'd be dressed in a black or dark blue business suit with a white blouse. This was the costume Wavering heard Augustus dictated for her to wear when she deplaned with the Fox cameras rolling and Augustus waving to the adoring crowds from the top of the disembarkation stairs.

Regina retained her Cirque physique. Svelte, as supple and lithe as a cat. She had a very white face——Wavering surmises there wasn't much sunshine in St. Petersburg where she grew up——and glistening black eyes. At least they glistened when she entered the cockpit and sat down behind Malcolm. On TV, when she stood off to Augustus's side, or behind him at the top of the disembarkation stairs, her eyes were as dull as lumps of coal. It was as if her body was there, but she wasn't. It disconcerted Wavering at times, but then he felt he understood. She had a job to do whether she was enthusiastic about it or not.

Wavering would slip one of his headphones to the side so he could hear Regina and Malcolm converse. Normally neither said much of anything. They were like that in public. When she descended the disembarkation stairs or reached the tarmac and Malcolm was standing watch, she merely nodded. Sometimes Wavering could pick up a shy 'hello.' She and Malcolm, he called them the 'inscrutables.' There was no way he could read what was on their minds. Were they born that way? Or had they acquired their inscrutability because they knew being with Augustus required it? Or, being aware there were hundreds of security cameras and microphones placed everywhere, had they developed the ability to express no more emotion than if they were made of granite? Wavering knew a lot of staff, including himself, did. That's how they kept their jobs.

As Regina and Malcolm conversed, Wavering could hear her clear, understandable English. But on those infrequent occasions when Augustus ordered her to say something at a formal dinner, she would say 'hello' or 'thank-you,' with a heavy Russian accent. 'Heeloo' and 'Tank-ou' with the 'a' sounding like 'ah.' Wavering thought Augustus wanted her to show how international he was. And how he had snatched a beautiful woman from a country that did not share his hatred of Muslims. Why that was important, Wavering could not figure out.

When Regina and Malcolm sat behind Wavering, Regina would sometimes interrogate Malcolm about his life. "What do you do when you're not on duty?" "Where do you live?" "Do you live with anyone?" "What do you do for leisure? I know you need it. We all do." "What TV movies and dramas do you like?" As if there was a choice outside the propaganda piped through Fox that was billed as entertainment. Her questions were so basic she sounded as if she had arrived from another planet and was conducting fundamental research on earth.

In his quiet way, he answered. " I read a lot." Wavering perked up on that. He knew reading was risky. And risky for Malcolm to admit. Wavering expected her to ask Malcolm what he read, but she did not. Like Wavering, she would assume he read banned books. Which, with her short leash, she could not. At least Wavering didn't think she could. "I go out to dinner quite often," Malcolm said. "I don't like to cook." To her question, "Do you have a wife?" he said, "No. I'd make a miserable husband. I'm hardly ever home. I have to be on call for the president."

What made her voice rise and her eyes grow brighter was his description of hiking and boating. "I take walks along the Potomac," he said. "When I have time, I drive down to the seashore. I watch the waves and the children and their parents and their dogs." At another time, he said, "I like to rent a sailboat on a lake. It's very relaxing. Just wind and sun and water." Wavering could see Regina's eyes glowing as if she were sitting at the seashore or sailing on a boat. Activities apparently she loved, but could not do. How could you with a bevy of secret service agents and be on call when Augustus III suddenly needed you?

Wherever she went, there was the bulletproof black limo with black SUV's fore and aft and a police escort on motorcycles with sirens blaring. She sometimes went shopping for clothes, something Wavering heard Augustus and her arguing about on Air Force One, with Augustus threatening her not to go out on her own. But she held her ground, and off she went to Gucci's or Niemen Marcus with the line of black SUV's and police escort. Anonymity was impossible.

As Wavering listened to these 'down home' conversations, he realized that Malcolm and Regina had something in common. They talked about activities outside the White House, away from Augustus III and the rest of DC apparatus. They were outcasts. He because he was African-American.

And Regina because she was an immigrant from Russia. Even though Augustus III pulled her away from her homeland, married her, and in one day made her a US citizen, she retained her Russian citizenship. Wavering saw her as a Russian. She wasn't a US citizen long enough to become addicted to Fox and Facebook and all the rest. Plus, he assessed her as a smart woman—she played both sides of the citizenship game. If Augustus dumped her as he did first ladies one and two, or imploded the United States as he also did, she still had Russia. At least what was left of Russia.

34

Mike holds the door open, and a slim hazmat suit enters. The face peering from inside the helmet visor is Regina's. She's smiling. Mike closes the door, leaving her to study Wavering, the empty swimming pool, the glass holding back the frozen fog. She sheds her hazmat suit and stands dressed in black leotards with a black turtleneck sweater and black sneakers. She dons a clear plastic air filter for her nose and mouth. Her black hair frames her white face. Her black eyes resting on Wavering sparkle. He has no idea why. He stands awkwardly. Even though III is not there, his nerves spark with apprehension that he should not be alone with the First Lady.

"Wavering, how are you?" she asks brightly. Wavering is speechless. She's never used his name informally. Around Augustus and his staff, Wavering was always 'Colonel Wavering.' It kept a formal distance lest she become familiar and Augustus's jealousy rush out of its cave. Wavering had seen that jealousy when wife number one, or wife number two, or Regina stared too long at another man. Or talked to one too long for Augustus's liking. Strange how he was supposed to focus on running the country and yet his radar eyes kept track of every move his wives made. But Wavering dismissed that as something any president would do.

How are you? Not a question Wavering answers very often. With the world destroyed and preparation for Genesis ever slow and Genesis itself being an interstellar gamble of colossal proportions, he doesn't feel good. Actually he works hard not to feel at all. Just tuck his feelings into some inaccessible niche and focus on planning for the journey. Or plan for a space-disaster, the thought of which creeps out of the niche too often.

"Maybe I shouldn't have asked," she says. Her eyes are intoxicating. There's a liveliness that shines brighter than what Wavering saw when she was in the cockpit talking to Malcolm. He's unnerved, he doesn't know what to do with his hands and arms or how to stand or what look he should have on his face. He has no idea how to relate to her.

Then she does something Wavering never imagined. She steps toward him, puts her arms around him, and gives him a hug. "It's good to see you," she says. She holds him for a moment, steps back and looks into his eyes.

This is such a sudden change in their relationship, Wavering has no idea what to say or do. She smiles and says, "Maybe I'm being abrupt." There's no apology in her voice. "It's good to see you. I've missed you."

When a relationship goes from icy, distant, and formal to a hug, and then she's dressed in those leotards and throwing her arms around him, her eyes glistening, her lips drawn in a sensuous smile, he's in shock. His brain has no ability to find words. He's had so few girlfriends he hasn't had much practice.

She turns serious, glances about. "He isn't here, is he?" Wavering knows who she's talking about. There's only one 'he' in the world she or Wavering take heed of.

"No," Wavering says. "He was here, but he left. Mr. Berwick has taken his place. But we are having issues with Berwick. We don't know what will happen to him."

"Berwick," she mumbles with disdain.

"The Reverend Doctor Jimmy Jones is here," Wavering says.

She pinches her brows. "Jones? He's that preacher. Why are you taking him on the rocket?"

Right, Wavering tells himself. Why are they taking him? What does he tell her? The truth, that there is no reason in the universe for taking him? He lives in a religious bubble of his own making, and there's no way anyone can jolt him into reality. He's made psychological dissociation a way of life.

Wavering recalls the peg he's hanging Jones on to qualify for the crew. He knows it's a weak one. Very weak. Jones gets physically fit enough to man a shovel or a pickaxe and helps build shelters and create gardens. Wavering says, "We'll need strong people to build what we need on Proxima b—that's our destination."

Regina stares at Wavering as if he's delusional. Such pretty eyes, even when they stare. "You've got to be kidding," she says. "You really think Reverend Talk Forever is going to do physical labor? I know you well enough, even though you may not know it. I know that you don't swoon to his angry God or Jesus waiting in the air." She pauses. "You may believe some of it, but you have to be a practical man."

Wavering smiles at her. Flying an airplane, yes, you have to be a practical man. Dreams, illusions, alternative or fake realities? They don't work. More so, they are dangerous. Planes crashed because pilots didn't focus, or for fleeting seconds were distracted, or failed to believe their instruments, or forgot to look through the windshield to see where they were going.

Wavering feels himself thawing slightly under her warm smile. "You've got a pretty good read," he says.

"I observe," she says. "I see a lot of things. I know that First Lady thing with my husband watching me gives the impression that I don't see and don't know and don't care. But you have to understand there's quite a bit of actress in me."

"Cirque de Soleil?" Wavering asks.

"All of us were actors. We danced with fake expressions on our faces. We contorted to express different emotions. With our bodies, we sent the message the artistic director wanted and the audience responded to." She pauses. "It was a lot of fun. But most of it was acting."

"But you left it for the president?" Wavering says. He has no idea what it would be like to be a Cirque dancer. He assumes the pay wasn't overwhelming. With the travel you wouldn't have a home life.

Regina lowers herself onto a chaise, one leg outstretched, the other bent and clasped in her right hand. After witnessing her cold rigidity when she was with Augustus III, Wavering can't adjust to the relaxed beautiful woman before him. He feels some affection. Guarded though. Why not? He's conditioned. When she entered the pool room and saw him, he expected her to spin away and leave, because that was her habit as First Lady. She seldom lingered and talked to anyone—other than her times with Malcolm. Wavering thinks Augustus did not expect her to have enough in her head to carry on a conversation for any length of time. A greeting. A farewell. Maybe a one-phrase soundbite. That was it.

"Put yourself in my place," she says. "Wouldn't you have left?"

Wavering glances at her body draped on the chaise. Put himself in her place? She's got to be kidding. There's no way he can stretch his imagination to identify with her. She's unique. Especially now, when he feels he's with a woman he never met before.

She doesn't wait for his response. "Maybe that's too much to ask," she says. "But you? Why did you go with him?"

Wavering concedes she has him there. She went with III, even though she knew what he was like. But so did Wavering. "If I'd known he was going to finish off the planet," he says, "I wouldn't have. But I didn't know." Who could anticipate that Augustus III would do what he did? "I was employed as an Air Force pilot. The Air Force assigned eight of us to Air Force One. It's a job. I'm under the orders of my superiors."

Regina smiles understandingly. "So you did your job. As you're doing now. You were given a role, as I was. We both played what we were given."

"I'm not sure I understand," Wavering says. "You voluntarily became his wife. You entered into a relationship."

Regina's lips turn upward, her face softens to a mirthful smile. She breaks into melodious laughter. "Oh Wavering, you're so innocent," she squeezes out. "A relationship? With Emperor Augustus Fluke III? You can't be serious. You really believe we have a relationship?"

Wavering hasn't been called 'innocent' for quite a while. But with the energy of her laugh he has to admit that to her he must appear totally out of touch. He knows how to be in touch with an aircraft, but with people, that's something else. Maybe he's no good at all.

"You did marry him," Wavering says. Although with Augustus making no announcement of the wedding in order to avoid giving gastric upset to Holiness Jones's horde of lemming followers, most people hardly noticed it. Those followers were so pleased to have right wing religion as the national religion and persecution of everyone who did not hue the line that they would have followed Augustus even if he destroyed the world. Which of course he did, but they did not know he would.

"It was an arrangement," Regina says. "A contract, although there was nothing written. I was like you. You're under a contract."

The question has been lurking, but Wavering has withheld until now. He's afraid he will upset her, but he can't hold back. "Do you love him?" he asks. "Or you did love him?"

She smiles at Wavering patronizingly. "Love? You can't mean it?"

"Well, you accepted his proposal when he went after you. There was a wedding, you are married. Usually there's love in there somewhere."

"Usually," she repeats. "Usually. But with him? Wavering, do you honestly believe he's capable of love?"

Wavering feels the conversation is veering into unknown waters. He reminds himself he is one of Augustus's pilots. They fly where he commands them to go. Everything is under his order. Love was never an issue Wavering thought about. Whether it was First Lady Number One or First Lady Number Two or Regina. Did III love any of them? Here is Regina asking him this question. Her guard, so impenetrable before, isn't just down, it's gone. For talking like this, Augustus III would have her executed.

"Whether he's capable of love is not a question I've ever asked," Wavering replies weakly.

"Well, ask it," she says. "Think. Love? Real affection? For me? For anyone?" She pauses. Wavering thinks she's waiting for him to wake up from his delusional state and see her point. He tries to look at Augustus not as Commander in Chief or President, but as a man. Take away the titles, his position, the pomp and circumstance of his public appearances and his demeanor to Wavering and others who serve him, and what's left?

It's not a good list. Greed. Entitlement. Narcissism. Brutality. Love? Wavering has to admit the only love III exhibits is for himself. Everything he does. Everything he says. Every relationship he has with anybody. All centered on his inflated image of himself. He wants adoration. He wants worship. He is like the Caesars who rose to such levels of self-aggrandizement that they demanded to be recognized as gods. Top dog human being in the world wasn't adequate. Neither is it for Augustus.

Wavering feels Regina will be disappointed if he doesn't get this right. He can only say what he perceives. "No, not love. I agree with you. No feeling. He has no empathy. There's nothing in him that can identify with other human beings. If he can't identify with them, if he doesn't see himself as part of them, no, he's emotionally dead."

Regina's body draped on the chaise stirs. "Well, hallelujah," she almost shouts. "Mister cool pilot of Air Force One gets it." She swings her legs over the side of the chaise, sits up, and faces Wavering in his white plastic picnic chair. "I told you Cirque de Soleil was an act. But First Lady? You wouldn't believe how much I practiced in front of mirrors. With President Self-Important not there. He dictated my makeup to suit him and the cameras. Clothes chosen by a committee to fit whatever role I was to play. Facial expression? Mirrors again. I'd try different looks. To meet foreign dignitaries. Military dictators. Banana-republic crackpots. A different face for each. And for women? My lips curved downward so they would know their inferior status. I was a total fake."

She says it with such resounding finality Wavering can't help but laugh. He's struck by the strange humor that surfaces when truth emerges from the fog of others' expectations. How refreshing to discover that behind the First Lady there has been a real person. That the fakery didn't erase her real self and replace it with an Augustus-dictated personality. If III were here now, he would not know her. Her glaring self-revelation would terrorize the bejesus out of him.

"Well," Wavering lets out weakly. "I take it that you didn't come here to be with him."

Regina laughs again. "Wavering, I want rid of him. I heard that he was here. Then I heard he left and was in the bunker. But I wasn't sure. I just followed the last thing I heard. Hoping, yes, he was in the bunker. I'm relieved. Greatly relieved. Can't you tell?"

What a rhetorical question that is, Wavering concedes.

"Can you imagine years and years in a bunker with him?" she asks.

Yes Wavering can. It's a recurring nightmare. III would never abandon his superiority and bullying because that's him. That's all there is. He can't change because he has nothing to change to. There's only one Augustus. But Wavering tells himself he can't get too euphoric. "I'm glad he's there and not here," he says. "But you do realize that until we launch, he could come back? Berwick did."

Regina's eyes harden. "But you wouldn't let him. Would you? If I can be on the rocket, you wouldn't put him there as well——so we'd be together? Because if you would, I'd walk out of here by myself and happily freeze to death."

"No you wouldn't," Wavering says.

"What do you mean I wouldn't?"

"You wouldn't walk out of here by yourself. We'd go together and we'd both freeze to death. Both happily freeze to death."

Her eyes soften, she smiles. "You know, Wavering, I like you. I always knew there was more to you than that silly uniform and 'yes sir,' 'no sir,' and all the rest." She stands. "Now, if I'm on board, how long before I meet the rest of the crew?"

35

"Can we talk here?" Regina looks about the inside of the elevator taking them from ground level to the silo bunker.

"Microphones, you mean?" Wavering asks.

"Yes. I'm always wary. The White House, The Winter White House. Everything everywhere, microphones. I think my bedroom had them too."

Wavering assures her there are none. "I know some of your crew," she says. "They'll lump me with the president. Now that everyone hates him, I'm not sure…"

"You're right," Wavering says. "There's a lot of tension. We were relieved when he left. No one except Olga would want him back."

Regina leans toward Wavering. "There's something I want you to know. But not the others. At least not now." She relates in low tones a role she had with the president Wavering never knew about. Never suspected. But he understands why she doesn't want it known. Even though it might endear her to the crew. Yet, like Wavering, she's lived under surveillance so long she can't assume she wouldn't be running a risk.

Regina and Wavering get off the elevator into the bunker. The crew members are sitting around the dining table. Wavering removes his hazmat suit, Regina takes off her stylist air filter. Heads swivel toward them. Conversation evaporates into thin air.

Regina waves her hand toward the silent crowd and says, "Hi everyone."

They look at her as if she's an apparition. Wavering can see her appearance is as startling for them as it was for him. As they continue to stare, Wavering thinks they're having difficulty identifying who she is. First Lady is probably not the first person to come to their minds. Nobody has mentioned her. Not Jones. Not Berwick. And not Augustus III when he was there.

It isn't just that she's there. Their eyes search up and down from her sneakers to her short hair with a sustained look of incredulity. Is this her? Is this the First Lady? I must be hallucinating.

Regina laughs. "Well, haven't we seen each other before? You do recognize me, don't you?"

One by one, the crew stands. But their tongues are tied. They're waiting for someone else to speak. Finally Olga stirs, "Honestly, First Lady, this is very unexpected." Her voice is icy, her glare cold. Wavering takes it that Augustus had Olga hanging around the White House, and Regina got more of her than she wanted. Augustus was like that with women. He could have been a sultan with a harem.

"Olga, how are you?" Regina asks.

"I thought you were away. In Russia. Visiting your mother." Olga softens not one bit. She spits out words as if she would be very glad if Regina had stayed in Russia visiting her mother.

"I was," Regina replies smoothly, with a light air. "But I came back. Well, not quite back. I came here."

"But the bunker?" Olga says. "Your husband is in the White House bunker. That's where he'll wait until conditions improve."

Regina glides closer to the table and looks at the faces. "I know," she says. "That's his choice."

"But he's your husband," Olga insists. "You should want to be with him."

"Thank you, Olga," Regina replies sarcastically. "I appreciate your concern for my well-being. But I am here. Here by choice. And I don't plan to leave."

She looks at Wavering, and he nods. "She's on board Genesis," he says.

There are no smiles on crewmembers' faces. Faces that remain stiff from shock. As if they've figured out who they're looking at, but can't get a fix on who she really is.

"Don't you think we should vote on that?" Gretchen asks. "If we take the First Lady, even without Augustus, aren't we still taking him? She's part of him." Gretchen's jaw is set. "The First Lady kowtowed to Augustus like a slave." Gretchen looks to Wavering. "Wavering, I disagree with your decision. I have an idea I'm not the only one."

Wavering opens up to the crew. "I know this is abrupt. Abrupt for me, too. I didn't know Regina was coming."

"First Lady," Jones interrupts him.

"Regina," Wavering says. "She and I have talked. Some of what she's said is confidential. You have to trust me that we can rely on her to be a full part of us."

The faces don't soften. Eyes are hard. Wavering doesn't know what more he can say. Berwick takes a graceless step toward Regina. "First Lady, it's good to have you here. You're very welcome." He smiles as a mouse would if it could when a menacing cat turns away distracted. Always the opportunist. If he sucks up to her, maybe she can get Wavering to change his mind and not send him to the bunker.

"Thank you, Mister Berwick," Regina says. She lets it go at that, not betraying Wavering has told her he's out of there. She looks away from him. "Why don't you all sit down. There's no president anymore. So there's no First Lady. As Wavering said, my name is 'Regina.' In Russian, it means 'queen.'" She laughs. "But I'm not a queen either. I'm just Regina."

The crew's glacial looks say they're not having it. Wavering knows what they're going through. The same as he went through in the swimming pool room at Motel Aurora Borealis. They can't make such a huge leap in a few minutes. She has been First Lady. She has been the queen to king Augustus Fluke III. She's sacrosanct. She walks on water. You defer. You bow. You do everything possible to show subservience and awe.

Regina walks around the tables and addresses each one. Those she knows by name. The others, she asks. She's ebullient, as if each is a warm friend. Wavering has never seen her like this. Apart from those conversations with Malcolm that Wavering overheard, she was always frozen with aloofness. Strictly obedient to Augustus, walking stiffly behind him, standing behind him. Never upstaging him.

When her eyes meet Malcolm's, there's more recognition than with the others. Do they notice? Wavering doesn't think so. They're still trying to break up the ice of their notion of First Lady.

Holiness Jones smiles and reaches for Regina in anticipation. Of what, no one can tell. His eyes gleam. "We need you," he blurts fawningly.

Regina halts rounding the table and looks at him. "Need me?" Her tone of voice is incredulous. "Need me for what?" she asks.

"Your support. Like you gave us as First Lady."

Regina pauses, forming her thoughts. "What are you talking about?" she asks.

"For the faith," he replies. "To maintain the national religion."

"National religion? Jimmy, in case you haven't noticed, there is no nation. So how can there be a national religion?"

"Religion is eternal," he replies. "It doesn't need a nation. All it needs is God."

Regina smiles condescendingly. "I don't mean to stand against God, but I would say all religion needs is a bunch of people who believe in it. And preachers who keep blowing high-sounding words into their balloon."

Jones stammers for words. "First Lady, what has happened to you? You were such a devoted follower."

Regina laughs. "Yes Jimmy, the First Lady was a devoted follower. Because that's what the First Lady was supposed to be. She devotedly followed the role she was given. The First Lady did that. But I told you. The First Lady is gone. So the devoted follower is gone." She stares at Jones for a moment to see if anything is sinking in.

The vacant look on his face tells Wavering it isn't. Here's a man who spent his life telling others the word of God and never listening to anyone. He had the truth, so why should he listen? No one else could possibly have anything to contribute.

"Jimmy, let's you and I be real," she says. "You had a role just as I did. You made it for yourself, or someone in your past made it for you. And it was good. Notoriety, cozying up to the White House, time with the president on Air Force One. On camera with him. In the headlines. You were one of the cardinals upholding the national religion. Maybe pope even. The money and fame were good. Always good. Can't sneeze at that, can you?"

Jones's eyes flit about as if he can't get God's attention to give him the words he needs. His lips flex, his cheeks quiver, his eyes grow more blank than the proverbial 'deer in the headlights.' It's as if he signed on for a tour of heaven and the bus went to hell. "But First Lady..." he blurts. He can't finish. He's off autopilot. His arsenal of stock phrases is empty. Or he never had one for a heretical First Lady. He developed a reputation for shoot-from-the-hip retorts, but he's bankrupt on this one.

Strange, because Wavering remembers how he loved to taunt, 'Do you really think my grandfather was a monkey?' So much for evolution. 'Don't you think God knows the weather is slightly warmer and we can leave it to Him to do something about it?' 'The Bible predicted nuclear war, so let's get used to it.' 'Those rocks the so-called experts say are a hundred million years old? Don't you think an all-powerful God can create rocks any age he wants whenever he decides to? And in six days six thousand years ago?' No scientific fact ever seemed to find a lodging in the ninety billion neurons caged in Jones's skull.

"First Lady was an act," Regina repeats. "First Lady bought your spiel because that's what a First Lady is trained to do. But Regina did not buy it. As a matter of fact, I found it loathsome."

Jones's arms flail. He seems suffused with an energy he can't control. He isn't used to being challenged. And by someone he was convinced was unhesitatingly loyal. It's as if he was promised an interview with Jesus and found Beelzebub sitting in Jesus' chair. "So you're not a believer?" he says accusingly.

"A believer in what you believe?" she says. "No. Never was."

"You're not a believer at all," he says. "What I believe is the word of God. There is no other."

Regina smiles as if Jones is a huckster selling fake handbags on Fifth Avenue. "Jimmy, you don't know much about Russian history, do you?"

"I prefer 'the Reverend Doctor Jones' if you don't mind," he replies.

"I'm not doing 'the Reverend Doctor Jones.' You're the same as the rest of us. Except you cover yourself with that holy look and that holy talk. I know many people bought it, but I didn't."

Jones sinks down in his chair. He isn't used to being lectured by someone he held in high regard but who now is knocking out his underpinnings. She's forcing him to 'come to the mountaintop,' a reference Wavering uses, thinking of Moses on Mount Sinai amidst the smoke and fire, confronting the voice of God.

"Leo Tolstoy pegged it," Regina says. "He was a wealthy aristocrat in the eighteenth century. But he had a heart for the peasants. He fought for their freedom and education. He fought for them to own land. He wanted the courts to grant them equal justice with aristocrats. But do you know what? The Russian church was in the grips of the government and the aristocracy. The money and prestige for the church and its hierarchy were good. So why not ignore the peasants and their suffering?"

"What's that got to do with me?" Jones asks. "I wasn't a Russian aristocrat."

"No, but you supported my husband to keep him in power. You were wedded to him. You joined with him to oppress everyone who did not bow to him and to your 'Christianizing' of the country. You gave divine sanction to whatever whim he had. You ignored the real Jesus."

"The real Jesus?" Jones gasps. "I believe in the real Jesus." His voice is weak, as if Regina is making him wade through theological quicksand.

"When you forced conversions? Jesus never did that. When you gave God's blessing to my husband's racism and misogyny, bigotry and xenophobia? To his sexual discrimination? To his eternally waging wars that he started and was losing but wouldn't admit it?"

Jones pulls himself up to standing. "First Lady, it isn't my calling to do those things. My calling is to convert people to the Lord Jesus and to save the world. To make everyone a believer so that God can bring on the Great Tribulation and Jesus can come again and the millennium of peace can begin."

Regina smiles with her glowing black eyes. "Jimmy, do you mind if I ask you a question?"

He nods assent.

"Do you have any idea what the world is like right now? What the world is?"

Jones squints at her as if she's talking rubbish.

She continues, "Who are you going to convert? Do you think we need an encore tribulation to add to the catastrophe we're in?

We will get a millennium of peace. We've got it now. Topside there's nothing but ice and snow and frozen air. And peace. Lots of peace. Because there's no one there."

Jones lets his eyes sink to the table as if it will tell him Regina is wrong and how. Will it give him words to combat her? But the table isn't talking. Apparently neither is God.

Regina says, "If Wavering insists on taking you on this rocket to wherever, you need to get rid of all your nonsense and prepare for what lies ahead. We don't need conversion. We will need strong bodies and strong backs and strong hands to create a civilization that won't follow wacko leadership and blow itself up." She pauses to see if Jones is listening. "If you won't do that, then I vote for you to go to the bunker and do your conversion shtick there."

Jones stares at Regina, but doesn't reply. Has the Holy Ghost deserted him? Regina turns to Wavering. "Sorry, Wavering, but I spent too many years nodding to the fake Jesus. I had to. But it made me sick."

Wavering looks at Jones and his sagging shoulders. What to do with him? He does need Jones the laborer, if there is such a man. But not Jones the preacher. If Jones got strong, he could contribute something. "Thanks, Regina," Wavering says. He thinks, if she can get Jones and the rest of them to deal with what they need to do for the journey, maybe, just maybe, they can pull off the impossible. That is, if they make it to Proxima b and land and etcetera. Why does he keep counting the risk factors?

36

Wavering is astounded at Sarah's expertise in rocket trajectories and the physics of rocket flight. He hates to admit what a disaster there would have been from the mistakes they would have made without her. Mistakes that, if Genesis got into space, would have sent them into black nothing to arrive at nowhere. But he still can't fathom her. Behind her pale face, who is she and what else is hidden in her complicated brain? Beyond Caltech and JPL, where has she been? When he enters the swimming pool room at one in the morning and sees her sitting at the plastic table with a lone candle flickering in front of her, a rendezvous she surreptitiously requested after dinner the previous night, he has no idea what he's in for.

Wavering enters the room and sits down. Sarah stares at the candle as if no one is there. One of her peculiar social skills Wavering has been trying to get used to. He has to admit, she spooks him. With Malcolm and his deep silences, and Regina the animated First Lady who may be real or may be acting--he can't tell, and Olga and the mystery of her seven dead husbands and formerly large bank account, there's a lot to get spooked from.

Sarah looks up. She's not smiling. Her look is hard, her eyes flit. "Thanks for coming," she says softly. She fidgets nervously with her hands, drops into silence. Wavering waits for some explanation why she wants to see him. At one in the morning. She looks at him. "I hope you don't mind." She pauses. Wavering shrugs, waiting. What's coming next? She's leaving? She has a shady past she wants to confess? In spite of her showing no interest in romance, she has a stirring? That would be hard to believe.

"I hacked your computer files," she says.

Wavering is stunned. He made it a point to protect the files with the most sophisticated codes and passwords he could come up with. At least he thought they were sophisticated. He's rested easily believing no one could hack them. He doesn't know what to say. Then he blurts, "You don't have a dragon tattoo, do you?"

She casts him a strange look. "Dragon tattoo? What are you talking about?"

Wavering pushes out a laugh, but it sounds fake, which it is. "There was a novel published near the beginning of the century, 'The Girl with the Dragon Tattoo.' The girl is Lizbeth Salander. She's strange and her mind impenetrable, but she has an almost superhuman ability to hack computers. You remind me of her."

He'd like to add that Sarah's appearance resembles her, although she doesn't have the facial earrings. But with her thick armor she feels to Wavering like a Salander clone that nothing can reach.

"Dragon tattoo?" she asks.

"It's a distinguishing mark she has. Although she's weird in so many ways, she doesn't need the tattoo."

Sarah nods. "Is that book in your collection?" she asks.

"Collection?"

"What I call the files I've accessed. I know you've got books and papers and art and music." Nothing in Sarah's eyes betrays guile. With her intelligence, it wouldn't take her long to survey the categories in which Wavering stored the material and scan some of the titles.

"I know it's all illegal," she adds, but not with any glee.

Wavering's nerves warn him this is an inquisition he never thought he would have. She's caught him red-handed, as they say. But what is the point? Extortion? Control? As one of Augustus

Fluke III's minions would if they could. But she doesn't seem that kind of person. "All right. You found it. What now?"

She smiles. "I don't mean to upset you."

"Upset me?" Wavering replies. "You know you could destroy me. Although since you can't pilot Genesis, I'm not sure what that would get you."

"You think I'm dangerous?"

Wavering thinks for a moment. Lizbeth Salander was dangerous. She bumped off her old man, but he was torturing her. No, that is not Sarah. "Not dangerous," he says. "But, Sarah, you are certainly a closed book that won't open. You must realize you've got impenetrable layers that I can't get through."

She leans back slightly and smiles. "Are you telling me you can't figure out who I am? Well, join the party. I'm as impenetrable to myself as I am to you. You know that saying that if you want to find yourself, go into a room, close the door, and you're in there somewhere? I tried it. I wasn't there. Never was there. I don't know where I was. But I wasn't there."

Wavering smiles. Lizbeth Salander all over again. Strange how a fictional character can come to life like this. He admits to himself that he finds Sarah intriguing. "Lizbeth Salander was abused as a child," he says. "There was a reason she was armored."

Sarah looks down at the table. "I'll have to read about her in your collection," she says. "She does sound like me. Was she diagnosed with PTSD?"

"No, no diagnosis that I can recall. But what she went through could have given her that disorder."

"I've been diagnosed," Sarah says. "It's hell. But it's who I am. I concentrate on what I can do. It's carried me this far."

"From childhood? Over time, doesn't it get easier?" Wavering asks. He recalls pilots who were diagnosed with PTSD. Some took their lives."

"Not easy," she says. "Never easy. But if I can stay busy. Like what I'm doing for Genesis. I have to occupy my mind, or else there are shadows. And bad memories." She seems about to go on, but doesn't. "Bad memories," she repeats and grows silent.

Wavering grasps her hand. It's thin and cold. He squeezes it warmly. She doesn't pull it away. She musters a tiny smile. "Thanks," she says.

37

The crew sits at the dining table in the Genesis bunker when the elevator door opens and out stumble six men in hazmat suits. What now? Wavering wonders. Why wasn't there some warning from the guards at the bunker entrance?

While the men are shedding their hazmat suits, Wavering goes to the intercom and calls the guard house. "What's this?" he asks.

"Sorry sir," comes the voice. "They're frozen stiff. The heater on their private jet failed. I was afraid they'd keel over from hypothermia. I didn't take time to warn you. I hope it's all right."

The guard has empathy, at least. Wavering appreciates that. "It's Okay," he says. "But who are they? What are they?"

"I didn't take time to ask. I've never seen them before."

Wavering faces the men in their dark blue and black suits with red ties and spit-shined shoes. They look prepared for a corporate board meeting. To reckon they're out of place is understatement.

The tall one steps toward Wavering. He's gray-haired and wears wire-rimmed glasses. "You're the one in charge here?" he asks.

Wavering isn't sure at this point he wants to be in charge. At least until he discovers what this visit from the frozen world to a drab bunker is about. Let Berwick handle them. They look his type. Wavering nods limply. He knows there's a querulous look on his face. He can't help it.

"Good," says the tall man. He hesitates, not sure what to say next. He and his entourage could be Jehovah's Witnesses or representatives of some other religious cult proselytizing for their faith. Although those and all other non-evangelical faiths evaporated under the heat of the Fluke succession's ban.

The men's faces are ghost white, they rub their hands together and tremble from the cold they've escaped. Wavering nods to one of the launch crewmen who holds up a coffee cup. "We'll get you some coffee. Won't you sit down?"

The men hobble to the table. They're like mannequins that flex only at their main joints. "What can I do for you?" he asks.

"We signed up for the Luxury Golf Tour of the Century to Mars," the tall man says.

Wavering stares at him in disbelief. Has he been living for so long in the Fluke succession's imaginary world that he has no idea about anything?

"Luxury Golf Tour of the Century to Mars?" Wavering repeats. "I don't think I've heard of it."

"We thought it might start here," the man says.

Wavering scrutinizes him. Is he sane? Where does he think he is? JFK? He's going to check the departures and arrivals board to see when his flight leaves and from what gate?

"We heard you have a rocket," the man adds. "We went to the president's bunker in West Virginia. They sent us here."

Well, Wavering thinks, that was generous of them. Anything to get them out of Augustus's hair. Nice of Augustus to inform the men that there is no trip to Mars and no golf tour. Since they didn't go to West Virginia to offer gold, frankincense, and myrrh, Wavering assumes they out-stayed their welcome as soon as they arrived.

"By the way, my name is Rupert," the tall man says. He stands, proffers Wavering his hand, Wavering shakes it. It's like grasping an icicle. Launch crew members arrive with coffee and hand it to their 'guests.' The guests seize the cups as if they will collapse if they don't drink immediately.

"We have tickets," Rupert says.

"Tickets?" Wavering says. Rupert really does think he's at JFK. Does he have a boarding pass? Has he gone through security? Did he check his bags? Wavering's mind is driving him crazy.

"They were a hundred million apiece," Rupert adds. He reaches inside his suit jacket, pulls out a glossy folder, opens it, and fingers a formal-looking sheet. He holds it up to show that it is indeed a ticket, with bar code, that entitles the bearer to one round trip to the planet Mars. Plus accommodation, four rounds of golf, and meals. Bar service is extra.

Rupert unfolds a glossy four-color brochure with the title, 'Luxury Golf Tour of the Century.' Inside are pictures of a gold-trimmed stucco clubhouse surrounded by green grass and populated by men in Ralph Lauren golf clothes. Standing near them are caddies in black uniforms lugging oversized golf bags.

There are pictures of greens and fairways and tees and happy golfers swinging here and there as if they're playing golf in heaven. Wavering has seen plenty of con jobs in his lifetime, but this one is truly extra-terrestrial. How in the world could these multi-millionaires believe there is golf on Mars? Even though spaceships have reached Mars and some have returned, it's still dicey whether humans can survive there. Wavering thinks of Mars as a planet-sized sand dune with no atmosphere. He would not consider visiting it.

"We've got clubs and balls on the plane," Rupert continues. "We're not sure what's available at the club."

As Wavering stares at Rupert and his friends, he recalls that Mars played a large role in the trophy room of Augustus Fluke III's successes. Fellow pilots, some of whom were on Mars missions, told Wavering that survival was still a question mark. But he guesses Augustus Fluke III, having run out of towers and taj mahals and other castles to build on earth, set his sights on the red planet.

Wavering once saw the Fox Travel channel puffing the grand opening of the Fluke Martian Golf Club. A talking head in a golf shirt warned that golfers should call for tee times well in advance of when they planned to play. Call? To Mars?

So, Wavering wonders, what does he do with six gaslighted links addicts? Tell them their brochure and Augustus's starry-eyed description and Fox Travel's footage are all fake? He should. It's the truth. But they won't believe him. They have their tickets and their brochure and Augustus's glowing assurances. To them, that is the truth. What a hack Air Force pilot says can't be trusted. It's got to be fake. What does he know about golf?

"Sorry, but our rocket is scheduled to go to Proxima b," Wavering says evenly.

Rupert looks at him curiously. "Proxima b? Never heard of it."

"It's out there," Wavering says. "Farther than Mars. In another solar system."

Rupert's visage falls. "Golf?" he asks weakly.

Wavering smiles. "No golf," he says. Rupert looks crestfallen so Wavering adds, "Sorry about that."

"No problem," Rupert says. He looks around. "Do you know of any other rockets? Something going to Mars?"

"Sorry again," Wavering says. "There were intercontinental missiles here, but they went bye bye to obliterate thousands of souls thousands of miles away. No way they would have gotten to Mars."

"I suppose not," Rupert says. "Is there someplace else? Someplace we've missed where there might be a Mars rocket?"

Wavering searches his mind. The rockets that reached Mars were launched from Cape Canaveral. But what is left of Cape Canaveral? Was it blown into radioactive dust like most other targets? And the runway for planes? Is it usable? Is the airstrip navigation signal still active? Lots of questions.

But Wavering concedes he doesn't need six golf fanatics

hanging around while they prepare to launch themselves to Proxima b. He's going crazy with the crew he's got. "Cape Canaveral," he says.

Rupert's visage brightens. "Cape Canaveral?" he repeats.

"That's where the Mars rockets launch from."

Rupert consults his ticket, then his brochure. "I don't know why they didn't tell us that," he says. "There's nothing here to inform us where to board."

"That's unfortunate," Wavering says. He assumes that whoever printed the brochure and sold the tickets figured they could fold up and disappear before these devotees discovered they'd bought a fraud. There were a lot of those. Business deregulation was so extensive there were no penalties no matter how big a scam someone perpetrated. Cons multiplied like bacteria.

If the law didn't go after them, why did perpetrators hide? Quite simple. With there being no restrictions on carrying guns, a number of the swindled dispatched the swindlers. If those who did the dispatching were apprehended and charged? No problem. 'Stand your ground' always worked. Even though the shooter was on the hunt and not standing any ground. Who knew? Who cared?

Rupert nods to his cohorts. They stand, thank Wavering, pull on their hazmat suits, and head for the elevator. "Your crew is fixing the heater," Rupert says. "Tell them thanks"

"I will," Wavering replies. "Have a great trip. Hit them straight."

Rupert and the other five hazmat suits nod in gratitude, enter the elevator, and are gone. Wavering suddenly feels guilt. He should have tried to attach them to reality. But who knows? Maybe there is a rocket destined for Mars. If there is, Wavering doesn't think that crew will take on six heavy golf bags and a supply of golf balls. But since they're all facing survival, Mars may be as good a bet as any.

38

Wavering is reading in the swimming pool room at the plastic table lit by a flickering candle. Silently the door opens, and Sarah enters. Wavering instinctively starts to hide his e-book, then pauses. Sarah casts him a shy smile, sits down opposite him. She sits silently. Wavering finds these situations with her awkward. Does she want him to start a conversation? Is she rifling through her brain for something to say? He knows she only speaks when she has something she thinks important.

"I have my own computer cache," Sarah says. "It's as illegal as yours. Maybe more so." There's a twinkle in her eyes.

"Books?" Wavering asks. He can't think what else she'd be talking about. How could they be more illegal than what he's stored? He thinks of how much he sweated fearing what would happen if he'd been caught.

"Samizdat," she says. "Thousands of pages of samizdat."

"Samizdat?" Wavering repeats with astonishment. He's heard of it. Samizdat was the illegal underground writing that emerged in the Soviet Union in the twentieth century. Books not approved by the Communist government were banned and burned. But some writers still wrote. Alexander Solzhenitsyn, who described the horrific life in the Soviet Siberian prison gulag, a cancer hospital, and a technical prison where skilled prisoners were forced to work for the state. The Soviet government expelled Solzhenitsyn, and he fled to Switzerland and then the United States.

"You don't know about it?" Sarah adds.

"I know the Soviet samizdat," Wavering says.

Sarah nods. "Mine isn't Soviet. It's American. Written about the Fluke regimes. What they did around the world. What went on inside the White House. But it was never reported in the news."

Wavering isn't surprised. He wondered many times if there were some who would risk defying the Flukes. But he never heard the Flukes complain that anyone did. Probably fearing that if they revealed concern it would encourage others. There had been times he overheard conversations on Air Force One that implied efforts were made to find and prosecute leakers of unauthorized information. But nothing specific.

"How in the world did you get it?" Wavering asks.

"Who was your dragon lady?"

Wavering nods. "Lizbeth Salander. So you hacked into the samizdat writer's computers?"

"A few. Even though they had good firewalls."

"But that didn't stop you?"

"It was a challenge, I'll grant you. But…"

"What did you find?"

Sarah stares off into space. "A lot."

"Such as?"

"Guantanamo for instance." Wavering remembers the notorious prison for terrorists at the east end of Cuba. Fox News frequently cheered that detainees were being sent there for alleged plans to bomb or shoot or destroy. Augustus III would say from time to time, 'We'll send him to Guantanamo.' Wavering thought it only meant imprisonment, but who was he to ask for clarification?

"It was expanded. Hundreds of square miles. There were thousands of prisoners. Immigrants suspected of being terrorists or having terrorist ties. Immigrants who came from countries on the Fluke hit list. It was guilt by origin. Guilt by religion. Muslims of course, Buddhists and the rest, also Presbyterians, Episcopalians, liberal Catholics. Those who didn't pass the evangelical litmus test."

Wavering recalls taking that litmus test and faking enough to pass. Holiness Jones helped create it. Augustus III enforced it. It contained what he heard from Jones about the six-day creation, the sun standing still, Jonah spending three days in the belly of a whale where he composed a poem. Events that seemed to Wavering to have nothing to do with following Jesus. Or flying Air Force One.

"I never heard of anyone being released," he says.

Sarah looks away uncomfortably. Her lips tremble. "It was like Nazi Germany. Fluke and his flunkies hid what was going on. There were mass executions. Some of the samizdat writers saw them. They had to dig graves, remove ashes from ovens. But this wasn't Nazi Germany, it was America."

Wavering can't think of what to say. Waves of nausea sweep across his stomach. He was one of those who piloted America's Fuhrer around the country. Around the world.

"Guantanamo wasn't the only prison," Sarah continues. "There were several in California's Owens Valley. New Mexico. Arizona. Remote places. Signs and identification on maps listed them as coal mines or salt mines, whatever they could think up. Even people living nearby didn't know."

"Russia?" Wavering asks. The Flukes were obsessed with Russia. "What did they write about it?"

"Plenty," Sarah says. Wavering remembers that throughout the Fluke succession, there was a close relationship with Russia. It went back to Russia providing loans for the Flukes and the Russian authorities having dirt on Fluke family members. Wavering doesn't know if it was sex or money or both. But the Russians seemed to have all they needed to extort.

"How did you find that?"

Sarah smiles sardonically. "Lizbeth Salander again."

"What did you hack?"

"I found where the Russians were hacking US computers. They didn't leave many footprints, but they couldn't fully hide."

"And you? How did you hide?"

"I put myself in their shoes. If I were them and saw that someone was watching their hacking, what would I do? When I figured out how they did it, I created disguises." Sarah pauses, smiles. "They had a name for me, or names. Jezebel was one, although I don't know who they thought I was subverting. They made up 'Rasputina' from Rasputin, that Siberian peasant who conned his way into the family of Czar Nicolas II. They were frustrated they couldn't find out who I was or where I was located."

A creaking noise startles Sarah and Wavering. They glance about. Wavering's nerves tense. With the candle flickering between them on the table, it's difficult to see beyond their circle of light. They hear the sound again, and realize it's a shift in the wind shaking the glass panels above them.

"The worst are the wars," Sarah says.

"The wars we were winning?" Wavering asks.

"Always winning," she mocks. "There's samizdat from the fronts. We weren't winning anything, never were. Every front was like World War I. We attacked, Muslim extremists dissolved into the countryside or disappeared into a half-wrecked city. Our troops thought they had prevailed. Then snipers appeared and were hard to hit. Improvised explosive devices blew up soldiers and vehicles, including tanks. People who looked like innocent civilians suddenly pulled out arms and fired. The lines went back and forth, back and forth. No progress. Not for the militants either. But what I've gotten indicates the jihadists were satisfied with that. Just holding off the mighty United States of America."

Wavering rifles his brain, but he's sure he heard nothing of this on the news. Augustus Fluke III never mentioned it on Air Force One. Surely he knew. "But wasn't Fox News there?" he asks.

Sarah laughs. "Fiction. Smoke and mirrors. The soldier-writers at the front never saw reporters, from anywhere. Reporters wouldn't have lived long if they went there. I don't mean just from the war, but because our advisors and special forces were instructed to kill them. They knew Fox wasn't there, so they didn't worry about getting the wrong ones."

What Sarah has in her possession is slowly sinking into Wavering's mind. He shudders to think, as maybe Sarah does as well, that prior to Augustus's ending the planet, if either of them were caught with what they had in their computers, they'd be in Guantanamo, and not just to be imprisoned.

"There's more," Sarah says. "There was someone in the White House. Maybe more than one. A mole. Or moles. They got out messages about the turmoil, the firings, about Augustus III blowing up and blaming everyone else for failure." Sarah pauses. "I can't believe anyone had the guts to do that. I don't know how they got away with it and didn't get caught."

Wavering freezes his face to mask what he knows. "Did the mole or moles have an ID?" he asks.

"Different ones. Always a number: '007,' '99,' '008.' Then random numbers. And I mean random. I ran them through my computer ad infinitum, but there was no pattern. Whoever did it knew the numbers betrayed nothing. If the moles had used words, experts might have been able to trace where they came from."

Sarah eyes Wavering closely. "Wavering, if you don't mind my saying it, I don't think what I'm telling you is news." She pauses, runs her hand through her hair. "Do you know something about this?"

Wavering feels her eyes x-raying his brain. He's unnerved by her perception, but does he tell her? With her rocket science, she's his copilot. He needs to trust her. He knows she trusts him. But if Jones or Berwick found out? Then again, what would they do? There's no police force to arrest them.

Wavering smiles at Sarah. "You're a rare breed," he says. "So quiet. So reserved. But does anything ever elude you?"

She cocks her head. "Probably," she says. "But if I don't know what it is, I wouldn't know."

"No, you wouldn't."

"So, the moles?"

Wavering smiles because even now he has a hard time believing what he was told. "I know of only one mole."

"A mole who sure got a lot of inside information. And kept it flowing." Sarah looks at him questioningly.

"You are brilliant, you know that," he says. "Who do you think it was?"

She shakes her head. "I have no idea what went on in the White House. You flew the president and his aides around. You were close."

"Yes," Wavering says. "But not that close. I didn't have a clue. I still have a hard time believing who it was." Wavering wonders if he's breaking an implied understanding. But Sarah? He has no doubt he can trust her. "The First Lady," he says.

Sarah's jaw drops. Her eyes light up. "My God," she says. "The First Lady? Regina? How did she get away with it?"

"I don't know. But she was confident the president wouldn't suspect her. With her looking like a statue, there was nothing about her that would make anyone suspect. You know how she was seen. A sycophant. An obedient wife. A slave. Never a flick of the eye to indicate she might not adore the president."

Sarah sighs. "That has to be the best spy job in history. The First Lady." Her brow knits, she looks at the frosted windows, shakes her head. "How did she get messages out?"

"I didn't know it at the time. Never suspected it. But it was on Air Force One." Wavering pauses to reflect. He doesn't want to compromise Malcolm without his permission. Regina must have slipped him mini flash drives when they met in the cockpit. Right under his nose. "If you don't mind, I'll let it rest there."

Sarah nods. "I understand. So what do we do with our illegal contraband?" she asks.

"We take it and we leave it," Wavering says crisply. "I've thought it through, because I knew this day would come. Taking it is in place now, since you've loaded what you've got into Genesis's computers. That will go with us to Proxima b. What we will do with it there I don't know. It isn't as if there's a media audience breathlessly waiting for breaking news."

But how do they leave it on earth? They need computers. They are in the Genesis silo control room, but what if that room is never discovered? With the prospect of a glacial age, every trace of the silo could be wiped out. The location they are in could even turn into the sixth Great Lake.

Then it occurs to him. "Air Force One," he says. "Plenty of computers. We can add what you've got to the files I've collected. No one would care what we put in, even if they did find out."

"How will the plane survive?" Sarah asks.

"I'm not sure it will. The ground crew will fly it back to the White House bunker after we're gone. It's well built. Even if it gets covered with ice, it should stay intact."

Sarah nods unconvincingly. Wavering knows what she's thinking. Someone may find Air Force One, but could they get anything from her computers?

"You're thinking we've got to get files stored in the White House bunker?" Wavering says laughing. "Can you imagine? Augustus Fluke III and his retinue living in quarters with banned works and samizdat?"

Sarah smiles. "It's the best way to assure they survive," she says. She pauses thoughtfully. "Don't worry. I'll figure out a way to do it."

Wavering looks at her in the candlelight. Lizbeth Salander? A fictional character? Not really. It's odd how on this wasted earth and in this bleak motel and the silo's tomb-like control bunker there's still a spark of life. Or is it an illusion? Like the absurd journey to Proxima b that they think they're going to make?

39

Sixty minutes to launch," the robotic timer announces over the speaker so everyone in the pre-flight room can hear. Wavering is clad in his space suit. The other crewmembers are trying them on for size and adjusting straps and Velcro fasteners to make sure the suits fit and are comfortable. If they are apprehensive about what they are about to do, they don't show it.

None of the space suits are made for a hulk the size of the Holy Reverend Jones. No one at NASA ever conceived of sending 300 pound men into space. But 300 pounds he is, and it's up to him to huff and puff and squeeze and pull until he's fully ensconced. Whether he'll be able to move about when suited, well that's his problem. Maybe Dr. Drone can put him on a diet while in flight so they don't have extra weight when landing on Proxima b. A secret diet, that is. Wavering doesn't see Jones as a weight watcher type.

Wavering reviews the countdown checklist which is several pages long and complicated. He did this several times when he was on the shuttle crew to the International Space Station, at least a while back it was called the International Space Station. When the notion of international fell apart, Augustus made certain they were operating the American Space Station. Goodbye Russia and Putin IV, even though Augustus loved Russia and Putin IV. Apparently he didn't love them enough to share the toys.

You might wonder how Wavering came to be commander of Genesis. He'd been a pilot since joining the Air Force at eighteen years of age. From the time he was a young kid, he was entranced with the notion of flying. He marveled at how birds could take off instantly, find air currents to glide on, land on a thin branch with never a miss. At a small airport near his home, he watched pilots train. Planes wobbling in flight, swooping up and down, landing hard or not at all. At the ocean, there were hang gliders that floated on rising air currents until pilots got tired of flight. Wavering thought he would never tire if he were one of them.

He went through the ropes of flight training from slow propeller trainers to the most advanced fighter planes. He fought in Afghanistan. He's not proud of that. The Afghan-Iraq-Syria war blasted and burned its way through decade after decade and who knows how many lives were lost? Wavering didn't go to Afghanistan to kill anyone, not if he could help it. But with the smart weapons they had and observers on the ground highlighting targets, all he had to do was push a button to unleash a candle with fire shooting out the back end and enough explosive in the front end to level a warehouse, dispatch a few hapless souls, and that was that.

Wavering heard stories of how some ground observers targeted relatives they didn't want to celebrate Thanksgiving with, or loan sharks who were calling in their debt, or a policeman who had given them a parking ticket and the like. But that did not deter Augustus and his generals from expending high explosives wherever they thought it would kill a Muslim or two. Even if the effort just produced a video clip on Fox News to convince the American people that their exorbitant taxes were worth paying.

After Afghanistan, Wavering was assigned to teach pilots how to fly more complex planes and run their armaments and defenses against enemy missiles. Then, when he qualified as a space crewman, he crewed and commanded several space missions. That was when the Air Force decided he was qualified to pilot Augustus Fluke III on Air Force One.

Wavering was hesitant, because he had no liking for Augustus

Fluke III. Maybe it was carryover from Fluke II requiring him to kill unknowing and innocent human beings in Afghanistan. And having Augustus Fluke III announce space launches publicly as resupplying the space station when actually they were deploying missiles with nuclear warheads to launch from orbit at whatever targets Augustus and his generals chose. Those missiles were fired as part of Augustus's response to the alleged Indonesian attack, but Wavering has no idea which parts of planet Earth they obliterated. With nuclear winter encompassing the planet, it made no difference.

40

The countdown continues when the headset in Wavering's helmet comes to life with the voice of one of the topside security officers. "Commander Wavering, Comm calling." Wavering assumes there must be a problem with the blast-proof covers over Genesis. They should open or retract under the launch crew's command. At some point in the countdown, they will open. Is there a problem?

"Wavering, copy that. Problem with the cover?"

"No," Comm says. "We've got a visitor, actually two." With the security officer's voice ragged from a lack of energy, Wavering's muscles tighten. Oh no. His brain ignites into flame. He must be asleep, this is one of those terrifying nightmares. Augustus Fluke III? Who else? This can't be happening. He must be dreaming.

"Don't tell me it's....," he says.

"It is, Sir."

"Who's the other one?"

"His daughter. Elena," Comm replies. Wavering detects a strain of doom in Comm's voice. It matches what he feels from head to toe. Elena is Augustus's 35-year-old daughter. Blond, willowy, she's a model and the CEO of the Fluke line of women's clothes—on a par with Gucci and the like, he's told. Leather pieces—handbags, belts, shoes. The one time he saw Elena's models on a runway showing off her latest designs, they wore leather stilettos with heels that looked like they had been sharpened and had a reputation for capsizing. Several models crashed to the floor. Sprained ankles, bruised knees. Wavering thought one ankle was broken. At least she had to be carried off the stage. Tough life, that being a model.

Elena had an office in the West Wing of the White House where she was designated 'assistant to the President.' Augustus referred to her often in news conferences. She was negotiating with China, she was seeking reconciliation between Israel and the Palestinians, she was monitoring the banking industry, she was meeting with business groups to determine how much deregulation was needed to assure jobs for everyone. Even though Wavering saw her once in a while, he did not know her well.

"So it's him and her?" he says.

"You've got it," Comm replies discreetly.

"What do they want?" Wavering asks. He doesn't really want to know. He can't get it into his skull that they're less than an hour from launch, and him and her are at the door.

There's a long pause. The communications officer is a friend. He and Wavering have been through a lot together. Wavering can sense the officer doesn't want to tell him. But: "They want on board Genesis."

"T minus 55 minutes and counting," says the automatic timer. Augustus Fluke III and his model daughter at the door? Wavering was so relieved when the VP came to tell III he was needed at the White House bunker. And then to see Augustus light up at making America great again, don his hazmat suit, step on the elevator, and disappear. Even with the nightmares, Wavering convinced himself he would never see August Fluke III again.

41

"You've got to let them in." The voice is like the bark of a Saint Bernard. It's Jones, who else. "After all, he is the president."

Wavering turns to Jones. "He isn't the president. In order to be president, you have to have a country." He stiffens as he reminds himself the absence of a country is all III's fault. He doesn't deserve to be on the planet. And Jones? How long does he live in his imaginary universe? Besides, Wavering warns himself, he must monitor the countdown or the launch could go haywire. "I don't have to let them in."

"You do," Reverend Jones says. "President Fluke the third is God's appointed ruler to bring order to the governed. As God's chosen, he must be respected."

Wavering looks at Jones. Where do you begin with this guy? Ruler? People who are governed? Wavering must respect him? If there was still a world and a world court, III would be found guilty of war crimes and flung into the slammer for life.

"Wavering, he's the one who authorized Genesis." The plaintive voice is Olga's. "Without him none of us would be here. There would be no rocket." Wavering concedes she might have a point. But without III they would not need a rocket. They would still have something called a planet. Rather nice to have. And the money that built Genesis came from the people, not Augustus. Augustus doesn't own it. And he sure as hell can't fly it.

Then there's that other problem. Wavering and the ground crew have been monitoring the weight limit. One empty seat makes up for the extra weight Jones is carrying. There's no way

Augustus comes on board without someone else leaving. And there is no place for Elena, as light as she is, period. Wavering looks at Jones stuffed into his space suit with sweat flowing down his fat cheeks. Jones or Augustus, which would Wavering dispense with? Is that a question? Get rid of them both. Get rid of their wacko ideas and the way they live in some reality created by Salvador Dali in an out-of-control phase of surreal insanity.

"All right," Wavering says robotically. He sends word to Comm, and a few moments later, Augustus and Elena enter the flight-ready room.

Frost cakes their eyebrows and hair, their faces are red, their eyes sag as if they haven't slept for days. In the condition she's in, Elena would not get access to a fashion runway. Augustus glances about at the crew, nodding smugly as if he owns them. He's reminding them that he chose them, so they're beholden to him. That beholden feeds his life blood. Gives him control. Augustus rests a contemptuous gaze on Wavering. "I'm taking over," he says.

Wavering notices signal lights have turned on at several switches. He throws the switches as the countdown proceeds. He turns back to Augustus. "You're taking over?" He pauses. "Haven't we been through this before? You're not qualified." Wavering admits that after years of 'Yes Sir, No Sir,' it makes him feel ten feet tall to defy his Majesty.

III glares at Wavering as if he's a subhuman African-American or Mexican. "I am the Commander in Chief of the United States of America."

Wavering pauses, then, "You were Commander in Chief, Mr. Fluke. You're not anymore. Because there is no United States of America. There is nothing but devastation which you caused. You have forfeit the right to be in charge of anything." III's face, red from the cold, changes hue as if it is heating up, his eyes flit about uncertainly.

"How dare you," III shouts. Wavering looks curiously at the red face and bulging eyes. There's thin-skinned, but III raises the bar to new heights.

"T minus 45 minutes and counting," comes the automatic timer. Wavering sets several dials and throws more switches. He feels vibration and can hear fuel flowing into Genesis's tanks in all three stages of the rocket.

"We don't have time to deal with this," Wavering says. "I can't take another oversized man. We've got to decide again who goes and who doesn't."

Augustus looks at Jones. Jones casts him a dog-like wrinkle of his brow. "The two of us will go," Augustus says pontifically. "And Elena. There's an empty seat."

Wavering sighs loudly. "It may look that way, but there isn't. The extra seat remains empty. With Jones, we're at the limit on weight. If we go over, we sabotage the mission by using too much fuel."

Augustus swivels his head to look at the other crewmembers. It would take two of them to equal one III or Jones. Wavering says, "Mr. Fluke, it's you or Jones. You decide which one of you goes. It doesn't make much difference to me." A lie, Wavering admits to himself. Of course it makes a difference. He'd definitely jettison Augustus. But then he's left with Jones. For sixteen years? No, not good.

"We're both going." Augustus's look is defiant.

"T minus 40 and counting." Wavering unzips his suit starting at the top. Pulls his arms out of the sleeves, shoves the suit down to his waist and over his hips.

"What are you doing?" Augustus barks.

"What does it look like I'm doing?"

"You must leave your suit on. You're the commander."

"I'm the commander? When you're deciding who is in the crew and who isn't? When you defy me when I make decisions?" He pauses to see if III might be thinking. The rigid body and frozen eyes suggest he isn't. "Someone has to go off the crew, so I'm taking myself off. Then both of you can go. Have a great trip." Wavering points up. "Your destination is up there. Somewhere. Good luck."

III's face puffs up like it's inflating. His breaths come in gasps. Wavering realizes he has no experience in handling challenges. Or stonewalls. "All right," III shouts. His voice in the small flight room echoes so loudly off the concrete walls and roof that he's deafening.

"All right what?" Wavering says.

III's body twitches, his feet shuffle involuntarily. Anger burns in his eyes. "You win." The words echo off the concrete. Wavering can't think how to respond. He's never heard III admit that anyone else wins. "What do we do?" III asks.

"It's simple. You and Jones decide which one goes. You can pick whatever reason you want, if you need one. I don't care."

Augustus looks at Jones. Jones looks at Augustus. Wavering suddenly realizes he might be looking at a stalemate. God's spokesman and God's supreme ruler at a crossroad? "Time is short," Wavering warns.

Eva stirs and steps forward. The white flight suit becomes her with her black hair and brows. "Let's take a vote," she says.

Wavering's spine chills. Again? They keep voting, and yet III and Jones are still here. Will this never end?

"No," Augustus shouts. "I won't have it." Veins bulge on his forehead. His eyes flit. Is he afraid he'll lose? Wavering knows III has never had to deal with a democracy. They've been without one for so long most people don't know what it is. Dictatorships come easy and die hard. Democracy comes hard and dies easy.

"T minus 35 minutes and counting." Wavering attends to

switches and dials and checks the scopes showing Genesis's status. So far, so good.

Wavering meets Augustus's contemptuous glare and says, "I call for a vote. But we've got to do it fast. As I call each name, if you are for that person staying, raise your hand. Is that clear?" He glances over the crew. The tension in their eyes shows they are not happy. But Wavering didn't bring on this mess. Do they think it's his job to make them happy? Maybe they do, but he's a pilot. He doesn't have a TV program where he listens to people describe their messed up lives and then gives them useless tips.

The timing voice interrupts: "T-minus 38 and holding. Wind." Wavering knows there's a low threshold for the launch. Crosswind could damage Genesis leaving the silo. They have only minutes before they lose the time window that will let them slingshot the moon.

Wavering calls for the vote. When he finishes, the choice is clear. Elena goes on Genesis. So does Augustus. Wavering guesses Jones's promises of rapture and God fixing everything and God taking care of all his people have lost traction. But Augustus is coming? The nightmare is alive and well.

The timer again. "Launch scrubbed. Launch scrubbed. Wind."

Wavering shouldn't be relieved, but he is. What a mess dealing with Jones and Augustus. Sarah and the trajectory team will have to reset the guidance parameters. But Wavering shares the letdown he sees on the crew's faces. On the other hand, if Genesis is going to blow up, maybe postponement has something positive going for it.

42

He hears a banging. Bang. Bang. Bang. What is it? He's well into a nightmare. He's commanding a space capsule with only three other hominids on board: Holiness Jones, Trillionaire Berwick, and President August Fluke III. He thinks the banging is his fists striking the only hatch on the spacecraft. He's trying to get the hatch open and flee to outer space. No more tribulations, no more world stock markets, and no more 'I'm the greatest ever in the history of the universe.' Cold, lifeless, dark outer space beckons.

The banging persists. He's waking up. The banging is real. "Colonel Wavering," comes a loud female voice shouting. "Open this door. Wake up."

He wrestles out from under his five blankets, staggers to his feet, pulls a blanket around him and hobbles to the door. He opens it, and there stands Regina, face red, eyes piercing. She appears angry. What has he done?

"You have to call a meeting," Regina says sharply.

"A meeting? A meeting for what?"

"A meeting to get Augustus off the rocket. You, Malcolm, Augustus, and me. Either Augustus leaves, or I do. I will not go on the rocket with him on board."

Wavering rubs his face, feels stubble, assumes there are wrinkles from the bedding. He must look a nightmare. "Augustus? You've told him we're having a meeting?"

"No. He won't listen to me. He especially won't listen to Malcolm. You are the commander of Genesis, so you have to tell him. He has to obey you."

Wavering remembers Regina said that if Augustus was on board, she would flee into the tundra without a hazmat suit and gladly freeze-dry. He joked that if she did that, he would go with her. Not thinking that Augustus would be back and then wangle to get himself on board Genesis. So much for joking.

Wavering goes to Augustus's room and pounds on his door. "Who is it," comes III's muffled voice.

"Commander Wavering," Wavering says with authority.

"Go away. I'm tired. Don't bother me."

"As commander, I order you. Open this door. Now."

Wavering hears rustling sounds from behind the door. It opens. III glares at him. "What do you want?"

"I'm calling a meeting. If you're to be on Genesis's crew, you have to meet with Regina, Malcolm, and me. In the swimming pool room."

"Hell no," III shouts. "Who are you to tell me what to do? I'm going. That's it." He casts Wavering a puff-eyed glare of contempt.

"Do I have to do it again?" Wavering says.

"Do what?"

"Threaten not to go. You follow my orders. Now. Do you understand?"

Wavering, Regina, and Malcolm sit at the plastic table in plastic chairs, wondering if Augustus will show up. Suddenly the door opens, and himself marches in. He cocks his head toward them. "You must know I'm the greatest president the United States ever had. George Washington? Can you believe he was an Army general, and he stood up in that boat crossing the Delaware River? Was he stupid or what? He could have fallen overboard. He could have been shot.

"And that dumb, 'I cannot tell a lie.' Over a cherry tree? What was that? Did that cherry tree deserve to live? A cherry tree? And he was great? Anybody who feels bad over telling a lie about a cherry tree is a loser. A real loser.”

Regina stirs. “Augustus, Augustus…..”

He refuses to look at her. He gazes off into the fog. “Abraham Lincoln. The Civil War? Totally unnecessary. Why? He could’ve negotiated. For every difference of opinion, there’s ground where you can make a deal. What did the South want? Slavery? Let ‘em keep it. Keep it. Just get the South to agree to put some regulations on it. A lot of slave owners were benevolent. They took good care of their slaves. Those slaves were better off on the plantations than when they were freed. Those civil rights marchers like Martin Luther King? King and all the rest got it all wrong. They were losers.

“If that didn’t work, there’s always money. If Lincoln had the smarts, he should’ve found out what it would take for the South to make a deal. Straight grants? Low-interest loans? Subsidies for plantations? Look, everyone is willing to make a deal. Everyone. But Lincoln didn’t try. He declared war, and that was it. Yeah, a real loser.”

“Mr. President,” Malcolm cuts in. “Mr. President. Mr. President.”

Augustus looks about as if he’s reading words off the fog. “Teddy Roosevelt? Look at all those parks. Look at the land he took away from the mining companies. Look at the land he took off the development market. Mining, oil, coal, developments, this country could have been so much greater. They were the life blood that made America great.

“You know, she once was great. Before Washington, before Lincoln, before Teddy Roosevelt. You make deals. Those deals profit the risk-takers who made America great. Forget Washington. Forget Lincoln. Forget Roosevelt. Think Andrew Carnegie, the Rockefellers, the railroad giants, think Wall Street. Where would America be without Wall Street? It’s money, it’s deals, that’s what made America great."

Wavering sighs. There's nothing new in this litany for Malcolm, Regina, or him. Augustus is like a CD disc stuck on one track. Wavering would think Malcolm, or at least Regina, would try harder to shut Augustus down, but they sit like criminal suspects in a police lineup. Wavering is sure Regina has tried many times. But with her having to live in Augustus's shadow, and Augustus having plucked her from Cirque de Soleil like she was an ornament for a Christmas tree, she carries no weight. Since Augustus didn't mention her after the world ended, Wavering wonders if she was ever anything more than a collector's item.

And Malcolm? A black? Forget it. Augustus always had show-window blacks in the outer rings of his entourage. And speaking for him on Fox whatever. They seemed natural, but after a while you heard the same words from each. Were they scripted? Does Wavering need to ask? They were Oreo cookies who learned the survival skill of acting more white than white people. On the one hand, Wavering felt sorry for them. On the other, didn't they see, didn't they understand how they were being used? And abused? Oh well.

Augustus's eyes bulge. "That Franklin Roosevelt. He killed off any hope America would be great. He killed it. He killed it. It was gone. Done away with. Socialism, that's what he did. Or Communism, what's the difference? He killed the entrepreneurial spirit. Self initiative. Personal responsibility. Gone. The welfare state. People didn't need to work. They didn't need to take care of themselves. The federal government would do it. He played to people's fears and laziness. He was the worst of the worst. A failure. A loser.

"John F Kennedy? Another loser. 'Civil rights?' What was that? It just gave lazy people the right to whine and extort the government to take care of them. Look at the fifties. Everything was fine. No demonstrations. No marching. Women at their ironing boards. Children were told what they could do and they did it or else. A chicken in every pot. What was that about? America never got great until the Flukes took over."

Wavering feels time has stopped. How often do they have to listen to this egotistical rant? He says, "Mr. Fluke, I thought it was Russia that was great. Did I miss something?"

Augustus's eyes drift over Wavering's shoulder. He never makes eye contact when someone questions him. "Russia?" III repeats. "Great country. Great country. Putin IV? One of the best. Maybe the best. Those Chechen Muslims? He slaughtered 'em. They deserved it. Muslims? A violent, brutal religion. People say Islam promotes peace and respect. Bullshit. It's the anti-Christ. That's what Jones says. Lots of others. All the others. Putin IV knows that. He's a great man."

"The loans Russia gave you?" Wavering asks. "When American banks refused you and said you were a bad risk."

"Losers, those banks. All losers. They only knew how to fail. They were cowards. They wanted collateral. They wanted guarantees. Well, when you're a very successful, very successful businessman as I am, that should be enough. Should be enough. Success should be more than enough. Just me. That's all they needed. But they listened to a bunch of nonsense from a bunch of losers, losers.

"They claimed they knew all about investing. They were idiots. JP Morgan, Chase, Wells Fargo, Citicorp, all a bunch of losers." Merrill-Lynch too, Wavering assumes, although they were Bank of America. III continues, "America! Can you imagine that? Bank of America, and they wouldn't do loans for the greatest president this country has ever had? Losers. Stupid. I should have liquidated them all and folded their assets into the government. Measly assets at that. Can you believe it?

"*Time* Magazine. The greatest magazine in the country. *Time* Magazine. Do you know how many covers I got? How many covers? Seventeen. Seventeen. Nobody in the history of the magazine ever got seventeen covers. And in a short time. Seventeen covers. Losers don't make covers on Time Magazine."

Time Magazine was taken over by Fox News and added to the Fox empire. Even now, if *Time* Magazine still existed, Wavering is sure it would extoll how great Augustus Fluke III was with the way he destroyed the planet. Nobody could have done it like he did. He is the greatest. Of course *Time* Magazine's offices and presses were incinerated and now float as particles in the fog drifting past the windows that enclose Borealis's swimming pool room with the empty pool.

"Mount Rushmore. What a joke. Washington who stood up in a rowboat. Lincoln who had no idea how to make a deal. Teddy Roosevelt who robbed America of oil and coal and gas and minerals that could have made her great again. Franklin Roosevelt, as bad as Stalin and the rest. All of them up there on that mountain. A bunch of losers. It should be called 'Mount Rushless.' Or 'Mount Worthless.'"

Or maybe it should be called 'Mount Confusing.' Wavering recalls Franklin Roosevelt isn't on Mount Rushmore. It's Thomas Jefferson. But that is a fact, and everyone knows what happened to facts.

"You know who should be up there?" Augustus continues. "Augustus Fluke the first, a great man, my great grandfather. He got that Supreme Court to do what it was designed to do, legalize everything the president does. Fluke II, he got rid of the killer two-party system. America only needed one party. One party. No two-party. Nothing got done. Put everything in the hands of great people, and great things happen."

"That leaves the fourth slot," Wavering puts in.

"Isn't it obvious?" Augustus replies. "Only the great should go up there. No losers. No losers. Not one loser."

"You?" Wavering asks. He feels likes he's in a mental ward talking to a patient who has become unmoored from everything. Here is the man who ended the world, and he believes he should have a place on Mount Rushmore? Wavering waits for a response, but Augustus seems to have run out of baloney. If he were a Roman Caesar, he could press for divinity. But maybe Holiness Jones would have some reservations about that.

Regina casts Wavering a look of impatience. No doubt she's had Augustus's sewer of greatness pumped at her many times. Her black eyes shine beseechingly. "Well, commander, what are you going to do?"

Wavering turns to Augustus. III's eyes bulge with self-confidence. His lips are pressed flat and wide in that smirk that leers from most of his photographs. His body leans forward, he thrusts his head at Wavering's face. Wavering knows he's looking at a man who fully believes everything he said.

As Augustus did of all his sycophants, he expects Wavering to genuflect before his greatness. How could Wavering not? Hasn't III just said there has never been anyone like him? Anyone in the history of the world? Yes, he does believe it. All of it. At least as long as he can repeat it over and over. And he'll do that for sixteen years?

Wavering's mind whirls. What does he say to III? Does he try to hide his loathing? Can he pretend that he is conciliatory? But he doesn't want to be a hypocrite. He looks III straight in the eye. III meets his gaze. The words come spontaneously, but Wavering says them slowly, "Mr. Fluke, you're fired."

43

III doesn't take it well. He stomps out of the swimming pool room and heads for the bunker where the rest of the crew is relaxing. Regina, Malcolm, and Wavering ride the elevator down with him and follow him into the bunker. They exchange no words. He refuses to look at them. He's so angry he breathes heavily.

"Listen everyone," he shouts to the crew. They turn their heads slowly and cast him looks that say, oh no. He launches into his litany of how great he is compared with all other presidents. Same presidents he trashed with Waverly, Regina, and Malcolm. Same words. He isn't known for creating new phrases. Or new ideas.

When he finishes, he gestures toward Wavering, but shouts at the crew. "This man. This man is denying me the right to a place on the rocket. Can you believe it? Can you believe it? I'm the president who made him. I made him a pilot on Air Force One. I gave him one of the most privileged positions in the entire military. I. I did it. And what does he do? He tells me I can't go on the rocket I authorized. The rocket I raised the funds to build. Me. He says he will not let me go. Can you believe it? Can you believe it?"

Wavering sees he's back with the Easter Island heads again. III might tug at Olga for support. Or Eva. Or Jones. But then Augustus would be begging, supplicating, something Wavering knows he loathes in others.

The silence is deafening. No one moves. No one speaks. Wavering's crewmates look at III as they would a street man talking gibberish to someone who exists only in his imagination.

Even from Olga, and Eva, and Jones, nothing.

"Good grief, Augustus. Get off it. You're a horse's ass." It's Regina. She's standing in her black leotards with her eyes glaring, her head pressed forward as if she's a panther about to attack.

Augustus's look of confidence deflates. "Why my First Lady, what has happened to you?"

"What happened to me? You happened to me. You. Yes I took the con. I took the bait. The president of the United States stalks a circus dancer and asks her for marriage? I took it. I thought you were what you said you were. When you talked about love, I thought you meant it. I didn't know you were incapable of love. For anyone other than yourself."

Augustus casts his gaze about at the rest of them. While he acts as if he ignores what people think, he seems to have a sense that his plea is not going well. His plan A is to win them over. What is plan B? He has one, Wavering is sure. Wavering knows him well enough to be aware that he never loses any battle to get what he wants.

III looks over at the launch crew sitting at their computers and monitor screens. "If Genesis flies without me," he says, "I'll be down here. There's nothing you can do if I sabotage the launch."

He's right, Wavering realizes. They are vulnerable.

"You wouldn't," Regina says.

Augustus smiles smugly. "Because you're on board?" he says. "Now that you've turned against me? Now that you've insulted me?" He glares menacingly at Regina, spins away, dons his hazmat suit, stomps to the elevator, and disappears.

44

Throughout Augustus's tirade, Elena, his daughter by First Lady the Second, sat looking and listening. Wavering thought she might defend Augustus as he heard her do before III pressed the button. But she sat as passively as the rest of the crew. Since she had the reputation as a runway clothes-horse, Wavering never thought there was much to her. Although he wondered if he was prejudiced because she was III's daughter.

After Augustus leaves, Elena stands thoughtfully, walks to where Wavering is sitting. He looks up. She says, "I'd like to be on board."

"Are you serious?" Wavering asks. "Without your father?" Wavering never saw anything that made him believe she'd break with him.

"Yes, and I know what I'm asking for," she says.

"Do you?" Wavering replies. "You'd have to work hard. We have to build a new civilization. Maybe from stone. You might need to become a new Eve. I'm not sure you would. But you'd be eligible." Wavering must admit he's saying this with a lot of reservations. Genetically she may be nothing but a money-hungry clothes horse. With no Gucci or Armani on Proxima b, her offspring could feel deprived all their lives. At least until someone set up a designer clothing business and put those daughters on the runway.

Wavering studies Elena's white face and blond hair. Since she isn't Regina's daughter, she isn't thinking of being with her mother. Elena knows Regina well, but Wavering has no idea what their chemistry is. She hardly knows any the rest of the crewmates. Malcolm maybe, since he provided security to the family.

Elena glances at Regina, then Wavering, and smiles. She takes a deep breath. "I know there's risk. But I do want to go. I mean it."

Wavering wonders, when will this crew get finalized? Fluke III is on. Fluke III is off. Fluke III wants back on. 'You're fired.' Ok, got that worked out. Berwick is on. Berwick is off. Jones is on. Jones is on? Jones is still on?

Now, what to do with a fashion-designer model? Wavering doesn't say it, but crew selection needles his mind. He has reservations about someone so spoiled being on board. There will be nothing she's used to. She'll go from pampered rich girl with servants for everything to a life as thin as camping. Something she's probably never done.

Then there's something bigger that unsettles his mind more. Augustus's threat to destroy Genesis on launch. Most people wouldn't take him seriously. But Wavering does. Wavering knows he's got a violent streak that he hides from most people. He's seen that he never relents trying to take out anyone who defies him. As Wavering did in firing him off the rocket.

But with Elena on board? Would he destroy her? He claimed he idolizes her. And with him off Genesis and Wavering thinking the White House bunker is hopeless to generate a new human race, she's the only candidate to continue the Fluke succession. He may think he can do it in the West Virginia bunker. But then he'd have to be a new Adam. Augustus a new Adam? There isn't a chance there'd be a new Eve to take him on.

Wavering looks carefully at Elena. She's young, she's strong. They need young people. He knows that. Maybe he's got her wrong. Does he refuse her? If she's the only one who could deter III from blowing up Genesis on liftoff? "If you really want to go, you're on," Wavering says. He waits for someone in the crew to object. Nobody does.

***

The next morning they are eating breakfast in the bunker when Augustus storms out of the elevator, wrenches off his hazmat suit, and charges toward the crew like an out-of-control tank. His legs are stiff, his arms swing as if he's gearing up for a fight. His eyes glare, his face is redder than usual, his lips press as if he can't find words fierce enough to express what's burning in his brain.

He stomps behind Wavering and grabs hold of his chair. "You," he shouts. "Colonel Loser." Wavering keeps his back to him and takes another swig of coffee. "I am talking to you. I am your Commander-in-Chief. You are under my command. Under my orders. I demand your attention. Now."

Wavering glances about at the rest of the crew. They look everywhere but at Augustus. If Augustus expects support, Wavering doesn't see it. Even Elena gazes down at the table as if it might provide a route of escape.

Wavering stands and turns to raging bull. Wavering wouldn't be surprised if III punched him. The launch crew, hearing the ruckus, silently moves in behind Augustus. "You want to talk to me?" Wavering asks quietly.

"Talk to you?" III shouts. "Talk to you?" He breathes so heavily Wavering wonders if he's about to have a heart attack. "Are you stupid? Are you an imbecile?"

Wavering stares but says nothing. III continues, "It's my daughter, you jackass. It's my daughter. My daughter Elena." He pauses as if Wavering is supposed to divine what this breakdown is about.

Wavering shrugs. "Your daughter Elena? What about her?"

"You are an imbecile. You are an idiot. Don't you know?"

Wavering remains silent. He feels III waiting to trash any answer he might offer.

"You put her on that rocket." He points to the wall beyond which he thinks Genesis stands. But he's a hundred and eighty degrees off. Smiles break out on the launch crew, but they stay silent. "What right do you think you have? She's a Fluke. She's mine. She doesn't obey anyone else. Do you understand? Do you understand?"

Wavering says nothing. What good would it do? He knows III never listens to anyone. He's never admitted that he was wrong about anything. "She does not go on that rocket," III shouts. "Not go on that rocket. She will not go. That is final."

Wavering wonders what is motivating III. If he were a normal father, it could be concern for her safety. Fear that Genesis is so high risk that she wouldn't have a chance. Not a bad worry. Wavering has it himself. But 'concern for her safety?' He's not sure about that.

Does he want her off so he can blow them to kingdom come during the launch? Is she in the way of his revenge against Wavering for firing him? Wavering knows that firing has to be eating his brain like Pac-Man crossed with a piranha. He'll never get over it. Even if he avenges, he has no ability to forget.

"I am going on that rocket." The voice is Elena's. She stands and glares at Augustus. "Wavering has nothing to do with it. I chose to go, and he agreed."

Augustus stares at her, then Wavering, then back to her. He seems uncertain which he should target. He settles on Elena. "You don't have my permission. You are prohibited. Banned. No, you can't go."

"I am going," Elena says strongly. "You want me to go to that bunker with you? I was there. I can't stand it. I'm claustrophobic. It's damp. It's depressing. Live the rest of my life there? No way."

She's crossing wires in his brain. He can attack Wavering with abandon. But Elena? Lose Elena's support? Lose her admiration? Wavering thinks she's draining the juice out of his ego.

III turns to Wavering. "I order you. Remove her from the crew. Take her off that rocket. Now. I command you. I am your Commander-in-Chief. I am the one who put you in the position you are in. I have every right to order you to do whatever I want."

Wavering's patience is growing thin. There's no way Augustus is going to stop his tirade unless he gets his way. Wavering looks him in the eye, but speaks softly. "You have two choices. Either you get your hazmat suit on and go to the motel. Or I will have you bound and taken there. I want you out of here. I want the launch crew and guards to ban you from coming back. They will take you food."

III's smirk returns. "You? Who do you think you are? Colonel Loser. Colonel never do well. Without me, you're nothing. My daughter comes off that rocket. I will order you to be bound and sent to the motel. Who are you to threaten me? Me? Commander-in-Chief. President. The greatest president ever."

He turns to the launch crew. "You," he shouts. "Bind him." He points at Wavering. "Take him to the motel."

Silence falls. Augustus's words echo off the concrete walls and die. The crew doesn't move. Then, suddenly, they surround Augustus, pin his arms behind his back. One crewman pulls out heavy plastic binding, slaps it around Augustus's wrists, tightens it until Augustus can't pull his hands apart. Augustus wriggles, bucks his head, tries to stomp on crewmen's feet. They grab his feet and lower him to the floor. Plastic binding around his ankles. Augustus lies there on his side. Wriggling. Groaning. Pathetic.

The crew loads him on a cart, wheels him to the elevator, and he is gone. Silence. What lightness Wavering feels. But then his eyes fall on Holiness Jones. He's been quiet, as if he could blend into the concrete walls and not be noticed. Wavering remembers he set conditions for him. Bag the religious shtick, get in shape, commit to working hard to set up life on Proxima b.

Wavering looks at Jones's dreamy eyes. He slumps like a kid in the back row of a schoolroom who doesn't want to be noticed. Doesn't want the teacher to call on him for an answer. Does Wavering tell him again he's waiting for Jones to give him a reply? How many times does he do that?

"Reverend Jones," Wavering says. "Pack up. You're going with your leader. You wouldn't want him to go without spiritual counsel, would you?" Wavering doesn't ask if Jones consents to that. He doesn't care.

Jones doesn't move. Has he developed sudden deafness disorder? Is he pretending Wavering didn't say anything. "Jones," he shouts. Jones's body jerks. He might have drifted into the sky to meet Jesus. Or he's duking it out at Megiddo, assured Armageddon has come and it's glory hallelujah time. "You're not going on Genesis," Wavering says. "Your commander-in-chief needs you."

Jones looks at Wavering as if he just arrived in the room. "You can go now," Wavering says. To force him to get out of there is the only way Wavering can be sure Jones understands. Jones rises to his feet, wobbles as if regaining balance. He looks about at the crew as if he's never seen them before. Even Regina, Olga, and Elena. None of them move a muscle to defend him. Or even say 'goodbye.'

He shuffles to the elevator, turns, and waits like a statue. The door opens, he enters. All right, Wavering thinks. At last he has his crew. He looks at them sitting around the table and nods with satisfaction.

45

The blast-off went perfectly. With twelve engines powering the first stage delivering twelve million pounds of thrust and the engines run prior only in test stands, there was huge risk. At engine ignition, Wavering reminded himself that he and the crew were guinea pigs. Never before had human beings been launched into space with so many untested rocket components.

Wavering anticipated the vibration. He'd been through it on other flights. But this time, the cockpit shook more than he'd ever experienced. Dials and switches blurred. In the seat next to him, Sarah monitored her instrument panel. Wavering glanced over from time to time to see how she was holding up. Her eyes never wavered. Shock waves rippled through both of them, but Sarah's head, her hands, she moved them not at all. Is she tough? Wavering wondered. Maybe she doesn't have the apprehension Wavering feels. Or is she just stoic? No matter. Wavering considers himself lucky to have her.

As always in space, Wavering has to reorient himself. In the launch silo, the control cockpit Sarah and Wavering sit in was at the top end of the spacecraft. In space there is no top and no bottom, only fore and aft. Below them, or what is now behind them, are the crew living quarters.

Concentrating on instruments during ascent, Wavering couldn't see his crewmates there. He knew they were in their spacesuits belted into couches. Couches that absorbed most of the vibration and kept them comfortable while pressed down with acceleration.

When they reached orbit and were weightless, they sounded the way Wavering and others did on their first flights. "Where am I?" "Where is up? Where is down?" "Everything is spinning. Does anyone else feel it?" Wavering told them to expect to be disoriented. He also said it would be like nothing they had known before. The inner ear and brain are screwed up. They're used to gravity, to an up and a down, and without it they don't know what signals to send. Also, your body has no weight. It has the same mass as on earth, but there's no force pulling it anywhere. Wavering heard loud thumps and smiled—bodies hitting the sides of the cabin. That, too, he knew.

Wavering recalls the only experience like space is being suspended in water. In a swimming pool and being able to move wherever you want—right, left, up, down. When you push off from a pool wall, you push hard. Water offers resistance. When you do the same thing in space with captive air that gives no resistance, you fly across the cabin and crunch into the opposite wall. Easy does it. Even though Wavering warned them, he knew they'd have to learn themselves. A few bumps. A few bruises. Oh well.

The third compartment is the sleeping quarters. Not that they need Beautyrest® or the like. Far from it. The room is equipped with sleeping bags. Anchored to the floor, the walls, they can be anywhere. The quarters are well ventilated. With no gravity, there's no circulation of heavier and lighter air, colder and warmer air. Your breath can hang at your face so you're inhaling more and more carbon dioxide. Not good. Oxygen deprivation can cause brain damage. Definitely not good. Although it occurs to Wavering that maybe human brains got oxygen-deprived on earth, and that was what made people follow a half-wit like Fluke III until he put it to the Indonesians. Just a thought, he concedes.

That sleeping deck is where they'll be when Dr. Drone administers the hibernation mickey. Wavering hasn't said anything to the others, but he doesn't look forward to it. He admits he's a control freak. Maybe he has to be to fly complicated planes and now this rocket. But to be asleep and let the spacecraft hurtle through unexplored space for years? Maybe he should try harder not to think about it.

Wavering appointed Regina crew chief. Piloting Genesis is more than a full-time job. Rocket flights he had been on before had several trained flight crew members. Even then they were all busy. Plus, Wavering has to confess again, he wasn't made for human relations. With all the coming and going before the launch, Wavering wondered whether they would ever get off the planet. And with a crew he could appreciate. As he looks at the crew now, is he lucky? He thinks so.

Regina especially. Not that the crew needs much supervision. Before launch, the women were concerned about how their space suits fit. They put them on, exchanged them with one another until all were satisfied. Malcolm and Buck? As long as they could get into theirs, they were fine. They only needed the suits for blast-off or if something went wrong. Went wrong? There Wavering goes again. Positive, Wavering. Think positive. Since they aren't blasting off now or facing something going wrong, the suits are off. Everyone is dressed in khaki pants, T-shirts, and sneakers.

Even Elena, although Wavering wonders, is she comfortable? Has she come to terms with the spacecraft? As the launch approached, she nervously asked what it would be like. Wavering tried to reassure her, but he doesn't think he hid his own apprehension. When he showed her Genesis from the outside, viewing it from the walkway that led from the silo wall to the spacecraft, she trembled. Well, she was looking down 500 feet into the silo and maybe there was a little vertigo.

But Regina helped her. "Look," she said to Elena. "It'll be like camping. Surely you went camping."

Elena looked at Regina with a squint. "Yes, one… once," she

said hesitantly.

"It wasn't too bad, was it?"

"It was awful," Elena said. "I was terrified."

"By camping? What was so awful?"

"I was in eighth grade. I was at like a private school. They took our grade camping in the Maine woods. Part of it was like they separated all twelve of us and made us stay forty-eight hours by ourselves. They left only a tarp and some water. It was like awful. I cried. I screamed. I curled up in a ball. Do you know how dark the woods can be at night? There were those sounds."

Wavering knows those sounds. Usually just mice, but there can be dozens of them crawling out of their holes because hawks don't do night shift. They can make a racket.

"I got no sleep at all," Elena says. "Of course I'd also done something stupid. I wore stilettoes. Can you believe it? Well, I did. Here I am on a dirt trail with nothing level and patches of mud. Then we're like crossing a meadow, it's wet, it's mushy. And one heel gets stuck in the mud. But I walk on. The heel pops right off the shoe. So I've got a flat on one foot and a stiletto on the other. The other kids laughed. But I didn't. It was like so humiliating. So I got mad and tore the heel off the other shoe, and that's what I hiked in. No, camping is awful."

Regina smiled. Wavering is sure she dealt with Elena before. It must not be easy. There's spoiled, and then there's royally spoiled. "Well, Elena," Regina said. "There's no mud here. You're not in stilettoes. They won't work on Proxima b anyway. And we're not going to put you forty-eight hours in the woods with creatures running around you. So this won't be that bad."

Elena's eyes softened slightly. Wavering guesses if you're raised by nannies, chauffeurs, private tutors, manicurists, pedicurists, and never have to clean your room or cook, you can get pretty indulgent. When Wavering heard Elena describe her childhood, he thought, what different worlds we live in. Elena's? Life on another planet.

46

At ten thousand feet, they break out of the frozen haze enveloping earth. Shafts of sunlight shoot in through the windows. They're blinded. Months of haze and holing up in bunkers have weakened their eye muscles. Sarah and Wavering put on heavy sunglasses, but they make reading the controls difficult.

As they're approaching the moon, and it looms larger and larger in their windows, Olga drifts in from the crew cabin. She peers out one of the windows. She turns to Wavering, her eyes pinched with shock. Wavering know what she sees. No sketchy 'man in the moon' they saw from earth. Plains and scattered rocks and light-colored soil radiating out from craters the size of London or New York from the air. Her voice grows shrill. "We're going to crash," she says. "We're going to crash."

Wavering has to admit it does look like that. The launch crew and Sarah set their course to maximize the moon's gravity to accelerate the craft. With no atmosphere offering resistance, they can skim the surface at a low altitude and then slingshot away under power to aim for the sun.

They draw closer. Olga's eyes pinch even more. "Do you know what you're doing?" she asks, trembling.

"I think so," Wavering says. He turns to Sarah. "What about you?"

Sarah glances at Olga's worried look. "Maybe we'll make it," she replies with a smile.

Olga points to the view in the window. "Maybe? Maybe?" she shouts. "We're going to crash. Do something."

214

They drop closer to the surface than Wavering has ever been. Dozens and dozens of small craters, boulders, mountain ridges that look as if they're as high as the Himalayas, although they aren't. Wavering doesn't know what to do with Olga. He says, "Relax. If you crash, I crash. We didn't put a crash in the flight plan."

Olga floats at the window, her body rigid. Maybe Wavering should put blinders on her. Or confine her to the sleeping deck where there are no windows. But he doesn't think she'd go. She'd rather stare and worry. He knows the type.

***

Wavering learned in school that the distance from the earth to the sun is 93 million miles. But he never imagined that one day he'd cover that distance in a spacecraft. They've jettisoned the third stage and are powered now and for the rest of the journey by a relatively new invention, an invention researchers sought to create for a long time, but found hard to achieve—a fusion rocket engine.

Using nuclear fusion the same as the sun's, the engine develops fuel as it burns. It can run indefinitely and will accelerate Genesis until they reach a velocity one quarter the speed of light. After leaving the moon, they'll be at the sun in just a few hours. Amazing. At least Wavering thinks so.

Some of the crewmates have their minds on other things. Buck comes to the control deck to check out Sarah and Wavering. He floats to a window and stares out. "Black out there," he says.

He's right. Without an atmosphere to spread sunlight and broaden its color spectrum, Buck is staring at ink black space dotted with brilliant stars. And then the sun, a yellow ball of fire. Beautiful, but not in a way that reminds Wavering of earthly sun and sunsets.

Buck pulls back from the window. "There's no treadmill," he says. He's in his white running shorts and white T-shirt and sneakers ready to do his fitness routine. "I thought there would be a treadmill."

Wavering shrugs his shoulders. "You watched too many space movies," he says. "They had treadmills, they had running tracks. In Hollywood, you can do that. But we're small, basic. Just enough craft to get us to Proxima b alive." Maybe they'll get there, Wavering thinks. Oh well.

"But our muscles?" Buck says with a hint of complaint. "We'll have no muscles when we get there. We'll be a bunch of jellies."

He's right about that. "Dr. Drone," Wavering says. "After we come out of hibernation, he's got rubber bands for us to exercise with. We'll need to do hard workouts to be ready for the planet."

"But now?" Buck asks. "What the hell do I do now?"

Wavering realizes that for Buck, to exercise is to be. He's got nothing else. Never did have anything else. Wavering feels like he's supervising a bunch of kids, and the play room has no toys to play with. Only Buck is a grown man. What to do?

"Do you have an e-book?" Wavering asks.

"I've got one. But I don't use it. Never got around to it."

"You don't read?" Wavering comments.

"I mean to. But with TV and phones and the like, who needs books?"

"But now?" Wavering says. "Without TV and phones and the like?"

Buck casts him a querulous look. Wavering doesn't think it has penetrated his gray matter that there is no TV and there are no phones, and he will never see them again. Life is tough. "We don't have books," Buck says.

"We do have books," Wavering says.

Buck looks at him like he's crazy. "Books?" he asks. "What

books?"

"E-books," Wavering says. "Thousands of them."

"Yeah. Books. Dull as hell. The ones the government gave us. How great America is. How it's the beacon of the world. The Fluke regime is the greatest America ever had. That's until… well…." He drifts off.

"Not those books," Wavering says. "Although we kept a few. To remember what it was like."

Buck's eyes brighten. "There are others?"

"Yes," Wavering says. "Sarah has them too." He nods to her. Wavering tells Buck they downloaded thousands of books. And samizdat, which Wavering explains is writing from those who opposed the Flukes.

Buck's eyes grow wide. "Do the others know?"

"Not yet. Why don't you tell them?"

Buck floats to the hatch and into the crew quarters. A few minutes later, the whole crew drifts through the hatch and crowds around Sarah and Wavering--behind them, beside them, and floating over their heads. "Books?" Regina asks. "You've got real books?"

Wavering feels he's with a band of pilgrims who crawled across a desert deprived of water and food. Their faces are eager. Even Olga seems to have lost her fear of crashing or whatever else was chilling her mind. Some of them have their e-book pads with them. Full of Fluke propaganda, of course.

"Real books," Wavering says. "Books that were blacklisted. Starting with the Greeks up to the imprisonment and execution of writers who didn't abide by the ban." Wavering points to a computer module at the edge of the control panel. "There. Plug in there, select what you want from the screen. Download to your heart's content."

They look at the module and hesitate. Don't they believe him?

Are they afraid if one goes first they'll look greedy? But greedy for books? They decide Gretchen should lead since she has the most knowledge in her head. The others stay in the control cabin and take their turns. If everything else fails, including they miss Proxima b and are doomed forever to float through space, at least they'll be the best educated dead castaways in the history of the universe. Or something like that.

47

Blinding sunlight streams in from the spacecraft windows. Wavering can't help but think of mythological Icarus and his solar duel. Now they are him. And, like Icarus, they are taking a huge risk.

Icarus's father Daedalus fashioned wings for himself and for Icarus from feathers and wax. He instructed Icarus to follow him in flight across the sea. He warned his son not to fly too close to the sun or the wax on his wings would melt.

Like many young men, Icarus treated the prohibition as an invitation. Euphoric because he was able to fly, he ignored his father's warning, took off and did soar too close to the sun. The wax melted, his feathers burned away, and Icarus, desperately trying to fly with his bare arms, plunged into the sea.

Hubris took him. Wavering ponders, isn't that what ended the human race? What were we thinking? That we could keep adding more and more people to a limited planet? That we could keep pumping carbon dioxide into the atmosphere and not pay a price? That we could survive countries run by psychopathic dictators and still achieve world peace? That we could develop nuclear weapons and nations could taunt each other with threats of attack, and someone not push the button that would end it all? From the Stone Age to the apocalypse, was it real progress?

Almost a million miles in diameter and approaching 10,000 degrees Fahrenheit at the surface, the sun viewed from the spacecraft is not the smooth yellow or orange or red sphere—depending on the time of day and density of the air--seen from earth. It is a boiling cauldron of fire and pyrotechnics. It is not uniformly one color or texture. There are black holes, not really holes, they're areas that are cooler than those surrounding. On earth they were called sunspots. Around each burns a ring of bright red fire. Outside that ring, flames burn orange and yellow, flaring and flashing as if the whole orb is trying to explode.

With his spine turning to ice, Wavering watches the flares, flares that could incinerate Genesis and its inhabitants in seconds. Atomic bombs, hydrogen bombs? Firecrackers compared with what Wavering sees directly ahead along the sun's horizon. Astrophysicists told him flares sometimes shoot 30,000 miles above the surface. They are awesome if Wavering can use that term. Awesomely threatening, too.

All is quiet inside Genesis. Wavering doesn't know if his crewmates are terrified witless and can't utter a sound. Or if they're mesmerized by the inferno that exceeds anything they saw on earth. Or they're saying their last prayers before they melt. Not melt like Icarus's wax and feathers, but the skin of Genesis soften, bend and twist as if in the grip of a giant hand, jagged holes erupt in the skin, and they perish. Nightmare stuff for sure.

Wavering has taken every precaution. Regina, Sarah, and he talked it over when the sun was still far ahead. Apart from flight-ending space debris, apart from missing Proxima b and floating through space forever, apart from crashing on landing, and apart from finding Proxima b has no atmosphere or it has surface elements toxic to human existence, this passing the sun and slingshotting away is the most dangerous part of their journey.

They are tightly clad in their spacesuits. When Wavering looks at Sarah in the seat next to him, all he sees of her face is the reflection on her helmet lens of the inside of the control deck and the dazzling light knifing through the windows. He has no idea if she is looking at the sun or her face is drawn up in terror.

Their spacesuits are hooked up to Genesis's air circulation system. Wavering set the temperature as low as it would go, so they are cold. At least they will be until they enter the arc above the sun's boiling surface that will accelerate the spacecraft. They are belted in their seats to prevent them from touching the inside of Genesis's skin. That skin will reach several hundred degrees. Centrifugal force from the rotation Wavering put Genesis in would throw them against that skin where they would die of burns or heat prostration. Genesis rotates like a roasting chicken on a spit in order to spread the heat evenly around the outside of the craft. Yes, like a chicken roasting on a spit, which could burn up if Sarah's calculations are off.

Sarah leans forward to stare more closely at a digital readout. It's the altitude above the sun's surface calculated by their radar. Wavering guesses terror is not on her mind. Although because she set the lower trajectory, he thinks she feels responsible if they incinerate. Not that there would be much time for apologies.

Wavering hears her voice through the headphones. "Right on trajectory," she says with some pride.

Wavering doesn't know how to reply. Because 'right on trajectory' might mean they're close enough to the surface to melt or bake to death. It is getting hotter. Beads of sweat run down his face, off his chin, he feels it collecting around the collar inside his suit. Not very comfortable.

"If you say so," Wavering replies. "I don't want to worry you. But if you check the temperature on the skin outside, is it what you projected?"

Silence as she shifts about to get a better look at the dials. "A little higher," she says with some reluctance.

"Can I ask how much? I mean might it go above the melting point? That could be an inconvenience, you know." Wavering doesn't want to alarm her, and to describe death as an inconvenience seems a bit lame, but he's concerned about her fragile side. At least he thinks he should be. It would also be an inconvenience in light of what they're trying to accomplish. He's not sure what he's thinking. Wavering takes a deep breath. Wow, it is hot, very hot.

48

He's being shaken. Someone has him by the shoulders and is shaking him. He feels he's emerging from somewhere deep underground. A bunker maybe? Is Fluke III there? He stiffens. He forces his eyes open. Blurry. A face. The shaking continues. He tries to raise his arm, but it's stuck. It's caught in the sleeping bag he's cocooned in. Finally he speaks. "I'm okay. I'm okay." The words come out as if spoken by a sandman. His lips are rough and dry. His vision clears. It's Dr. Drone's face peering down at him. Wrinkles on his brow.

"Boy," he says. "Were you gone." Wavering nods. Gone. But in the bunker? No, not that gone. "The timer went off," Dr. Done continues. Wavering thinks. Timer? Ah, Proxima b.

"We're getting close?" he asks. Dr. Drone nods. Wavering feels for his stomach. There's nothing there. His abdomen is caved in like that of a dead man. Yes, he is hungry. He envisions grilled salmon, barbequed pork ribs, New York strip steak. A stemmed wineglass cupping the deep red of cabernet sauvignon.

Dr. Drone hands him a granola bar. He looks at it. The wineglass disappears. He attacks the bar with his teeth. Dry, like grit. His taste glands are tuned up for flavor. If there ever was flavor in the bar, it must have escaped three lightyears ago. But as he munches he consoles himself that the bar is something to eat. At least it's not beans.

He glances about the sleeping cabin. Other sleeping bags are stirring. They look like butterfly chrysalises breaking out of their cocoons. Arms and legs struggle with the bags, eyes blink. Voices are so dry and weak they are incoherent. Wavering wriggles free of his cocoon and swims through nothing into the cockpit. Sarah is belted in her seat as if she's been there for four lightyears. "Did you sleep at all?" he asks.

She laughs. "Hey, I wanted to get back in here. I like doing this stuff." She concentrates on a screen showing nearby stars.

"How are we doing?" he asks. Here they are hurtling through space toward what? His brain is fuzzy. Toward what? Proxima b? He can't picture it. 'Rock,' they said. Just rock.

"ETA looks just over a month," Sarah says. "Two weeks to braking burn."

Gad, Wavering responds, she is on top of this journey. He shakes his head. He's got to get a grip. And stop thinking about rock. He looks at his hands, nails definitely need trimming. He touches his face. Tries to touch his face. His beard gets in the way. He looks at his reflection in a window. Scary. Bushman with wild hair. Doesn't Sarah notice? Her eyes stay fixed on the instruments. She writes down numbers on a pad. He doesn't think she notices anything else.

His eyes are so weak the cabin lights blind him. He glances through the forward windshield. The three Proxima suns. The way auto pilot has Genesis positioned, Alpha Centauri burns white to the left, Beta Centauri to the right. He looks for Proxima Centauri. Being the red dwarf it is, it must be the dim reddish object almost equidistant between Alpha and Beta. That's what the astrophysicists told him to expect. But that much dimmer? What kind of life could it support? Oh well.

Regina pokes her head through the hatch. She looks at him, but doesn't react to his scary-man look. She's kind. "The crew is coming along," she assures him. He nods. Wavering just wishes he was coming along. Thank goodness for Sarah. Regina glances at Sarah, but doesn't disturb her. Wavering reminds himself that the approach to Proxima b will be dicey. Sarah will give him the numbers he needs to tweak their trajectory. Do they really know what they're doing?

Wavering floats through the hatch to see the crew for himself. "Hey Skipper," Buck says. "How's it goin' up there?" He's shaved and pedicured himself, showered, and put on clean pants and T-shirt. He looks ready for a workout. Of course there's no up there, Wavering thinks. At least until they've landed on Proxima b, but Buck has an unvarnished way of seeing things. He also has a sunny disposition that doesn't seem dimmed by the risk they're taking. Maybe he doesn't think about it. Wavering wishes he could do the same.

"Great job you guys are doing," Malcolm says. Smiling broadly, he raises his arms to stretch elastic exercise bands that reach from his wrists to his feet. He takes conditioning seriously. Buck, too. As they all should, including himself. Wavering takes a band, stretches it between his wrists, and moves his arms out and in. Pain stabs from his wrists to his shoulders. He's a wreck.

With a month on their hands and nothing else to do, they read. The crew cabin is quiet and looks like a public library. Some of the crew are tethered to the walls. Others are belted in chairs. Or just float, their e-books either held, or floating motionless in front of their faces. Wavering prefers belted in a chair and holding his e-book now loaded with Don Quixote. As Wavering accompanies Don from one crazy scene to another, he finds he identifies. How happy Don was in his imaginary wonderland.

Wavering's distracted by Elena, who looks at him with a querulous expression.. "Did you find something interesting?" he asks.

"Some of these books," she says. "They seem to understand me better than I do myself."

Wavering nods. Books can do that. Isn't that one reason he read them? Entertainment too, of course.

"Vanity of vanities," Elena says. "Vanity of vanities." Wavering waits for more, but her dreamy look says she's lost in thought.

"What about it?" Wavering says.

She laughs. "I could tell you thought I was a showboat." Righto, Wavering thinks. But he wouldn't tell her that. It wouldn't be nice. "I was," she continues with a note of finality. "Do you know what it's like to walk the runway with hundreds of people looking at you? Adoring you? And you look so good, so sexy?"

Wavering tries to imagine himself as a fashion model on a runway. "I can't say that I know what it's like," he says. Runway? Yeah, he knows a runway. It's a two-mile slab of concrete he lands an airplane on.

Elena looks off. "The praise was so intoxicating. I think it made me drunk. Like a booze drunk, I had to get more. And more. But more was never enough. Did I know what I wanted? Where was I going? No, don't answer. I was going nowhere. And I didn't know it. Nowhere. Just more clothes, more runways, more adoration. I was a clothes-aholic. I was a praise-aholic. But more didn't get me anything. I had nothing inside me." She pauses, nods. "Vanity of vanities. All is vanity."

"Elena, don't be too hard on yourself," Wavering says. "You didn't choose the life you had."

Her eyes harden. "I didn't choose it. But how could I not have noticed? Was I that blind?" She smiles. "You don't need to answer that."

***

Eva floats about the cabin. Wavering has seen she's reading the Bible. She looks at him as if she's seeing a vision and says, "Almost all the people in here are Jews." What did she think? Irish?

Chinese? Samoan? "And there are no Jews here to be part of the new human race."

Everyone falls silent. She's right. Wavering knows why there's no Jew. Along with the racism and xenophobia and misogyny and sexual discrimination and anti-immigrant hysteria there was the dark nemesis of anti-Semitism. When the neo-Nazis held their demonstrations, usually like those nighttime torch parades to celebrate Adolf Hitler's rule as the Fuhrer, on Fox TV—every channel—there were snaking lines of black-leather-clad marchers with swastika armbands holding torches and shouting, "Death to Jews. Death to Jews." Was this from Unter den Linden in Berlin where Hitler's marches took place? No. Germany didn't allow it. But all over America. Crowds lining the streets cheered and joined the chant.

Regina pushes off the floor. She and Eva circle opposite each other as if in a three-dimensional dance. There's a smile on Regina's face. She and Eva keep circling the cabin. Wavering loves watching them. They could be sisters having a crazy time.

"Eva, you're wrong," Regina says.

"Wrong?" Eva asks. "What do you mean?"

"That there is no Jew among us."

They all pull their faces out of their books and glance about. What is Regina talking about? Augustus would never put a Jew on Genesis. Or anywhere else. Finally Wavering fixes his gaze on Regina and her lovely face. "You?" he says.

She smiles. She really is beautiful. The black eyes hypnotizing. She touches the wall and launches herself into slow summersaults. "I can't believe it," Wavering says. "The president..."

She laughs. "He never knew. You know, I don't have... I don't have the circumcision." Her contagious laugh spreads to the others. "So he couldn't tell. He never asked about my background. You know. He saw me at Cirque. He decided he needed me for his collection. He got what he wanted. You know when he decided he wanted something, he was not a man to ask questions."

Elena breaks out laughing. She shakes her head. "My goodness, Regina. I can't believe you. He spouted his anti-Semitism and never knew." Elena's face glows. "If only he could hear you now." Elena floats into the center of the cabin. She joins hands with Eva and Regina in their aerial dance and the three of them glide in a circle. Wavering shakes his head. What next?

49

At forty-six thousand miles per second, they are closing the gap to Centauri Proxima. Alpha and Beta Centauri are moving wider apart. Through their windows, they see Centauri Proxima growing larger and brighter. Not much brighter, but its red disk stands out clearly against the stars behind it. Wavering tries to work up some enthusiasm for Proxima, but he does wonder if real suns Alpha or Beta would have been a better choice. So the astro boys said they had no evidence either had a planet that might be in 'the habitable zone.' What if there were a small one? The astros wouldn't have seen it. Oh well.

Wavering has so much time to think that he wonders what it means that Proxima b is in the habitable zone. It may mean nothing. Nothing. There might be water There might be air. There might be something resembling soil to grow things in. Would the astrophysicists have prepared a four-color brochure like the one those golfers had? What if there's no atmosphere at all? The brochure would depict something like The Stone Desert in Libya—with a pitch black sky. Nobody would go to a place like that. Maybe he's thinking too much. Be positive, Wavering. Be positive.

"Reverse thrust in two minutes and counting," Sarah says. Her nose is in the screens in front of her. She throws switches, tweaks dials. She presses buttons to give her the readouts she wants. The variables that depress Wavering don't seem to distract her. He activates the maneuvering jets and turns Genesis one hundred eighty degrees. "On course," Sarah says. Wavering throws the

229

switches to raise the engine to full power. He's jerked back into his seat, his head presses against the backrest.

"This is a long burn," Sarah says. Wavering nods. He looks over at her. She stares at a handheld transponder with a readout of their course. Nerves? He doesn't notice any. He says to her. "I hope you don't mind if I ask." She looks at him expectantly. "You're doing so well. Maybe I sound trite. But, your PTSD? This is stressful stuff we're doing."

She cocks her head thoughtfully. "When I'm navigating, I don't feel depressed," she says. "I lose myself. Especially when I know my projections mean life or death."

She pauses, then, "There's another symptom most people don't know about. They call it a foreshortened sense of the future. I guess you might call it a sense of doom. When anything happens that threatens change, I tense up. It used to happen when the phone rang and I didn't know who would be on the other end. Or when I went to a party and wasn't sure I would know anyone. Even when I went to shop in a store. Not knowing what kind of people I would run into."

"I don't have PTSD, Sarah, but right now I can identify with you if you're talking about fear of what might happen in the future."

"You?" she says. "We're doing very well. Why would you be worried?"

"Why?" Wavering replies. "Should I count the ways? You know them all. We've got to approach Proxima b at an angle and with a velocity that will insert Genesis into an orbit that will hold. No slingshotting past. Not so steep that gravity accelerates our descent." And no crashing, Wavering thinks, but he doesn't see any good mentioning it. "Then if we get to the surface…"

"When we get to the surface," she says.

"When?" Wavering says. "What happened to your

foreshortened future?"

"You're a good pilot, Wavering."

"What does that have to do with it?" he asks.

"I don't feel fear," she says. "I don't know why. Maybe it's a sixth sense—if there is such a thing."

Wavering says. "Well I've now got a sense of foreshortening. But I guess you won't join me."

Sarah laughs. "I know you have quite an imagination. Maybe hard to control." She glances about, her voice grows wistful. "I want to tell you, Wavering, this trip has been great. I know we can't predict how it'll turn out. But I've never had an experience like this. No one ever trusted me with so much responsibility. Since we're trying to be optimistic, but, you know… I want to say 'thank you.' Is that all right?"

50

Wavering tries to ease the stress he feels in his neck and muscles as they draw closer to Proxima b, but he can't keep his mind from speculating. It isn't just that the name 'Proxima' eats at him. It sounds as if astrophysicists found the planet so undefinable they couldn't figure out what it is or what to do with it. Proxima seems so tentative. He assumes they were just being honest. They detected a planet orbiting Centauri Proxima. The orbit is in the zone that could support life. Could support it. That's only the orbit. Not much to go on. Good luck.

Then Wavering jumps: if we do manage to set up life, what will we call ourselves? 'Proxi-mates?' Or 'Proximites?' he takes a deep breath. Maybe the oxygen level in Genesis has dropped and he's obsessing with stuff that's unimportant. But it does take his mind off landing. He has no experience landing a rocket on a site that hasn't been scoped from orbit. Normally there are pictures taken by robots on the ground. They won't get ground. But they should get orbital. What will the pictures show? So many 'what ifs' he doesn't want to know.

They slow Genesis to 17,000 miles per hour and enter an orbit 250 miles above Proxima b's surface. With the accuracy of Sarah's projections, a piece of cake. All of them crowd to the windows to take a look at the planet. It's like they're approaching fogged in LA or San Francisco on an airliner. Fog. Nothing but fog.

They swing around several orbits, clearly see the reddish light side and the dark side. And the twilight zone between. Maybe the entire planet is having a foggy day. Day? He's got to get over that.

Give the planet some time, and they will see clouds breaking up.

Genesis is stable in its orbit. They could go on indefinitely. But from the solid cloud they see skimming beneath them, it looks like 'indefinitely' might not change the view. He feels chilled. Proxima b from orbit looks like wrecked planet earth that they left. Wavering recalls the endless clouds he saw from Air Force One. All cloud. Everywhere. Wrecked earth and Proxima b look like Venus. And Venus, if he recalls correctly, does a pretty good job of matching a literary description of hell. Temperatures up to 800 degrees Fahrenheit, a cyclone that never relents keeps stirring up the planet's atmosphere that is mostly carbon dioxide. Lightning storms not caused by lightning as we know it, they're explosions of sulfur dioxide.

Wavering sees no explosions in the clouds beneath them, but is this what they've come four light years to find? Another Venus? Sarah's eyes are fixed on the radar screen and camera images. She glances out the window as if hoping the images are false, so Wavering doesn't bother her with his turmoil about Venus. "Well, skipper," she says hopefully. "Where will it be?"

Wavering glances out the window. Where? One part of solid cloud is as good or bad as another. He sees no holes, no crease in the clouds that would indicate a front, a change in the weather. Just cloud, cloud, cloud. He's landed Air Force One in poor weather conditions, but he had an instrument landing system, he had radar on the ground confirming course, altitude, and speed. He could bring the plane down to fifty feet before seeing runway landing lights. But here? Nothing. Absolutely nothing. He doesn't tell Sarah his concern. His spine is turning to ice. His brain overworks with images of landing on a jagged mountain or in an ocean where they have no sight of a shoreline. Or they crash. He could go on, but he's morbid enough already.

"Take your pick," Wavering says to Sarah.

Sarah laughs. How can she can do that in this situation? Doesn't she get it? "You mean a friendly part of the cloud?" she asks.

"If you can find one," Wavering says. "Otherwise we drop through at the twilight zone and..."

"And?" she asks with a grinning querulous look.

"Your life insurance paid up?" Wavering asks. He's acting crazy. But if he were to get serious, he'd open a hatch and drift off into space—without a spacesuit. Or would crashing be better? Instant lights out? It does have some appeal.

"I upped the coverage before I left," Sarah says. She's as crazy as he is.

***

Wavering instructs the crew to don their spacesuits and prepare for landing. His mind flits back to Air Force One. "Put your seats in an upright position. Seatbelts fastened and tight." All routine back then, except that Augustus Fluke III never put his seatback upright and never bothered to fasten his seatbelt. That was only for mortals. Oh well.

Wavering fires a long engine burn. The craft slows, they are pressed back in their seats. Wavering watches velocity, altitude, and attitude so they will back down vertically to the surface. That is, assuming there is one. Sarah is glued to radar screens and camera images. They've prepared how to communicate if they break through the clouds and see the ground before they hit. If they don't break through the clouds before they hit, well it's like Vegas or Wall Street. You take your chances.

"Hold," Sarah says. "We're through, but we're over mountains."

Wavering halts the descent, hovers, and waits. Sarah swivels one of the cameras for a side view. "Three o'clock, slowly," she says. Wavering slides Genesis to the right. "Slower," she adds. "Looks flat enough. Hold here. Now, down slowly. I'll watch as we go in."

Wavering reduces thrust. Their descent is so slow he can hardly feel it. Suddenly dust swirls outside the windows. They drop lower, the dust disappears. He sees through the window a dirt surface with scattered small stones. It looks firm enough to support their landing struts. They touch down gently, Genesis settles level. Only now is Wavering aware of the tightness in his chest. He takes a deep breath. Sarah nods and smiles. He gives her a high five. A rather lame celebration after sixteen years and risk beyond the imagination. They hear the crew cheer. We're here, he thinks. Should he believe it?

51

Wavering gives Proxima b a new name: 'Earth II.' Not because they've landed on a pristine planet with a Garden of Eden. Nor a Stone Age with hominids running around in animal skins and hurling wooden spears with stone points at mammoths or unicorns or each other. Nor empires like those of the Egyptians, the Greeks, or the Romans. At least they had empires until they fought too many wars and wasted too much money and too many people. Nor a Medieval dark age with draconian kings and priests suppressing the poor. Nor a Renaissance, nor the Industrial Revolution. Nor an Atomic Age nor a Dotcom Age nor an Artificial Intelligence age. No, now that they have disembarked from Genesis, what they see reminds them of none of them.

They stand on the edge of the plateau they landed on and look in the direction where the cloudy sky is brightest—the eternal sunny side. Beneath that sky and below where they stand there appears to be a desert. Dunes that look like ocean waves extending to the horizon. Some are high with long ridges. Between them are troughs that look like they've been carved out by the wind. The wind. Moderate but steady. No gusts, no lulls.

They pick their way down a slope strewn with boulders. At the bottom, their feet sink into what they thought was sand. But it isn't sand. It's dust, large-grained dust. At the bottom of the troughs between the dunes, they see faint outlines of roads and highways, maybe freeways. The concrete is eroded, pockmarked holes expose rust-covered metal reinforcing rods. Drawing closer to the dunes, they discover they conceal the ruins of buildings. Pieces of stone, pieces of concrete walls push out from the dust. Metal beams, too. The debris makes some of the dunes look like porcupines that have lost some of their quills.

Among the dunes and troughs, not a sign of life. Nothing moves except clouds of dust and dust devils that pirouette from trough to trough. No sign of death either. Destruction must have taken place so long ago that whoever built the place and then was destroyed, or destroyed it, has joined the dust. Bones, too. Not much for archeologists to work with.

Astrophysicists said Proxima b is two to three hundred million years older than earth. That must have given her a head start over earth on civilization. And a head start on ending civilization. Wavering feels sad to think that another planet went through what they did. He doesn't say anything to the others. They all stare in silence and grieve in their own way.

Malcolm says, "Well, it looks like we weren't the only ones to develop nuclear weapons. And use them." That doesn't feel much like consolation. To leave a ruin and sixteen years later to arrive at another ruin? Wavering has no idea what to think. Is this trip a total waste of time?

Gretchen, scientist that she is, doesn't look on in despair. She's looking at the instruments she's brought. "There's oxygen," she says. "It's equivalent to twenty-thousand feet altitude on earth. Over time, like the Nepalese, we could adjust. If we have babies, they would develop larger lungs and their blood would hold more oxygen molecules. They would get along fine. But there's still us." She pauses thoughtfully. "I'm not sure we can adapt."

"There's methane, too," Gretchen says. Maybe they could get used to that. As industrial progress toasted the earth's climate to the point where species died and millions of people became refugees fleeing the growing deserts, climatologists told them they were breathing more methane. The warming earth became a methane well. How bad it was for them Wavering didn't know.

The temperature where they are on Proxima b is warmer than what they left on earth, it hovers just above freezing. They're not sure what that will do for Gretchen's vegetables and fruits and trees and her maybe genetically engineered something like a chicken or a pig. After all, what do they feed animals or themselves if nothing will grow?

"Pits," Malcolm says mildly.

"Bitch," Buck says. "How am I going to set up a running track in a place like this?"

Wavering looks at Buck with his shoulders bent in despair. Does he have tunnel vision? A normal person would think about food and water and shelter, things that would keep them alive. It seems a stretch to complain about the lack of a gymnasium, weights, and a running track. Maybe a hot tub and sauna, too.

"Well, everyone," Regina says with a sigh. "You have to admit it was a great ride."

Wavering looks at her and expects to see sadness in her black eyes. But he doesn't. He just sees resolve. Here she is looking at this Mad Max of a city and expressing a sense of gratitude. She's right, of course. They did get along well. They loved the discoveries of books and art and music. And the views? Stars and galaxies, the sky unobstructed by an atmosphere, so brilliant Wavering can't imagine the stars and galaxies are lightyears distant from each other and yet form a canopy of light. As he reflects on what they saw, his chest swells with gratitude.

"Well, captain, what do we do now?" The refrigerator voice is Olga's. She's such a champ at blowing the air out of euphoria. If only she could get Reverend Jones's 'God will provide' or 'God moves in mysterious ways.' Anything to take her mind off the reality that they have traveled sixteen earth years, and they might be back where they started.

Wavering turns to Olga. "Hate to say it, but my contract is up. My job was to get us here. We are here. Thanks a great deal to Sarah. From now on, I'm one of the rest of you. We have to plan together."

Tears well in Olga's eyes. Wavering has no idea how to buck her up. "Genesis will keep us well for a while," he says. "I've banked the engine. It will provide us with light, heat, and a working galley stove." He pauses, searching for more. "Our dried food supplies should last for a while." But only for a while? Then what?

Poor Olga. She's so dependent. She looks at him with sheepish eyes that remind him of a bulldog he once owned who gave him that look when he was starved for attention. The dog got on his nerves. So does Olga. He'd tell her to start working on her problems herself, but he's not confident there's one neuron out of her 90 billion that has any intention of moving her in that direction.

Wavering has a thought. "Olga, do you know how to cook?"

She wrinkles her brow as if he's asked her to rob a bank. "Cook? No. I never had to cook."

Ah, the luxurious life some of his crewmates had. "Look," he says. "Cooking on Genesis, as you know, is just add water and heat. Can you do that?"

Her brow is still wrinkled.

"Olga," he says. "You need to do something. If not cook, then explore?"

She sets her lip, looks about at the dirt plateau, the rocky ridges in the distance. "I'll cook."

52

Each morning—morning by earth clock—Malcolm and Elena put on long underwear, thick, warm pants, and turtleneck shirts which they cover with sweaters. Warm gloves and lugged hiking boots. Carrying a pick and shovel, they set off toward the twilight dark. They chatter with each other as if they're lifelong hiking members of the Sierra Club—before Fluke III's gestapo shut it down, that is. Wavering reminds himself this is the Elena of stilettoes and silk dresses and leather handbags and jewelry. Maybe some people can change.

And Malcolm? Wavering understands why he gets along with Elena. They were both rigorously trained on how to act. With TV cameras focused on Elena so much of the time, her trainers warned her there was no room for a screw-up. Especially with Augustus's obsession with appearance and his lack of patience.

Malcolm, Secret Service agent that he was, when he was on duty with the president, he had to be razor-focused, always searching for a potential attacker. Looking for a hand hidden in a pants pocket or slipped behind a jacket lapel. Or a bulge that could indicate a bomb. At Fluke III speeches, he faced the crowds, scanning for unusual movement. In SUV convoys, he rode ahead of or behind the president's bulletproof, blast-proof limousine watching for some fool—or maybe they were patriots, who knows—to fire a gun or hurl a grenade intending to relieve Augustus of his obligation to live.

On golf courses—Augustus loved to golf although he claimed he played not at all—Malcolm never allowed himself to look at the

240

grass and trees. His eyes scanned hedges and bushes from which a gunman could jump and race toward the president. Or a sniper taking aim with a rifle from the leafy branches of a tree.

One day Malcolm and Elena come to Wavering with a request. "An electric drill and some wire," Malcolm says. Wavering has no idea what they're doing and they don't volunteer one, but he doesn't question them. When they return later in the day, Wavering sees in the distance there are three of them. Three? As they draw closer, he sees tall Malcolm on the left, slender model Elena on the right. Between them, they hold up a full skeleton of the strangest-looking hominid Wavering has ever seen. About four feet tall, with a disproportionately large head. He resembles no skeleton of a pre-hominid figure he had seen on earth.

"We found the bones in a cave," Elena says. "We wired them together to see what our friend looked like. There were bones of others. Malcolm and I call them 'people.'" Smiling, she looks at their new-found friend. "Malcolm thinks a group of them hid in the cave. Like Augustus and his friends holed up in the White House bunker. But they ran out of food."

"Do you have a name for... I don't know what to call your...?" Wavering asks.

Malcolm says, "We call our new friend 'Proxie.'" When Gretchen arrives and studies him, she declares he's a male. But being so small, is he a child? At four feet tall, his body, apart from a larger than earthling rib cage, is dwarfed. But his head, it's human-sized at least. So Proxie and his fellow-citizens must have had 90-billion neuron brains that could build a civilization. And destroy it. Wavering wonders, is this a pattern?

Proxie's face looks normal except for eye sockets the size of baseballs. "Look at those eyes," Wavering says.

"It's the dim light," Gretchen says. "Proxima Centauri's sunlight is so weak these creatures had to have bigger eyes to let in more light." Wavering recalls from his collection of art images an artist who painted children. They all had big eyes, maybe twice the size of normal. Eyes that were curious or sad or happy. But those kids didn't have a red dwarf sun.

53

Regina and Wavering set out to cross to the far side of the dust-entombed city to see what's there. They weave their way through the dunes, keeping the brightest sky before them. When they start out, they are clad in heavy pants and sweaters. But as they navigate dune after dune, they find they are sweating. Off come the sweaters and heavy undershirts. She's in a tank top and Wavering in a T-shirt. But the heat continues to rise. The air becomes heavy with humidity. While the sunlight is so dim it doesn't bother their eyes, they agree that to try to live on dry dirt and in such heat would be a struggle. Back to the twilight zone.

***

Regina joins Eva, Buck, and Sarah, and they set out day after day—earth day, that is—to explore what lies at the lower end of the slope that sinks into darkness. Wavering doesn't know what they're looking for, but they step off with energy and much conversation.

One day, the four of them return, and their walk is more jubilant than usual. Maybe they found some moonshine. Or a wine cellar. No, Sarah holds in her hands what, with imagination, Wavering identifies as a fish. At least something that looks like it swims in water. Or did. But it's repulsive, it's dried stiff with rot holes. It should put off a foul odor, but he thinks it's too dried out for that. It has a slender body and a large head with big red eyes. Another creature that evolved to live in infrared light.

"There have to be living ones," Buck says with enthusiasm.

"Did you see any?" Wavering asks. Pragmatist that he is, he likes to have empirical evidence.

"No," says Eva. "We sat on the beach for a while, but saw nothing. I don't think it means anything. On earth, water could be teeming with fish and none came to the surface. We need to dive."

Eva casts Wavering an inviting look, but he's not biting. "If we did suit up one of us to dive, how could we see anything in this light?" he asks.

"Don't we have a light that will work underwater?" she says.

Yes they do, but Wavering's not enthusiastic. There may be live fish, but there may also be live sharks and who knows what else? Maybe Proxima b had no cataclysm to kill off dinosaurs like they had on earth. A swimming dinosaur? Would it have teeth? Although for Wavering, sharks are enough. A Proximite version of Great Whites? Wavering feels no impulse to take the first dive.

54

Wavering's monitoring Genesis while the crew explores isn't giving him enough to do. Enough, that is, to keep his mind from speculating on how they will be able to survive. And propagate? He's not anxious to go there.

Wavering feels chronic exhaustion. Exhaustion that isn't from lack of sleep or too much exertion or work. He thinks it's from the task of getting them to Proxima b. And the preparations and all that yammering with Augustus Fluke III and Berwick and Holiness Jones. It was stress. It wasn't just the blather that he thought would never end. It was the dread that one or all of the big three would be on board Genesis. It would have been like packing the Devil on a pilgrimage to Mecca, or wherever pilgrimages went.

Since Genesis doesn't take much of his time, Wavering does a lot of reading. Especially history, a subject he avoided while in school. He didn't think what people did in the past was important. But now as he reads it, he hopes he can figure out how humans got to self-destruction. Wars. So many wars. He doesn't know if historians were obsessed with wars, but they spent a lot of time writing about them. Or was it that there were a lot of wars, and they made up much of history? At first, he was hoping not. But he's not sure.

From time to time Wavering looks over at Proxie propped up in a niche on the crew deck. Wavering takes in his big eyes and little body and wonders what his life was like. Did he have a pretty wife? Did he have beautiful children whom he loved? Did he have a job that satisfied and fulfilled him? Was he sent into battle as Wavering was with the assignment to kill other Proximites? Citizens living on his planet that he not know and had no assurance they were intent on killing someone and not celebrating a wedding or an anniversary or a birthday? Did he have a dictator bent on violence? Rich men who paid to keep brutal leaders in power? Were there religions that sanctioned killing and war? Proxie's empty skull and dead eye sockets reveal nothing.

Wavering would like to think they can create a civilization free from killing and war and genocide. But the more history he reads, the more pessimistic he is. Why should he believe what advanced beings on two different planets did was an anomaly? Obviously it wasn't. A lot of neurons in a lot of brains devoted themselves to devising ways to hate and kill. It's as simple as that.

The hatch opens, and Regina and Gretchen enter. They shake dust off their boots and glance at his e-book. "Interesting stuff?" Gretchen asks.

"You might say that," Wavering replies.

"You look... what is it? Melancholy? Sad," Regina says.

Wavering smiles at Regina's perception. "Melancholy," he says. "That's the right word."

"A sad book?"

"It's just history."

"Sad history?"

"I'm finding history is sad. You're the Russian expert. You know what your country went through."

Regina glances away. "I don't like to think about it," she says.

"Well, our history was bad, too," Wavering says. "It makes me wonder about our future here. We were so ginned up over the prospect of a new Adam and a new Eve. Founding a new human race."

"You don't think we can do it?" Regina asks.

"The Adam and Eve part, yes," Wavering says. "It's just

biological. At least that's what Eva said."

"Isn't that enough?" Regina asks.

"To make babies," Wavering replies. "But what about those babies? If they turn into Cain and Abel and the cycle starts again? Reading this history, I keep asking why it had to go the way it did. It wasn't that people didn't realize that despotic leaders and dictatorships led to wars. Despots kept rising and people kept supporting them. It's as if the human race was bent on suicide."

Gretchen examines a flat of seedlings she's growing under artificial light. She gives them a light sprinkling from a small watering can. She sighs. "Well, Wavering, if we didn't get it figured out on earth, how do you think we're going to do it here?"

"That's what's on my mind," Wavering says. He had anticipated a new civilization on a new planet. But that hope is fading—fast. He feels a growing dread. "I hate to burden us. But how do we start anew and yet avoid what happened on earth? I know I sound pessimistic, but don't you think we need to ask that question?"

Regina and Gretchen fall silent. Wavering thinks they're getting infected with his melancholia. He's sorry about that. "So, what do we do?" Regina asks. "We've come a long way. We're doing well."

She's right about that. After they left earth and Fluke III and his moneyed and religious supporters, life has been different. His crewmates don't seem to have the suicidal instinct. They get along very well. They make decisions without rancor. "We thought democracy was the answer," Wavering says.

"It is," Gretchen says strongly. "It worked. Until we gave it away, that is. Free speech became money. Equality and happiness for all gave way to domination by the richest." She pauses thoughtfully. "People who shouted the loudest that they were Christian supported political leaders who appealed only to animal instincts. Maybe I shouldn't say that. Most animals treated each other better than we did."

"You remind me of something I just read," Wavering says. "I found this quote from president John Adams: 'Remember, democracy never lasts long. It soon wastes, exhausts, and murders itself. There never was a democracy yet that did not commit suicide.' Adams didn't know that one day we would throw away the democracy that he and the other forefathers created. Unfortunately he was prescient."

Regina perks up. "Let's get out of history and look at ourselves. With your help, we are a democracy."

"Yes," Wavering says. "But remember that if we had Augustus or Berwick or Jones here, we wouldn't be."

"Wavering, they aren't here," Regina says. "But we are. We can start a civilization if we choose to. Then leave it to the new civilization to decide whether to thrive or... or kill itself off."

55

Several days later, Wavering is trying to surface from his gloomy non-reverie when Regina enters the crew cabin and casts him a cheery smile. He loves seeing her. She's still lithe, willowy, alluringly shapely in her black leotards and black turtleneck sweater. Black and white. In her face too, with her smooth skin and those shining black eyes and black hair. Yes, he's smitten. Who wouldn't be?

"The crew had a meeting," she says. There's a lilt in her voice. Wavering is not expecting bad news. But what? The thought of a meeting doesn't pull him out of his non-reverie. "What was it about?" he asks.

"We're trying to decide what to do next," she says.

She reviews what she got from her team of Malcolm, Olga, and Elena. They used fishing gear from the cargo bay and actually caught fish. Fish not like what they knew on earth, but fish. They had Gretchen examine them for toxins. There were some, but not enough to make the crew sick. They cooked some of the fish. Wavering knew that already from the odor wafting from the galley. They concluded that if they could live on fish, the planet would sustain them. There might be seaweed too, for salads, or as a vegetable.

Wavering sighs. At least not beans. Perhaps better tasting even than their freeze-dried rations. As long as Genesis lasts, they have the ability to purify water, including remove salt if it's in the lake or ocean giving them the fish.

"What do you think this means?" Wavering asks.

Regina tilts her head thoughtfully. "Malcolm, Elena, and I want us to stay and try to make life here."

"And Olga?" Wavering asks.

"She wants to go back to earth. She says she's homesick."

"Homesick?" Wavering asks with astonishment. "For what?"

"I think she's delusional. She says maybe by the time we get back earth will recover."

"Recover? Recover what?" Wavering can't imagine what Olga has in mind, beyond a larger selection of eligible husbands. That is, if there is anyone left.

"Be like it was. You know. Before everything was destroyed."

Wavering feels again the numbing cold at Motel Aurora Borealis, sees the gloom from the clouds, chafes at the time they spent holed up like rodents in the missile bunker.

"She thinks people will rebuild. Niemen-Marcus, Nordstrom, Tiffany, Saks Fifth Avenue, Harvard, Yale, Stanford, The Empire State Building, I-95, Emirates Air Lines, you name it."

All Wavering can think of is ice and snow. None of the ice ages lasted less than a thousand years. The recollection of what he'd read about them chills his bones. "If you're asking me, no way."

"We agree. At least you and I and Malcolm and Elena agree. We told Olga she was alone in wanting to go back."

"And she said?"

"She looks to Malcolm. He told her she was crazy. I think that put an end to it."

Good for Malcolm. Wavering only hopes she's not thinking she'll make him husband number eight. Her radar never seems to stop searching for an eligible man. Maybe that's okay. Better than lobbying for everyone to return to earth.

"There are the others," Regina goes on. "Apart from Doctor Drone."

"Okay," Wavering says. "Four others?"

"Gretchen, Sarah, Eva, and Buck."

Wavering is thankful for them all. Even Buck, whom he considered to be a man-sized mosquito when he got to know him at Borealis. But with books feeding a brain that was never stimulated enough to mature, he's become a thoughtful and rather deep individual. Not that he's backed off on the running track he outlined with small stones on the dust-covered plateau or the weights he gruntingly lifts to keep himself fit. Actually the rest of them should emulate him.

"They want to move on," Regina says.

"Move on?" Wavering says with surprise. "Move on where?"

"Another planet," Regina says.

"Another planet? And face the dangers of space again?" Wavering asks. "Just because we made it here doesn't mean we'd survive another transit."

Regina cocks her head thoughtfully. "They like traveling on Genesis." Wavering has to admit he did too. But did they become too comfortable? Since they weren't destroyed by space debris, too complacent? They did approach Proxima b and land in good shape. Could they do it again elsewhere? He's not ready to deal with a challenge like that.

"Sarah searched the astronomy files and found a planet called 'Kapteyn b.' It's larger than Proxima b, which she thinks is okay. But it also has one of these red dwarf suns like Proxima Centauri. Sarah warns us that most stars are red dwarfs. Suns like we had are rare and too distant." She pauses. "I know what you're wondering. Maybe thirteen light years."

"Four times as long as it took to come from earth. How do we do that?"

"Dr. Drone says we can hibernate in stages. Four years for each stage, maybe three. Wake up for a while, make sure we're fit and healthy. Then another hibernation."

Wavering didn't expect this. Maybe he's become content with the life they've got on Proxima b. Could it be that he just enjoys this crew and doesn't feel a need to keep traveling?

"We took a vote," Regina adds. "It's four to four with Dr. Drone abstaining."

"Can't you tell him he needs to break the tie?" Wavering says.

"I did. He says he's here to take care of us, not lead us. Frankly, I don't think he cares."

"What do you suggest?" Wavering asks.

"As I said, I'm for staying. But we want to be democratic."

"Four to four doesn't work," Wavering says. So they've appointed him to break the tie and decide where the human race takes its stand? Yet, whatever they do, wherever they go, they're still the human race. They carry with them the seeds of a new creation and the germs of self-destruction.

Something Wavering read in a comic book that got into his book collection pops into mind. "We have met the enemy, and he is us." Thinking back how the world and the United States became more and more divided and dictators like the Flukes proliferated, how true. So how can they prevent becoming the enemy?

"Wavering, what are you thinking?" Regina asks. "Not that I expect an immediate decision. We have plenty of time. But which way might you lean?"

Wavering takes in her shining black eyes and smooth skin. She really is beautiful. He's content to sit there and look at her. For a long time. But he does need to be practical. Is flying on to another unknown planet through hostile space feasible? Who knows? Maybe his mind is failing. He doesn't want to have to think about anything anymore. Yet he still has one thought. He smiles at Regina. "I'm in favor of our having a party," he says. "With grilled fish. Served on a bed of sautéed seaweed. Garnished with spices." He pauses. I noticed we still have some bottles of sauvignon blanc.

Chilled of course."

ACKNOWLEDGEMENTS

I want to thank Judy Golden and Don Beless for their helpful insights and comments. Jay Scherberth for his professional assistance preparing the book for publication. Wes Pierce and Heidi Blackie for guidance in finalizing the cover. And thanks to my late wife, Lynn, whose relentless and tireless communications with politicians expressed her commitment to justice, mercy, and love. You left a legacy that is a challenge to follow.

ABOUT THE AUTHOR

Bruce Blackie currently serves as an advisor to a fund that supports civil rights, the environment, world hunger solutions, the defense of threatened journalists, cancer and primary mental health research. He resides in California.